PETE BARTHOLOMEW—Odd jobs are his specialty, but his latest piece of work is as bizarre as it gets. He's trying to figure out if the eighty-eight-year-old grande dame of Nashtoba Island is an angel of mercy . . . or a cold-blooded murderer.

CONNIE BARTHOLOMEW—She's never run from a challenge in her life—even a second marriage to Pete. But this latest mystery is so full of twists and turns, she may end up losing him again . . . permanently.

SARAH ABREW—At eighty-eight, she's had a lifetime of experience in the art of repressing, suppressing, and covering up the truth. But even a confession of murder won't keep the most shameful family secret of all from coming out.

JOANNA ABREW—For thirty years, Sarah's daughter has been haunted by a moment of utter terror and humiliation. Now, the shocking hidden truth is rising to the surface, dredged from the past by an act of passion and revenge.

CARRIE SUGGS—Sarah's cleaning woman is a young single mother who has made almost every sacrifice imaginable in the struggle to survive. There is, however, one compromise she's unwilling to make . . . no matter who pays the price.

WEBSTER SUTTON—An old hand at financial trickery and sexual blackmail, he's finally paid for his sins with his life. But his murder is only the beginning of the strange and sordid tale about to unfold on Nashtoba Island.

ROUGH WATER

"It's smooth sailing for Gunning, who does her usual fine job of story unraveling. . . . *Rough Water* is fun, it's fast and . . . a good read."

—*Sunday Cape Cod Times*

TROUBLED WATER

"A fine addition to a thoroughly enjoyable series."

—*I Love a Mystery Newsletter*

ICE WATER

"Sally Gunning is building an audience for her Peter Bartholomew mysteries, and her newest release shows why."

—*Rave Reviews*

UNDER WATER

"Loaded with red herrings. . . . A most entertaining mystery. . . . Well deserves the full complement of five [cats] (highest rating)."

—*Murder Under Cover*

HOT WATER

"Sally Gunning brings a deep understanding of small-town life to her first novel, and an unforgettable cast of characters sure to bring readers back to the next Peter Batholomew mystery."

—*Mystery News*

Books by Sally Gunning

Hot Water
Under Water
Ice Water
Troubled Water
Rough Water
Still Water
Deep Water
Muddy Water
Dirty Water

Published by POCKET BOOKS

For orders other than by individual consumers, Pocket Books grants a discount on the purchase of **10 or more** copies of single titles for special markets or premium use. For further details, please write to the Vice-President of Special Markets, Pocket Books, 1633 Broadway, New York, NY 10019-6785, 8th Floor.

For information on how individual consumers can place orders, please write to Mail Order Department, Simon & Schuster Inc., 200 Old Tappan Road, Old Tappan, NJ 07675.

DIRTY WATER

A PETER BARTHOLOMEW MYSTERY

SALLY GUNNING

POCKET BOOKS

New York London Toronto Sydney Tokyo Singapore

This book is a work of fiction. Names, characters, places and
incidents are products of the author's imagination or are used
fictitiously. Any resemblance to actual events or locales or persons,
living or dead, is entirely coincidental.

An *Original* Publication of POCKET BOOKS

POCKET BOOKS, a division of Simon & Schuster Inc.
1230 Avenue of the Americas, New York, NY 10020

Copyright © 1998 by Sally Gunning

ISBN: 1-4165-0318-8

This Pocket Books paperback printing May 2004

10 9 8 7 6 5 4 3 2 1

POCKET and colophon are registered trademarks of
Simon & Schuster Inc.

Cover art by Ben Perini

Printed in the U.S.A.

In memory of E.M.A.

Acknowledgments

Alack, what trouble was I then to you!

My thanks to William Shakespeare's *The Tempest* for the above quote and those prefacing each chapter.

Much love and *muchos gracias* to John "Hurricane" Leaning for sharing his wealth of research on storms, to Ellie Leaning for naming my hurricane after her favorite spider, to Sport Carlson for the usual insightful reading-in-the-rough, and to Tom, for the usual everything.

1

What have we here? A man or a fish?
Dead or alive?

Sarah Abrew stood on the cracked mud floor of the old Indian tower, eyes closed, gun in hand. *Think, you old fool.* The sound of a gunshot ringing around the old stone walls would rattle anyone, young or old. It was only natural she'd be standing here, feet rooted, mind blank. Well, she'd best make it a short blank. She was already listening to the silence as the industrial-strength vacuum cleaner shut off in her house not fifty yards away. That was the tip-off. Her cleaning woman had heard the shot. Hard not to, with every blasted window in her house wide open. Septembers were mild on Nashtoba Island, but this one was milder than most, all those tropical depressions, one after the other, it seemed, coming up from the south. So the cleaning woman, Carrie Suggs, had heard the shot and any minute now she'd come running. Or would she? Hard to tell, the modern response being what it was today, but if Sarah knew Carrie Suggs, she'd come running. But did Sarah know Carrie Suggs? No. Not really. Still, best to proceed according to plan. Some plan. So Carrie Suggs will come running. Then what?

So think.

This was no time for what brain cells she had left to go out to lunch. Sarah forced her eyes open and looked around. The Pilgrims had built the tower on this particular rise of land a few hundred years ago, as a lookout for Indian attacks. It made no sense, considering the minute the Pilgrims had landed on Nashtoba the Indians had welcomed them with gifts, but then again, who said the Pilgrims made sense? And who said anyone around these parts had improved things since? The selfsame folly that had been built of Pilgrim stone and mud had been sanctified and fortified by Historical Society cement so that almost four hundred years later, it still stood.

And here Sarah still stood.

And here lay Webster Sutton.

Dead.

So think.

The body lay kilted against the foot of the circular stone wall, legs splayed, head twisted sideways. From where Sarah stood, or maybe because of her pathetic eyesight, she couldn't see the hole in Webster's temple, but she knew it was there, on the left. She could see the blood-darkened stones on the wall above and behind him just fine. She forced her eyes over the rest of the corpse, making detached note of the big, sagging belly, signs that he'd lived too well for too long a time. But when Sarah's eyes hit the undone belt buckle she looked away. No, he had not lived well. And it was that fact that had caused him to die. That fact, no other. She'd do well to remember that.

So, think.

Sarah looked down, saw the gun still gripped in her knobbed, arthritic fingers, and almost laughed out loud. Was she going to forget about the gun? Now that would be a cute trick. No. The gun was the easy part. It was Webster Sutton's gun, it belonged in Webster Sutton's hand. She took a step toward the body and was surprised to find her knees steady, her step sure on the clay floor. Good Lord, she was going to pull this off. She may be half-dead and half-blind, but she had more steel and sinew than most people a third her age. And she still had all her marbles. All right, maybe she was shy a peewee or two. She could not, for example, ever seem to remember that fool mailman's name. But there were enough marbles still rattling around in there to match wits with the police chief anytime.

So think.

Webster Sutton's wound was on the left side. Nothing for it but to put the gun in his left hand. Sarah wiped the gun on her skirt, braced herself with one hand on her knee, and leaned down. She pressed the gun into the fleshy fingers of Webster Sutton's hand and straightened cautiously. It wouldn't do to pitch over onto the corpse at this late date. She took a careful step backward and had just turned, hand outstretched to brace herself against the ancient stone wall, when there she was, the cleaning woman, Carrie Suggs, standing in the tower door.

"Mrs. Abrew? Is everything all right? I thought I heard . . ."

She saw. She shrank back against the door.

"Mrs. Abrew," she whispered.

"It's all right, Carrie. Or, rather, it isn't, but I am." She stepped forward. Carrie's hand stretched out for hers and Sarah couldn't help a moment's gloating. Here was Carrie Suggs's twenty-four-year-old hand, trembling badly, and Sarah Abrew's, eighty-eight last January first, steady as a stone.

"What . . . what happened?"

"It was an accident," said Sarah firmly. "We must notify the police. If you would be so kind as to help me home."

She was in the doorway when she finally stumbled. It was the natural place to stumble because of the wood sill that jutted out of the clay floor, but it was also a handy place to stumble. Sarah was able to grip the doorframe and steady herself with one hand, while Carrie Suggs's arm came around her to help her through the door. As if she'd scripted it, thought Sarah, and again she almost laughed out loud, but poor Carrie didn't appear to be in any laughing mood.

"Here," she said stiffly, "sit down on this log. You're much too shaken to walk. I'll get my car." She eased Sarah onto the log, but continued to stand there, looking around her like a field mouse in the shadow of an owl. "Mrs. Abrew," she finally whispered again, as if Webster Sutton could hear. "Mrs. Abrew, are you sure? You're truly all right? I just don't know—"

"I'm all right, Carrie. Please. It's an excellent suggestion. Get your car."

The younger eyes searched the older ones and seemed to find whatever they needed in the way of impetus. She jogged off through the trees and Sarah was again alone. Thank the Lord. Carrie Suggs was good and strong. It had felt nice back there in the doorway to borrow that sturdy arm. In the course of their day-to-day housekeeping interactions she had seemed level-headed enough, too, but right now the woman was a nervous wreck, and what Sarah needed was someone who was cool and calm.

And someone who could drive a car.

She heard it long before she could see it, in the woods on the opposite side of the tower, coming way too fast over the dirt track that accessed the tower from the main thoroughfare. She heard the car stop, heard that peculiar, grinding whine of a laboring gear, another stop, then forward again, then stop, reverse, stop, forward, it seemed to Sarah to go on for years.

Really, Carrie.

At long last, there was the car door. Next Sarah heard the crack of twigs, the rattle of old leaves, as Carrie crashed through the woods toward her. Sarah got to her feet and steadied herself, but she didn't dare proceed over unfamiliar, rough terrain alone. She waited where she was.

Calm. Cool.

When Carrie arrived Sarah let her take her arm, let herself be guided toward the waiting car. Carrie had swung in beside and just ahead of Webster Sutton's car, a big, substantial, dark thing, just the kind Sarah would have expected a man like him to drive. Carrie Suggs's car was small and light, but boxy, just roomy enough for the equipment she had to drag around. And was it gray or light blue? Sarah's eyes weren't up to the nuances these days. She let Carrie open her door, help her inside, find her the seat belt, even for the short ride, a cautionary move that surprised Sarah, somehow. Carrie closed her in and circled to her own side. As she slid in behind the wheel she spoke for the first time since she'd left to get the car. "I drove in as far as—"

"The sand," Sarah finished for her. "Got stuck, didn't you? I could tell. Well, I'm sorry for the trouble, but I appreciate the help. Lucky for me it's your cleaning day. This has been a dreadful accident. Shall I tell you how it happened?" And without waiting for further words from Carrie, Sarah began. After all, she could use the trial run. She listened to her own voice, calm and strong. Too calm and strong? She attempted a sentence in a weaker register, felt it come across sounding querulous and old, nothing more. All right, the devil take them all. She would be strong. She would sound so strong they would see at once she was fighting tooth and nail to create the illusion of strength, realize at once that she was near collapse, offer her tea, tuck her into bed like any normal, doddering eighty-eight-year-old.

Or, better yet, they might just leave her alone.

The ride seemed long for one so short, to Sarah's sensitive ear the car sounding tinny and unreliable. If she'd had her druthers she'd have preferred Peter Bartholomew's clankity old truck with Pete himself at the wheel. But no, Sarah corrected herself. That wouldn't do. Wouldn't do at all. The boy knew her too well. Was too fond of playing by the rules. Connie, perhaps? No. First, of course, was that ridiculous sports car of hers. Second was the fact that any rules Connie might agree to break were bound to be the wrong ones. Sarah and her cleaning woman would have to go it alone.

The minute the car drew to a halt Sarah opened the door and swung her feet to the ground. She was a good quarter of the way up the walk before Carrie reached her, but this time Sarah brushed away the helping hand. This, at least, was familiar ground, and she needed to take the next steps fast, before Carrie or her own second thoughts could turn her around. She opened her front door, headed right to the kitchen, reached up to the wall for the phone. She dialed those newfangled numbers the way Pete had drilled her.

Nine-one-one.

Better the old days, when the operator knew who you were and who you wanted and whether or not you'd be apt to find them in. Now there was nobody on the line to discourage her. The next voice she heard was the police dispatcher, Jean Martell, speaking knee-deep in the middle of a yawn.

Well, this should wake her up some.

"It's Sarah Abrew," said Sarah. "There has been an accident. Webster Sutton has been shot. That's Webster Two, not Webster One. One's already dead, as you might recall. I believe young Three's still off at school. But Webster Two is in the Indian tower. Don't bother with the ambulance, he's past that now. Blackout Bernie's hearse will do."

She hung up the phone feeling pretty well satisfied with the job, but when she turned, she found Carrie Suggs, still looking anxious, hovering in the hall. "They should be here in a minute. Thank you for your help, Carrie. Now you may go home."

Carrie gave her a blank look. "Home?"

Sarah ignored her, moving doggedly past and into the living room. She couldn't stand around waiting for the woman to remember where she lived. Suddenly she truly did need to sit down. She dropped into her favorite chair, the wood so old it was the color of tar, the back so high it made her feel like she was on a throne.

Sarah closed her eyes.

Soon she heard Carrie's heavy tread enter the room, heard the creak of the couch as Carrie sat down.

Sarah opened her eyes. "What in thunderation do you think you're doing now?"

"I'm going to wait with you. Until the police come."

"At your usual exorbitant hourly rate, I suppose?"

Carrie said nothing, but Sarah could see her chin come up.

Well, good. Let her sit there, then.

"Mrs. Abrew."

"I'm in no mood for chitchat, girl."

Sarah closed her eyes once more.

Carrie didn't speak again.

It seemed a long time before they heard the brisk knock on the door, which barely preceded its opening. Will McOwat dwarfed everything in the room the minute he entered it, including Sarah's throne, and for a minute she was taken aback. She'd forgotten the police chief was so large. But his tread, his voice, were gentle. He came straight to her chair and leaned down. "Are you all right, Sarah?"

Ironically, those were the words that gave her her first real pause. She had also forgotten how much she liked this man. For a minute she found it hard to answer. Perhaps, just possibly, none of this had been necessary after all?

"I believe you're inquiring after the health of the wrong party," she said finally. "It's Webster Sutton who's faring poorly. Is dead, as a matter of fact."

"I know. I've seen him. I'm sorry, Sarah. I take it you found him?"

"You take it wrong." She gave herself a minute. She closed her eyes, rubbed her hands across them. She heard the creak of leather. The chief's holster, perhaps? Next she heard the thrum of a couch spring, the *thwap, thwap, thwap* of an approaching pair of shoes. When she opened her eyes the police chief had squatted in front of her and Carrie Suggs stood hovering behind, hands fluttering in the air.

Sarah dropped her eyes from Carrie's to the chief's. "You take it wrong," she said again. "I didn't just find Webster Sutton. I killed the man."

2

'T was a sweet marriage, and we prosper well in our return.

Peter Bartholomew began his second day of married life by opening his eyes to clouds. Clouds? No, not clouds. Roses. White roses. Then he remembered. The canopy bed. He'd felt like a fool when he'd seen it. He'd told Connie. There was no way he was going to be able to properly perform his husbandly duties lying under a canopy of white roses.

Wanna bet? she'd answered.

Shortly thereafter, of course, he'd forgotten about the roses.

Weird how the whole thing seemed so new when it was far from it. They had, after all, been married to each other before. Before Connie had run off. Before Pete had divorced her.

And here they were twelve years later, married

again, on a honeymoon again, somewhere in New Hampshire. Or was it Maine? Pete didn't know and didn't care. They'd driven along the old coast route till they'd seen a place that had made them feel like stopping, marched up to the desk of the first presentable inn they'd seen, and booked a room. Pete supposed it was his own fault about the roses, since he was the one who'd mentioned the word *honeymoon*. But it was a nice invention, the honeymoon. Say the magic word and the world leaves you alone. Not that the world had had a choice in their case. Pete and Connie had left no forwarding address behind them.

And here they were. Here *Connie* was. But against what odds? Connie's eyelids fluttered open. The white roses seemed to give her pause, also, until she rolled over and saw him. Something in his face must have shown his thoughts. "See? Still here." She smiled.

"And guess what. No one else is. No friends, no family, no Factotum customers."

"One customer, maybe. If I can believe your logo. You are a person employed to do *all* kinds of work?"

Pete opened his mouth on hers.

And somebody opened a fist on their door.

Pete groaned.

"Wrong room!" called Connie.

Bang, bang, bang.

"It's the wrong room," said Connie. "Isn't it? It has to be. Nobody even knows we—"

"Mr. Bartholomew?"

Pete drew back, looked at Connie. "No, thank you," he tried.

"Mr. Bartholomew," said the voice, more confidently. "I'm sorry to disturb you, but you have a phone call."

"Look, you've got the wrong—"

"It's a Mr. McOwat. A Chief McOwat, actually. I'm sorry, but he insisted I wake you."

Pete shot up. Willy? The police chief? It could only mean one thing. Somebody had died. His father. No, his mother. Or Connie's mother, she was the one with the heart thing. He ripped back the covers and by the time he'd found the discarded jeans and yanked on a sweater he'd run through the usual long list he dragged out each time the phone rang. After their parents came his sister Polly. Polly'd gotten into a car accident. Or worse yet, a new boyfriend. Or maybe it was his partner, Rita. Or Rita's daughter, Maxine. Or Maxine's boyfriend, who at last tally had been Pete's sole remaining employee, Andy Oatley. By the time Pete had flung himself out the door and practically pushed the blinking young man down the stairs ahead of him, he was busy contemplating the unlimited types and sizes of catastrophes that could have been generated by Andy.

The lobby was empty. A phone receiver lay dangling on the front desk. The young man pointed to it and tactfully disappeared. Pete snatched it up. "Willy?"

"Sorry about this," said Willy.

"What is it? Who died?"

"Webster Sutton."

"Webster Sutton? What is this, a joke? How'd you find me?"

"I'm a cop. We're supposed to be good at these things. I knew you took the west road, but I admit you got farther along than I figured. It took me ten calls to find you. And it took me a whole day to decide to try. But it's not who's dead, it's who killed him. Or who says she did. Your old friend Sarah Abrew."

Some time must have gone by during which Pete tried to figure how Sarah had inadvertently slipped down his worry list to a spot somewhere behind Andy Oatley.

"If you're waiting for the punch line, there isn't one," said Willy finally.

Pete looked at the clock on the wall. "I'll be at Sarah's by two."

"I'll meet you," said Willy.

"I knew it," said Pete, once they were packed up and on the road. "I knew something like this would happen. Things were going so great."

"This didn't happen to us, it happened to Sarah," said Connie. "And she didn't ask us to come back, you know."

Pete looked sideways at her.

"All right. I know. But I'm warning you, she won't thank you."

No, thought Pete, as he bore down on the accelerator, she certainly wouldn't thank either of them. Sarah Abrew was, as the chief had said, an old friend, but she was an even older Factotum customer. She'd been one of the first to hire the brand-new, sixteen-year-old entrepreneur over twenty years earlier to read her the morning paper once her eyesight had begun to fail. The intervening years had brought them together over a variety of tasks on an almost daily basis, minus, of course, those days when they weren't speaking to each other. It figured that right now it would be those arguments he remembered. It also figured he couldn't remember ever winning one.

Pete shot a second look at Connie. By now her head was back against the seat and her eyes were closed.

She possessed a certain nonchalance about her appearance that usually left her looking slightly storm-tossed and today was true enough to form—she'd gotten straight out of the shower, slicked the wet hair back from her face, thrown a short denim jacket over a long T-shirt, cuffed up a pair of Pete's jeans. Where the hair had already dried it fell forward like gold leaves, tangling in the dark lashes. Pete gazed at her fondly for as long as he dared before returning his eyes to the road. Connie was one argument he'd been happy enough to lose to Sarah—it was Sarah who had managed to convince him to give it another go.

The next time Pete looked sideways she met his eyes with her own telltale sparkle of sea-foam green. "Will you stop looking at me like you expect me to evaporate? Do something useful and tell me about this Webster Sutton."

"There used to be three of them, father, son, grandson. They called them One, Two, and Three. It looks like we're down to Three, now. Web One died a while ago. He was an accountant. So was the one who was killed, Webster Two, only he had a few more letters after his name, called himself a financial consultant. He had that ugly office on Cold Storage Road. Sutton-Fitch Financial Services. I don't know much about Web Three except that he's still in school."

"What's the connection to Sarah?"

"Got me. I'll tell you this: I can't believe she . . ." He stopped.

Or could he?

Connie reached across and collected his free hand. "It's some crazy screwup, you wait and see. Or there's an extenuating circumstance. It'll get explained somehow."

* * *

When they got to Sarah's they found two cars in her drive—the police chief's brand-new Ford Explorer and an unfamiliar blue Honda Civic with most of the shine gone. As Pete walked in it occurred to him how different it felt to be here—usually Sarah's tiny half-Cape, built low and steeply pitched to ward off the northeast weather, welcomed Pete like a safe harbor. This time the sight of it filled him with dread. What could possibly have happened to make Sarah gun a man down? He supposed they'd find out soon enough. They trudged up the walk and went in.

The tiny living room seemed full—Sarah in her usual chair, looking small and still and alone, the police chief, looming large on the couch by comparison, and a long, lean young woman with old hands, dark eyes, and an ink-black ponytail, lurking by the door. The minute they saw Pete and Connie, all three people came to life.

The police chief stood up. The ponytail backed up. Sarah spoke up.

"What in the blue blazes are you two doing here?"

"Oh," said Connie. "Second honeymoons. You know."

Sarah fixed a cloudy eye on Pete as if she were trying to remember where she'd stashed her marriage manual. The police chief crossed the room to her chair and hovered protectively, but to protect whom? Them from Sarah? Sarah from them? "I called Pete and Connie," he explained to Sarah now. "Since you refused to call your daughter. Or a lawyer. This is Carrie Suggs. Ms. Suggs, Pete and Connie Bartholomew. Ms. Suggs was the unfortunate Johnny-on-the-spot at the time of the . . ."

"You might as well say it," snapped Sarah. "At the time of the murder. And you two might as well go right back where you came from. Nobody needs you here. Leastways I certainly don't. Do you need him, Chief? You usually do, it seems."

She doesn't miss much, thought Pete. How many other people knew how the out-of-towner police chief turned for local aid to Pete, the native son?

"Since we're here," said Pete, "why don't you tell us what happened?"

"Why not tell the whole world? Why not hang up a sign somewhere?"

Carrie Suggs, at least, seemed able to take a hint— she excused herself and left the room—but the police chief merely crossed to the couch and sat down.

Sarah glared at him. "You can't mean you want to hear it over again? You're just like my daughter and the three bears. If I had to tell that fool story once, I had to tell it a thousand times. 'Mama, tell me about that little girl and those bears.' Mind you, she could never remember the name of the girl. She called her Goodipots. Now that I think of it—"

"Sarah," said Pete gently, "what's gone on around here?"

"Simple enough." Sarah cast the chief a withering look. "Simple for some of us, anyway. Sit down, sit down. I can't abide people hovering."

Pete and Connie sat down on either side of the chief on the couch.

Sarah surveyed them like a preacher surveying her congregation, then removed an embroidered handkerchief from the cuff of her blouse and coughed into it twice. "All right, you wanted it, here it is, but I warn you, it's not pretty. Yesterday. Ten o'clock, it was. Or close enough not to matter. Carrie was here cleaning and making the usual ruckus with that god-awful vacuum of hers, so I decided to take my usual walk early. You know, along that path you cleared out, through the woods to the Indian tower. It was a nice warm day yesterday. Today's a mite cooler. I hear it's supposed to warm up again by the end of the—"

"You went to the tower," Pete prompted.

"Hang on to your horses, why don't you? A man in that much of a hurry, no wonder you're back from your honeymoon. Yes, I went to the tower. When I got close I heard voices. I looked inside, and there was Webster Sutton. The accountant. You know him?"

Pete shook his head, remembered Sarah might not be able to see it, said, "Not personally, no."

"Lucky for you. He was in there, just inside the door, almost blocking the door so it would be hard if not impossible to scoot past him. And there was a young girl, up against the wall. Bright red hair and plump as a pigeon. I'd say not more than sixteen or seventeen years old. Not a girl I'd seen around here before. And Webster Sutton was standing there in broad daylight, exposing himself to her." Sarah coughed once more into the handkerchief. "Did I mention he had a gun in his hand? His other hand, that is. Well, I wasn't about to stand there with him waving everything around in that girl's face. I picked up a stick and marched up to him. I hollered and swung the stick at him. I don't mind telling you I wouldn't have objected if I'd knocked a few of his teeth down his throat, but I did not intend to kill him. Still, it seems I did. The stick must have knocked the gun hand, the gun went off, and it killed him. End of story. I must say, I think Goldilocks and the three bears is a better one."

Pete got up off the couch and crossed to Sarah.

When he drew close she closed her eyes. Pete picked up her hands. Sarah's hands were usually so warm they felt hot, but today they were like ice and, just for a minute, they clung. "It was a rotten accident, Sarah. There are things you'll have to do and I'll help you every step of the way, but I think we should call Joanna."

"And a lawyer," said Willy.

Sarah's eyes snapped open. "They will be no calls to any daughters or any lawyers."

"I don't see why she'll need a lawyer," said Connie. "It sounds pretty cut-and-dried to me."

Carrie Suggs reentered the room, carrying a teacup. Connie jumped up and moved a small marble table closer to Sarah's chair. The chief caught Pete's eye and motioned him toward the door.

Pete followed him out. The chief led the way along the path to the Indian tower, but it was a familiar enough route to Pete. As Sarah had said, he was the one who had originally cleared it for her and had trimmed it faithfully every spring, cutting back errant limbs from scrub pine and oak, ripping out any bullbriers or roots that threatened to trip her. Now the path rose smooth and unfettered over the long rise to the tower. As soon as they reached the stone fortress Pete said, "All right, what's bugging you?"

The chief waved Pete ahead of him through the tower door. The tower was not unassuming if you thought in terms of early seventeenth century—two-foot-thick walls soared fifty feet in the air, with several small rectangles cut through at irregular intervals for lookouts. A larger rectangle at ground level was embedded with crusted hinges attached to a thick wooden door. Pete ducked through the entrance into the dim interior and smelled earth and must and other, unidentifiable things that didn't belong there. In the bright patch of light from the door the stain on the wall stood out clear against the pale stone. Suddenly Pete pictured Sarah standing there with a dead man at her feet and a weeping young girl behind her. He stepped hastily back through the doorway and into the damp air.

Willy followed.

"So what's bugging you?" Pete asked again.

"I'll start with first things first. We can't find that redheaded pigeon of hers. Sarah says she ran off through the woods after the shot." Willy waved an arm in an arc along the empty woods. "We've searched and we've asked and we've even run through the census. I even brought down a sketch artist from the state barracks, but considering Sarah's eyesight, we didn't limit ourselves to more than the generalities—young, plump, red hair. Still, we found only three who matched that description. One was getting her hair permed. One was on her way to Middleborn with the school band. One was taking her driver's test. All verified."

"So you can't find the pigeon. That sounds like your problem, not Sarah's."

Willy shot Pete a look he didn't much care for. "Number two. Sarah says she knocked Sutton's gun arm and the gun went off. When we found him the gun was in his left hand."

"Don't tell me—he was right-handed. So he had a sprained thumb."

"With the gun in his left hand," repeated Willy, "which corresponds to the shot through the left temple. Yes, he was right-handed, but that's only half the problem. The other half is that if Sutton was holding the gun when it went off, it means the shot had to come from a distance less than or equal to the length of his upper arm. And a shot at that close range would have left tattoos. Powder burns. There weren't any."

Pete opened his mouth, closed it, opened it again. "Whose gun is it?"

"Sutton's. He had a permit. His wife says he kept it in a drawer at the office. There was often a fair amount of cash lying around."

"Prints?"

"On the gun? Webster Sutton's. One neat set. Only."

Pete decided to ignore the emphasis on the word *only.* "And in the tower?"

"The usual elimination prints—Sutton, Sarah, Carrie Suggs—some we can't identify."

"What does Carrie Suggs say about all this?"

"Pretty much what Sarah does. She was at the house, cleaning, Sarah took off for a walk to the tower, and when Carrie heard the shot coming from that direction she ran after her. She says she walked into the tower and saw Sarah standing there near collapse, Sutton dead on the ground, gun in hand."

"Left hand?"

"Left hand. The woman was observant. She also noticed the man's pants were undone."

"Did she see the redhead?"

"She saw no redhead. She says when she was running through the woods she thought she heard someone else running deeper in the woods, but it could just as easily have been her own echo. That happens out there."

"The road. It's all dirt. There must have been some tire tracks."

"Useless ones, mostly the Suggs woman's. She pulled her car around to drive Sarah back to the house and got stuck in the sand. Spewed up everything."

Pete set off along the path back to the house. The chief fell in step beside him. For a while neither man said anything.

"You see my problem?" said Willy finally.

"I see your problem. See if you see mine. Did you call me home to help Sarah or to help you?"

A shadow of an old, familiar grin cracked the chief's long jaw. "What makes you think it's not one and the same? But I'm beginning to think that, of the two, I need it more. She's a tough old bird."

"She's not as tough as she sounds. She's been through something; whatever it is, I can tell. It will hit her soon. I don't like the idea of her staying there alone."

"You think I do? The Suggs woman stayed with her last night or I would have called you before now. But the worst Sarah looked through all this was when I offered to call her daughter. I would have called her anyway if I couldn't reach you, but I know how tight you two are. That's the first reason I called you. The second reason is this: I've still got to come up with some plausible answers, and short of locking up an eighty-eight-year-old . . ." Willy stopped and gave Pete a sheepish look. "Well, would you? If it was a choice between that or going the longer, easier way around—"

"The longer, easier way around being . . . ?" asked Pete, but he was pretty sure he knew. The longer, easier way around was straight through him.

"Look, you know her better than anyone. Talk to her. Find out the truth about what happened back there."

"How the hell do I know what the truth is?"

"You should be good at this by now. You'll know when you hear. And other than that I can only tell you this—we haven't heard it so far."

3

〜〜〜

*You cram these words into mine ears against the
stomach of my sense.*

Sarah Abrew was finally forced to admit she was
running low on steam. Yesterday had been bad
enough, but today was turning out worse. First she'd
had to come face-to-face with the two people in the
world she least wanted to lie to. Then she'd had to tell
the whole hideous tale one more time. Now she was
struggling to fend off Pete's and Connie's so-called
solutions to the so-called problems. First it was this
calling-Joanna business again. Then it was Connie's
offer to bunk in upstairs. And now here was Pete,
freshly returned from God only knew what skulk-
ing and prowling with the police chief, chiming in
with the worst suggestion of the whole lot—that he
and Connie would bring Sarah to their house for a
few days.

No. That would not do. Number one, Pete and Connie knew her a darned sight too well. Number two, they were supposed to be on their honeymoon. Married two days and Sarah had already destroyed their lovely trip, but she wasn't about to destroy the rest of it, whatever time they could find to be alone. Not only did those two deserve a rest, but honeymoons were invented so people could practice up on how to be a pair without the whole world looking on. There were still aspects of pair-hood on which those two could certainly use a refresher course. No, it was not the time for an old hen to perch in the nest between the doves.

But at all cost they must not drag Joanna here.

What to do?

And then Sarah's eye fell on Carrie Suggs, hovering as unobtrusively as she could in the hall. Carrie Suggs, one of those single mothers you kept hearing so much about these days, living in a half-room someplace and working day and night with nobody's help but her own to support herself and her little girl. But thanks to either a kind Fate or a bit of clever planning on someone else's part, the child was spending the weekend at a friend's. Carrie Suggs was available, and Carrie Suggs could use the cash; and although Sarah neither wanted it nor needed it, Carrie's presence here would keep the various people who loved her home where they belonged. It wasn't quite fair to Carrie, of course, to finagle the whole thing without telling her first, but it wasn't the first and it certainly wouldn't be the last thing in Carrie Suggs's life that wasn't fair.

"Carrie!" Sarah called. "Come along in here."

The young woman came through the door like the last Christian to face a stadium full of lions. Sarah gave her what she hoped was a reassuring nod, but if there was any beneficial effect, it was lost to Sarah's poor eyes.

"Carrie and I were talking this over not long ago, weren't we, dear?" she began. "Carrie had very kindly agreed to stay with me last night, and she offered to stay tonight, too. At first I said no, but I'll admit to you now that as the day wears on, I seem to be wilting a mite." Good Lord, thought Sarah, what blather would she come up with next? But there were times when blather did the trick. She could see Pete and Connie exchanging looks, glancing at Carrie. She imagined she could see relief all around.

Except from Carrie.

"You will be compensated at your usual reasonable rate, of course," she added quickly. "Agreed?"

Pause. "As I mentioned before," said Carrie finally, "I'd be happy to stay until I pick up my daughter tomorrow after school."

"Good. Then it's all arranged. Perhaps this would be as good a time as any for you to collect any extra things you might need from home. And you could pick up something nice for dinner on the way back. Lamb chops, perhaps."

Carrie left the room and Sarah wasn't so blind she didn't notice Connie slip out after her. Probably checking up to see if the arrangement was really to Carrie's liking. Well, check away, my girl. Now if the police chief would only follow suit . . . Yes, very nice, there he goes, making his farewells, and pretty gracious ones considering the circumstances, too. Three down and only Pete to go. He was standing. He was moving. She was going to make it. She was going to do it.

But Pete didn't move toward the door, he moved to

perch on the hearth next to Sarah, and with his first words, she heard all her well-laid plans come crashing down.

"I've talked to the chief, Sarah. When you feel up to it, maybe you and I should have a few words, too."

"And when you feel up to it you should go home and make it up to your wife for that pitiful honeymoon. Sometimes I don't know what this world is coming to. Here you sit—"

"I've got the rest of my life to make it up to Connie. I think I can spare an hour for you."

"Well, excuse me while I get out the violins."

Sarah was disappointed when Pete chose to ignore that one. She'd thought it was one of her better efforts.

But no, he just mowed right along. "I'd like to discuss a few things that cropped up while I was talking to the chief. When you feel up to it, as I said before."

Up to it. *Up to it.* It had to be one of the most annoying expressions known to man. Well, she wasn't up to it and she wasn't ever going to be up to it, but she might as well find out right now what trouble that fool police chief was going to cause. Although that might be the whole trouble in a nutshell—that the fool police chief wasn't so much a fool after all.

"Well? What's he been saying to you?"

"He's been outlining the problems."

"Such as?"

"Such as Sutton was right-handed. And the gun was in his left hand."

"And we all know what he had in the right one. But you make an interesting point. Which one would you have put in your good hand?"

There, that slowed him up some. Sarah almost

chuckled. Really, Pete was a bit of an old woman, at least when he was sitting in Sarah's living room. And he had his ideas about how old women should act, too. Well, Sarah wasn't above using that to her advantage now and again.

But by now Pete had recovered and was plowing on. "And the chief can't find this red-haired girl you mentioned."

"I'm not surprised. Who has the chief got to work with? That infant sidekick of his, Ted Ball. Ted couldn't find his own fanny in a fog. How's he going to find some young redhead who might not take too kindly to being found at all?"

"Last but not least," said Pete ominously, "if Sutton was holding the gun when it went off, if it had been fired from a position that close, there would have been tattoo marks, powder burns on his skin. There were no burns. So it seems pretty clear to the chief that the shot that killed him came from somewhere farther off."

Sarah withdrew her handkerchief and coughed for a spell. All this coughing was giving her a sore throat—she was going to have to come up with something else to stall with pretty soon. She replaced her handkerchief and gripped the arms of her chair, hoisting herself to her feet just seconds before Pete could get there with a hand under the elbow. All right, so she wasn't run completely dry after all. "I certainly hope the poor man solves his problems soon," she said brightly. "Now if you'll excuse me, it's been a long day and I believe I could use a short nap before dinner."

Ah. That stopped the badgering. That was one of the things Sarah had always loved about the boy—he knew how and when to leave her alone. But he did help her out of the room and down the hall and Sarah had to admit she was glad of the use of a strong arm. She'd even go a step further. Despite the risks involved, she'd have to admit she was glad he'd come home. Much better than Joanna—Joanna, who flew off the handle these days if she so much as burned toast. Not that any of this was easy on Pete, though. For a moment Sarah was filled with compunction. She peered up at Pete, wishing she could see his eyes more clearly. They used to tell her everything she needed to know. As he helped her onto her bed and fussed her under her afghan, she reached up and patted his face. She could feel the smile spring up readily enough under her hand and she sighed with relief. He always managed. Despite everything she'd dumped in his lap this day and all the others that had gone before. But as he moved toward the door she said, "Peter."

"Yes, Sarah?"

"If it had been left up to me I wouldn't have troubled you over this. Not now. Not for all the tea in China."

"I know. That's why I'm glad it wasn't left up to you. I'll stick around awhile in case you need anything."

"I won't. Besides, Carrie's back, I heard her car a moment ago. You take your wife and go home."

She could see his teeth gleam at the word *wife*. "I'll see you tomorrow, then. You have a good sleep. You look like you could use it."

Sarah didn't argue with him, but once his long shadow had disappeared she sat up. What did he think she was, ninety-eight instead of eighty-eight? She wasn't about to lie here in bed in broad daylight. The last time she'd done that she'd been four years old. Sarah listened and heard him in the hall, saying something to Carrie, something she didn't catch the whole of, but something that ended with some sort of query.

Whatever Carrie answered seemed to satisfy him. Soon after, Sarah heard his car pull away.

Gone.

Sarah folded back the afghan and got to her feet. She was less steady than she'd have liked, but on the other hand, she was still moving, not something she could say about most of her contemporaries. She walked down the hall and into the kitchen.

Carrie turned from the sink where she was washing lettuce, wiped her hands on her blue jeans, and said without preamble, "They don't believe you, you know."

So it was going to come from all sides, was it? Well, she could head this one off in a hurry. "If you know what's good for you, you'll keep your nose out of it."

"I'm only telling you what I heard. The police chief and your friend, Peter Bartholomew, is that his name? They were talking and I heard them. They don't believe you and I thought you should know."

"Is that so? And what do you suggest I do about it?"

"I suggest you tell the truth."

Oh, really, thought Sarah. But all she said out loud was, "And when do you pick up your daughter?"

At least the woman seemed to recognize a pointed conversational turn when she heard one.

"Tomorrow at two-thirty," answered Carrie.

She went back to her lettuce and left Sarah alone.

Connie gazed at Pete, more looking than listening as he drove and talked. She still couldn't believe it, that they'd managed to turn the clock back. Or was it forward? Forward, she decided. It was all so different this time. For one thing, there he sat, rattling away about murder, and here she sat, admiring his chin. She'd always liked his chin, nothing showy, just enough to balance off the face, but all of a sudden she couldn't seem to stop looking at it. Or him. It was this honeymoon thing, she decided. Really, people should do it more often. She reached over and ran a hand up his neck into his hair.

"Mmm," he said, and kept talking.

Now that was something you never really noticed about him, she thought. His hair. It was just dark. There. It was the eyes that stopped you, like a good strong dose of sodium pentothal. You noticed the nice teeth, too, but only on those rare occasions when he forgot to hide them.

"Well?" he said suddenly. "Can you?"

"Can I what?"

"Can you believe the luck."

"No," said Connie truthfully, thinking of her own, but suddenly it dawned on her she was supposed to be thinking of somebody else's. "I mean . . . whose luck?"

"Willy's. Ours, too, I guess. Mine, anyway, since he's dumped it on me. Granted, finding the redhead's his problem."

"He can't find the redhead?"

Pete glanced sideways and the teeth flashed. Briefly. "See that? Married one day and you've already stopped listening."

"But only because I was sitting here admiring you. It's okay now, though, I was coming to the dangerous parts. You know, you're in pretty good shape for a man your age."

"It must be all that great food you don't cook me."

Connie's fingers, which had lingered in his hair, grabbed the short hairs at the nape and pulled.

Pete yelped.

"So Willy can't find the redhead. What else?"

"The gun was in Sutton's wrong hand, for one thing."

"You're kidding."

"No, I'm not. And not only was the gun in the wrong hand—which, as Sarah was quick to point out to me, could be explained by the fact that we tend to put the best foot forward, so to speak, when it comes to our more personal machinery—it was also fired from farther away than the length of Sutton's arm. Hence, it's highly unlikely it was Sutton who fired it."

"You're kidding."

"Would you stop saying that? I'm not kidding."

Connie stopped saying much of anything. She was too busy thinking. So if it wasn't Sutton who fired the gun, Sarah was lying. And if Sarah was lying . . .

No. *No.*

Connie was still tossing around variations on the same one word when Pete pulled into their driveway. She wished she could say it felt good to be home, but even so, she had to admit their little cottage looked inviting. Squat and square, except for the new dormers on the second story, and beyond the house, the green and gold marsh, beyond the marsh, the sunflecked Sound. She noticed the mud along the creek through the marsh, the wash of pale green across the Sound. Low tide, then. As she got out of the truck she could smell damp exposed sand, dried salt, wet seaweed. It smelled good, much better than Maine or New Hampshire had.

Much better, in fact, than the house as they walked

into it. The house smelled stuffy, as if they'd been gone a lot longer than a day and a half, but of course they'd closed it up as if they'd be gone a few weeks, which had been their original intention. Connie ran around opening a few strategic windows as Pete unpacked the car. Next she opened the refrigerator, which was empty, but that had little to do with the fact that they'd planned to be away. The refrigerator was always empty. She pulled out two Ballantine ales and took them out onto the screened porch. When Pete came out he dropped into the rocker, popped the can, and raised it, not in the usual direction of the water, but in her direction. "Happy honeymoon."

Connie raised her can, too, trying to conjure up the one night they had managed to squeeze in and a few of the things they'd managed to squeeze into it, but the images were unfairly clouded by one of Webster Sutton exposing himself to a plump, redheaded teenager. She felt suddenly and violently sick and told herself, again, *no*. She wouldn't let one disturbed individual ruin this for them. She kicked mentally back in time to that moment at the town hall on Saturday when those eyes and teeth she'd been so recently admiring had grinned at her and said those two little words. *I do.*

And he will, too, she thought. And so would she, if it killed her this time.

Yes, she felt better now.

She raised her can higher. "Happy anniversary."

They grinned at each other, until almost at the same time, it seemed, it began to feel wrong. They had, after all, just come from a situation where grins didn't go.

"Tell me this," said Pete finally. "If that had been

your mother in the Indian tower and I knew about it and didn't call you, what would you do?"

"I don't know. Divorce you, I suppose."

Pete's face went funny. He got up and went inside. Connie took a last, lingering look at the pristine world before her and followed him in. He sat at the kitchen table and reached for the phone, but when he had it in hand he hesitated. "Or maybe I should call a lawyer."

Now he had her doing it. For a strange, disconnected minute Connie actually thought he was talking about a divorce lawyer. But she looked down at the ring on her hand and her brain instantly cleared. "Maybe Joanna already has a lawyer."

"True." Pete thumbed through his address book, picked up the receiver of the old black rotary phone he'd stubbornly refused to trade in, and dialed Baltimore. It was immediately clear by his stilted tone that he'd gotten an answering machine. He left a message, unalarming, succinct: a situation that required a conversation. Please call.

"We might not reach her, you know," said Pete. "You think that Suggs woman's all right over there?"

"She said so. Until her kid comes home tomorrow." The word *kid* seemed to ring extra loud in her ears. Connie had miscarried two months ago. She wondered if Pete reacted to the subject of children this way these days, too. She watched him sip his beer.

No, she didn't think so.

The sat in silence for a while, each lost in his or her own particular web, until the phone finally rang. That, too, seemed loud. Connie could tell this time that Pete had gotten Joanna's husband, Dennis. He tossed out the choice tidbits, got something back that he had to confirm by repeating the word *Thursday* over and over. Finally *Thursday* turned to *Wednesday*. Then *Tuesday*. Then suddenly, out of the blue, *noon on Monday*. There was discussion about a confirmatory phone call and Pete hung up.

"Neither of them is at home, but Dennis picked up the message and thought he'd better call. He'll try to reach Joanna."

"Like when?"

"I'm not sure."

"Where is she?"

"I'm not sure about that, either."

"Where's he?"

"He didn't say. It was all pretty vague. But he thought he should be able to get here by noon tomorrow."

Pete and Connie looked at each other.

"Odd," said Connie.

"Add it to the collection."

Silence.

"Pete," said Connie finally. "About Sarah. You don't think . . ." She stopped.

The creepy thing was that Pete let her leave it there.

4

In troops I have dispers'd them 'bout the isle.

Rita Peck sat at her desk in what used to be Pete's living room before Factotum had encroached, and stared at the phone. It had rung nonstop for the first fifteen minutes this morning—what was the meaning of this unexpected lull? Better not to ask why. Better simply to take advantage. She snatched up the receiver and dialed her daughter Maxine's number. Maxine, much to everyone's surprise, had plunged last-minute into summer school, completed her one missing credit, and raced off to college three weeks ago. Fletcher College. It could more aptly have been named Flunker's College, thought Rita, but beggars couldn't be choosers. She was grateful anyone had wanted her troublesome child at all.

The phone in Maxine's dorm room rang and rang,

unanswered. Rita had actually begun to hope that Maxine had gotten up for her eight o'clock Monday class, for once, when she heard the phone picked up and set down again. So the little creep thought she'd sleep in, did she? Rita clenched her teeth and redialed. Not that she had anything crucial to say to her, but it had been three weeks and she hadn't heard one word from her. It would be nice to know she was at least alive and breathing.

The phone rang less long this time, but this time after it got picked up it got left off the hook.

So the heck with her.

Rita plunked down the receiver and almost as soon as it hit the cradle it began ringing. She snatched it up. "Factotum." She looked up and saw Pete coming down the stairs. "Persons employed to do all kinds of work," she added sweetly, and was rewarded with a gag motion from her partner. So the car in the drive hadn't lied. So they were here. The question was, why? Oh, she supposed she could guess why. The whole island was jabbering about the why. The more pertinent question would be, how had he heard? Even Rita hadn't known where they'd gone. But all she could do now was point Pete to his usual corner of her desk with a sternly extended finger that meant *stay there* while she continue her discourse with Avery Phelps via phone, regarding, what else? The weather.

"Mr. Phelps, really," she interjected mid-forecast. "I am well aware that there is a hurricane off—"

"The Bahamas," said Mr. Phelps.

"Correct me if I'm wrong, but I believe I just explained that we're—"

"Short-handed," said Mr. Phelps. "I do understand. It's only that I have this tree problem."

"I'll have someone out there to assess the situation as soon as—"

"It's just that she's now off the Bahamas," said Mr. Phelps.

"And the Bahamas are a thousand miles away, aren't they? We'll be out as soon as we possibly can. Good-bye, Mr. Phelps."

Rita hung up. "Honestly, I've only been here half an hour and I'm already sick of the word *hurricane*. They know you're gone and they're panicking. Or they think you're gone. I'm almost afraid to ask. What are you doing here?"

Pete explained about the call from the chief yesterday morning. Rita tried to keep the relief from her face. Despite the Sarah news, she'd still managed to form one of those worst-case scenarios for herself the minute she'd seen their car—marriage gone bust first day out. She supposed she should have more faith in the man. She supposed, by now, she should also have more faith in the woman. But suddenly the real reason he was home seemed to sink in and she knew whatever relief might have shown in her face a minute ago was now replaced with the more appropriate expression.

"Poor Sarah."

"No 'poor Webster'?"

"I'm sorry, no. He handled my ex-husband's accounts. He managed a nice little disappearing act with most of the money just before the court order got there. Consequently I don't tend to count Webster Sutton among my friends." But as she gazed at Pete her eyes softened. Here was somebody she certainly did count among my friends. "Your beautiful new honeymoon, Pete. I'm so sorry."

"Yeah, well. We'll try again later."

Yes, thought Rita, but how much later? She glanced at the pad on her desk and the ever-lengthening list she'd been compiling. Surely they'd put off any further attempts at honeymooning at least a week. And in a week they could get caught up. Or almost. At least they could if they started immediately. Like a cheetah on the trail of some poor dumb wildebeest she asked brightly, "And what are your plans for this morning?"

"Sarah's, first. After that, I don't know. It depends how things are over there. But I'd kind of hoped Connie and I could make ourselves scarce for a while. Do you think you can still get by with Andy?"

"Certainly." Rita tried to say it with confidence, but the truth of the matter was, she knew their sole remaining employee, Andy Oatley, a little too well. Andy was getting better—at least his mishaps tended to draw less blood than formerly—but without Pete and Connie, things were going to get dicey.

And apparently she hadn't fooled Pete any. He sighed. "All right. Let me talk to Connie." He pointed to the phone. "I take it it's been busy?"

"They're calling from five states. They think you're Moses, that they can build a house on a dune and when the flood comes you'll part the water for them. That's not to mention the boats. They don't want to haul them because they want to fish next weekend, but just make sure they don't get swamped or washed ashore. Oh, sure. Fine. Certainly."

Rita's tirade was cut short by what sounded like a small colonial militia practicing on the town green but was in fact Connie coming down the stairs. She looked damp around the edges, like she'd just come from the shower. She also looked like she wasn't too sure whether it was night or morning. Or, for that matter, whether it was here or there. Wherever *there* had been.

"Welcome home," said Rita. "I think."

"Yeah, thanks. I think."

"What's your vote?" asked Pete. "Are we working or playing?"

Connie peered over Rita's shoulder at the day's list. "It looks like we're working. What's going on around here? Earthquake coming?"

"Hurricane," said Rita. "Charlotte. And I'm not going to pretend we don't need you and neither am I going to pretend it's my fault. Haven't I been telling you we need more help? For two years. No, three. More, if you choose to count—"

"All right," said Pete. "Then we'd better get moving. At least I'd better get moving. Who knows who Sarah will decide to kill this morning."

Rita didn't laugh, but then again, neither did anyone else, so she didn't have to feel as she sometimes did around those two, that it was her own personal sense of humor that was lacking. Honestly, the things those two could laugh at sometimes. She admonished Pete to check in as soon as he was through with Sarah and handed Connie a short list to get her through till lunchtime—the Ameraults' windows, Betty's Bud Boutique, Avery Phelps's tree problems, whatever they might be.

The newlyweds moved to the door and Rita picked up the phone, but she paused before dialing, transfixed by the scene in front of her. Connie was actually kissing Pete good-bye. Now that was a new one. Pete seemed to think it was odd, too—he burst into laughter.

"What's so funny?" demanded Connie indignantly.

"Sorry. I felt like Ward Cleaver."

"Oh, yeah?"

Connie kissed him again.

It didn't look like June and Ward to Rita, but then again, it was only recently that Rita had come to feel somewhat expert on the subject herself. As Pete and Connie exited she found her own thoughts turning to her gentleman friend, Evan Spender, and certain pleasurable yet unforeseen aspects of middle-aged life.

Oh, well, she thought. Whatever else the day might bring, at least they were all starting it smiling.

As Pete pulled up to Sarah's he saw Carrie Suggs in the bushes in front of the house, washing the kitchen windows. Pete strolled close enough to speak without inside ears overhearing. "How did it go last night?"

Carrie jumped and pivoted, simultaneously squeezing the hair-trigger on the Windex bottle. Pete took most of it in the ear.

"Oh, sorry," she said. She made a move to dab at him with a paper towel, but must have decided she didn't know him well enough. She handed him the towel instead.

As Pete mopped up he tried again. "How's Sarah?"

Carrie's face went long. "She didn't sleep well. I heard her up several times in the night. And she hardly touched breakfast."

Pete sighed. "I'm trying to reach Sarah's daughter. You're okay here in the meantime?"

"I have to pick up my own daughter at two-thirty. I could bring her back here if you think—"

"Could you?" said Pete, relieved. "I'm sure as soon as I reach Joanna she'll appear, but I hate to leave Sarah on her own until then."

"No," said Carrie instantly. "She shouldn't be alone."

Pete went inside, his resolve bolstered by that definitive second opinion. He didn't care how much she squawked, Sarah was not going to railroad him this time. He found her sitting in her usual chair in the living room, listening to the radio. As Pete walked in she held up a knobbed finger, commanding Pete to listen.

Pete listened.

"What have you got for us on the weather, Bob?"

"Well, Jeff, we've got Charlotte. One of those rare Cape Verdeans. Hit hurricane force before it reached the western Atlantic."

"Which is where she is right now, I understand?"

"Oh, we know where she is, we just can't say where she's going to end up. Right now we're concerned about that northwest veer. If it keeps on that course, that means we're in for some weather. But if it follows the track of the last Cape Verde, it will miss us completely. Which leaves us—"

Sarah switched off the radio in disgust. "Which leaves us looking out the window, same as usual. And what are you doing here? I thought I told you to take a honeymoon."

Pete ignored her. He'd learned to do that a lot over the years. But while he was ignoring her, he also tried to get a bead on her. She looked, he decided, like she was dead tired and trying not to show it. The white hair that usually flew every which way was neatly combed and she sat in her chair with her back poker-straight, ankles neatly crossed, looking around brightly.

"No chief of police with you?" she said. "I thought you traveled in tandem now."

"I'd be happy to get him if you've got something to say to him."

"Yes, as a matter of fact, I do."

Just like that. The bluff called. Okay, thought Pete, keep cool. "Like what?"

"Like something I've recollected. Or perhaps *recollected* isn't the exact word. Something I'd like to correct. Yes, that's better. Having thought better of it. Having received some excellent advice from an unusual quarter. Having wised up, to use your vernacular."

Pete peered at her.

"Well? Did you grow roots or are you enjoying the view? Go fetch him, why don't you?"

Pete left the room and went to the phone. The dispatcher, Jean Martell, gave him a suspiciously short grilling that led Pete to suspect the state of the chief's usual even keel. But when he came on the line all he said was, "What?"

"I'm at Sarah Abrew's," said Pete. "It seems your lead suspect would like to amend her story."

"I'll be there in five minutes," said Willy.

He was there in four and a half, looking far less bright-eyed than Sarah and already possessing more furrows in his forehead. Then again, the farther the hair retreated, the more forehead there was to furrow. And it looked like Sarah was well on her way to giving him another deep one.

"Come in! Come in!" she chirped. "Find that young girl yet?"

"No," said Willy. Not only did he look tired, but he sounded tired, and as Pete heard the fatigue in the chief's voice he could tell Sarah heard it, too. A little of the brightness left her.

"Never you mind, young man. Don't see what you needed her for, anyway."

"You had something you wished to tell me?" said Willy.

Sarah unfolded her hands and gripped the armrests of her chair. She uncrossed, then recrossed her feet. She inhaled and exhaled once, deeply. "I wasn't entirely truthful with you before. I would like to give you the corrected version. Sit down, sit down, both of you. If there's one thing I can't abide, it's these tall men who think they have to loom over you. Now where was I?"

"Telling the truth," said Willy.

A flicker of a smile twitched the corner of Sarah's mouth. "Ah, yes. That was it. You may not appreciate the fact that I did it all for you, Chief, but that's the truth right there. It seemed so much simpler the way I laid it out the first time. I thought to myself, why confuse the poor man? But as I was reminded last night, it's always best to tell the truth, as far as you can without hurting anybody else. That's always been my rule. So here it is. Are you taking notes? All right. First, there was no stick. Pete didn't mention that you didn't find a stick, but as far as I know, there wasn't one. When I saw what that demon was up to I marched right up to him and snatched the gun away from him. I must have surprised him plenty. I don't suppose he expected a wasted old shell of a woman to go on the attack that way. But once I had the gun, you see, he came lunging after me. I warned him to stay back, but he didn't. So I shot him." Sarah stopped and waited.

So did the chief.

After some seconds he said, "And?"

A shadow—doubt? puzzlement?—darkened Sarah's

features. "What do you mean, 'And'? I tried to back away and he came after me. So I shot. I'm not quite ready to cash in the old chips yet. He fell down dead and that's the end of the story. If I don't sound more remorseful, I'm sorry. He was exposing himself to an innocent young girl and he most likely would have killed me."

"So you'd call it self-defense," said Willy.

"How in the blue blazes do I know what you'd call it?" But she paused, considering. "All right, yes. Self-defense. I'm sure a jury will understand, even if you don't."

"And the other charges?"

Again, the flicker.

"While you were so kindly simplifying things for me by returning the gun to Sutton's hand—I assume that was what you were referring to? I'm sure it never occurred to you that this was also against the law, that you were tampering with evidence."

Sarah cast her eyes downward, apparently duly chastised. "No, it didn't occur to me. And I'm sorry for any trouble it caused. I don't mind telling you I'd rather not go to jail. I'll be eighty-nine next January." Her head came up. "But I also don't mind telling you I did nothing I'm ashamed of. Due to circumstances entirely of his own making, Webster Sutton got himself killed. I saw no need to go making heavy weather of it. It was his fault. I gave him back his gun to prove it. Seemed simple enough to me at the time."

Again they waited. This time Willy looked down at the notebook he'd written nothing in. "A few more questions, if you don't mind," he continued finally. "And this might be a good time to suggest again that you are entitled to call a lawyer, that you don't have to—"

"How many times do I have to tell you? I don't need any lawyer to prove what any damned fool should be able to see plain as day if he used the eyes and ears God gave him."

Willy glanced at Pete, a glance Pete found unreadable. "Then I'll proceed with my questions?"

"Proceed," said Sarah. She repeated the crossing and uncrossing ritual, but this time she left off the deep breathing exercise.

"You say you approached the Indian tower and saw Webster Sutton. And the young girl?"

Pete counted two seconds, using the one-Mississippi, two-Mississippi system, before Sarah answered.

"Yes, the young girl. Bright red hair. Plump, very plump. Short, too."

"And when exactly did the girl run off? The minute you walked in? Or after you grabbed the gun?"

"She ran off the minute she knew that beast wasn't going to shoot her," said Sarah briskly. "I'm sure that's why Carrie didn't see her."

"So you walked up to Sutton and grabbed the gun. Was this inside or outside the tower?"

Four Mississippis this time.

"Inside. He was inside. I was inside."

"So you grabbed the gun. He came toward you. What did you do then?"

"I backed up. What in tarnation did you think I'd do, go forward?"

"And when you finished backing up, were you both still inside?"

"Of course we were inside. Didn't you see him? He was lying up against the wall."

"So you were both inside, but the girl had run off. And when you fired at him, how far away was he?"

Six Mississippis. "I don't recollect the exact distance. I was backing up, as I say."

"If you think it would help we could return to the Indian tower and walk through it again."

For a minute, only a minute, Pete half-rose out of his chair, of a mind to put an end to this, to get Sarah that lawyer. Then Sarah drew a gnarled hand across her face and the gesture rang so false, was so obviously theatrical, he sank back into his seat.

My God, he thought, she's *enjoying* this.

"I'm afraid my stamina isn't just what it should be these days," said Sarah. "When you're about to turn eighty-nine come January, young fellow, maybe you'll understand what I mean. No, I'll remain in my chair, if you don't mind. I will tell you what I remember, however, which is this. I backed up. He came after me. I spoke to him. I warned him if he came any closer I would shoot. He continued to move toward me. Not being completely devoid of the usual garden-variety survival instincts, I shot him. Is that sufficient? Am I excused?"

"He was still approaching as you shot?"

"Of course he was still approaching. If he wasn't still approaching I wouldn't have shot. I am not a cold-blooded killer. It wasn't till he lunged at me that I pulled the trigger."

"So let me make sure I have the picture complete. You walked in and saw Sutton exposing himself to a short, overweight, redheaded sixteen- or seventeen-year-old girl. You walked up to him and grabbed his gun. So you would have been standing quite close to him."

"Didn't I tell you I backed up?"

"Yes, you did, but at the particular instant that you

grabbed the gun you would have been within arm's length, isn't that correct?"

"Correct," snapped Sarah.

"So you grabbed the gun and you back up. How many steps backward would you say you took?"

"You show me someone who counts his steps when he's backing away from a loaded gun and I'll show you a bloody fool."

Was that a glint in Willy's eye? Pete thought so.

"Let's try it this way, then. Let's say that for the sake of argument Webster Sutton was standing as far away from you as possible. We'll say he was even up against the wall. You grabbed his gun. He came toward you. Let's say we count that as step one. He was a large man, he probably took a reasonably good-sized step, let's say it brought him forward a yard. You backed up. Just for the sake of argument we'll say you backed up one yard to his one, shall we?"

"We shall. Certainly we shall. Considering that if I hadn't I'd be roadkill right now."

"Fine," said Willy calmly. "And at this point you say you told him to stop, but he continued to move forward. To *lunge* forward, I believe was the exact expression you used. So that would bring him at the very least an additional yard away from the wall, but more likely a good bit more than an additional yard. A lunge would be longer than a normal step, wouldn't you agree?"

Ten Mississippis. That was a lot of Mississippis. When Sarah finally spoke, Pete was sweating. "I believe I told you before I do not have the foggiest notion where he was when I shot him," said Sarah with dignity. "And I am equally unable to comprehend your apparent difficulty. Perhaps if you give some thought to the degree of my distress on this occasion? Add to that the fact that my memory is not what it should be. And neither, might I add, is my eyesight. In that poorly lit area—"

"And yet in that poorly lit area you could apparently see well enough to notice that he was exposing himself. I believe that was the expression you used?"

This time Pete got all the way to his feet. He was about to speak when Sarah's eye gave a telltale twinkle.

"I don't know about your experience, Chief McOwat, but it's been mine that some things are more noticeable than others."

With that the police chief seemed to run out of questions.

Either that or he was afraid of the answers.

5

. . . you'll lie like dogs and yet say nothing neither.

Carrie Suggs entered the room. "Mrs. Abrew, your lunch is on."

Sarah rose unsteadily, and Pete hurried across the room, alarmed, but the helping hand was not accepted gracefully. Still, Pete refused to be shook off. As he escorted Sarah to the dining room he could see the chief in his peripheral vision, snapping his notebook shut, heading for the door.

The back one.

Once Pete had Sarah settled at the dining table, Carrie Suggs hovering nearby, he backtracked after him.

Pete could just see him through the trees, on the path to the Indian tower, like a trolley in its old, familiar track. Pete caught up with the chief just as he ducked under the tower doorway and disappeared into the dimness. Pete did likewise. He waited while Willy looked around.

"I guess you know she's still lying," said Willy finally. He pointed to a dark spot at just about head height on the old stone wall. "See that bloodstain? Sutton was up against that wall when he was shot. Look." The chief walked Pete to the wall, pointing, explaining. The pattern of the blood. The nick in the stone where the bullet had met rock. The marks in the ancient mud, marks that the chief said were caused by Sutton's fingernails. What had Sutton been doing, trying to claw his way out? By the time the chief was through, Pete felt sick.

"In short," said Willy, "Sutton wasn't lunging toward his shooter, he was going the other way. He was cowering against the wall, face turned away, when the bullet got him."

"Which means . . ."

"Which means she's lying," said Willy. "And I'd give a lot to know why. Any theories?"

Pete had no theories, but he did have another sudden desire for some air. This time, instead of backing out the door, he swung himself onto the old wooden stairs and took them two at a time to the top of the tower. He walked to the edge of the wall and looked out, first toward Close Harbor. He could see a smattering of boats, the fringe of trees on the far shore, even a fine ribbon of Atlantic ocean beyond. Next he looked down. The ground swam. Other than Sarah Abrew's tiny house and neat lawn, nothing but forest stretched below him. A young girl, alone, on foot, couldn't she be anywhere in there? But surely someone would have reported her missing.

The floor behind Pete groaned as two-hundred-plus pounds of police chief eased onto it.

"I suppose somebody's checked those woods."

Willy nodded. "With dogs from the barracks."

"I don't get it," said Pete. "It's not like Sarah to lie."

"There's one other thing."

Something about the way the police chief said it told Pete he didn't want to hear it.

"I began to wonder about the gun the minute I saw that one neat set of prints there. Sarah obviously wiped it clean, then put it in his hand. But that's not all she wiped."

Pete waited.

"His belt buckle. One of those polished brass military types with the sliding catch. Impossible to undo without leaving some kind of mark."

"And?"

"And there's nothing. The buckle was polished clean. Which makes you wonder whose prints were on it that she didn't want us finding there."

"Hold it."

"Say someone else undid the guy's pants to make it look like he—"

"Wait a minute. Are you trying to tell me Sarah Abrew . . ." Pete stopped.

Willy said nothing.

After a while Pete said, "You'd better find that redhead."

Willy squinted at him.

"I'm telling you," Pete said, "there's no way Sarah Abrew gunned down Webster Sutton in cold blood. At least not without good reason."

"So find me a reason."

"She gave you a reason."

Another squint.

"All right," said Pete. "What now?"

"You're her big chum," said Willy. "Talk to her."

Sarah Abrew sat at the dining room table and watched, or listened, as Carrie Suggs slapped her china around. If she had to be stuck with somebody, why couldn't it be somebody with a little grace, a little panache, not this long collection of bone jarring on sinew? True, it was better than having Joanna here, or Pete here, or Connie here, but this was still danger of another sort. Let Carrie stay around long enough and Sarah would get used to her, would lose the will to go it alone. Still, she couldn't let the woman go yet. She could tell by the tension coming off Pete in waves that it was way too soon.

It had started badly, this morning. She knew it had started badly. For a minute there she'd thought she'd lost. The poor chief. She'd even sensed he'd thought he'd won. Perhaps he still thought he'd won. Oh, well, the worst was over now. What was done was done. What was said was said. Nothing for it but to sit tight and see which way the man would jump.

Carrie Suggs brought Sarah's tea, pulled out the chair across from her, sat down.

"Thank you, dear," said Sarah. "This looks lovely. I'm afraid you're spoiling me." She picked up the sandwich and bit down. Tuna fish. Not her favorite. "Mmm," she said politely.

"I saw you talking to the chief again this morning," said Carrie.

Sarah set down her sandwich. "Go ahead. Ask, why don't you? You want to know if I told him the truth. Well, I told him as much as I could."

"Which is how much?"

"As much as I could without hurting anyone."

"Including you?"

"Yes," snapped Sarah. "Including me. What's your problem, girl? You think you know something I don't?"

Carrie took a bite of her tuna fish, chewed, swallowed, set the sandwich down. "I know they still don't believe you."

Blast this woman. "What did you do, creep around behind them with a tape recorder?"

"I was doing the back bedroom windows when they came out of the woods. They were talking. They didn't see me. They still think you're lying. Both of them. I'm sorry, but I think you should know."

Sarah pushed away her lunch plate. The smell of the tuna was almost making her ill now. "Do you like egg salad? I've always been fond of a nice egg salad. Or cream cheese and olive. On whole wheat. Untoasted. The egg salad on toast, but the cream cheese—"

"Mrs. Abrew," said Carrie. "Peter Bartholomew spoke to me this morning. He's concerned about you staying here alone. He's trying to reach your daughter."

Sarah's heart sank. She should have known. The interfering old . . . No. She couldn't speak ill of him. To his face, certainly, but not behind his back. But it was sure and certain if he once got hold of Joanna and told her what was going on she'd be here camped out for the duration. And that wouldn't do. That wouldn't do at all. Right now Joanna needed to be home.

"Mrs. Abrew," said Carrie again, "I don't think you realize the full extent of what you're doing. Each time you lie to the police chief you're committing a crime. Do you realize what could happen?"

"Certainly I realize what could happen. And I

realize what's not going to happen, too. In addition to that, I also realize what to do. Tell me, Carrie, dear, didn't you mention something about possibly losing your apartment?"

The woman was slow as molasses. She blinked those big, hollow eyes and stared across her food. "I'm two months behind in the rent. I expected to catch up this month and I told the landlord so, but . . ." She stopped.

But, thought Sarah, catching up is easier to say than to do. She'd been there herself a time or two. And it was no way to live, not with a small child to worry about, she knew that, too. And what in tarnation was that little girl's name? Sarah was highly aggravated to realize she couldn't remember. It had been told to her more than once, and not long ago. Oh, well, no matter. Leastways, not right now. "I have a proposition for you, Carrie, dear. At all cost we do not want my daughter hovering around here, or Peter Bartholomew, for that matter. Not now. But they will, one or both of them, unless I do something and do it now. I have one empty room upstairs. You're welcome to it, free of charge. All you have to do is what you've been doing. Hold it together around here. You do that and we'll keep the wolf from the door. Do you think you could manage something like that, child? It won't always be easy. But I believe it would be best all around. I believe we could make a good team, we two."

"You've forgotten Lucy?"

Lucy. That was it, Lucy. "I have not forgotten Lucy. I'm counting on Lucy to liven things up around here. I never had any grandchildren, you know. There are two beds up there. So what about it? Will you come?"

The pause seemed long. "Yes, I'll come," said Carrie finally. "But Mrs. Abrew, there is an easier way for you to keep that wolf away."

"There's always an easier way, but it's seldom as much fun. So. That's all settled, then."

After some time Carrie said, "Yes," and after some more time, almost in a whisper, "Thank you, Mrs. Abrew."

"Maybe you'd best call me Sarah now."

The phone rang. Carrie got up and went into the kitchen. Sarah could hear her answer, just like a maid on one of those PBS shows. "Abrew residence. Yes, she is. One minute, please."

She came around the corner with the phone held out. Sarah took it from her, cleared her throat, said, "Hello?"

"Hello, Mother," said her son-in-law. "How are you?"

Connie could have predicted the Factotum clients that were on her list for the day, all of them from the pound-of-prevention school. The Ameraults, for example. A hurricane off the Bahamas? Beat the rush and get the windows taped now. Preferably by noon. Connie mounted the stepladder and began to cross-hatch the plate glass as Ethel Amerault, a pruny-looking woman who seemed to be worrying herself into a new wrinkle a minute, hovered below.

"Isn't this awful?" she sang out at three-second intervals. "A hurricane on top of everything."

"Everything?" asked Connie finally.

"You know. Everything that's been going on. Webster Two."

And here Connie had been thinking of Webster

Sutton as their own personal little problem, never as anyone else's. Not even as anyone else's news. But on an island as small as Nashtoba, with a year-round population that had yet to reach the four-digit mark, this was big-time news. Hell, for all Connie knew Ethel Amerault was Webster Sutton's sister or cousin or illegitimate daughter. She took a closer look at Ethel. Or mother, even. Whatever, it was too good a chance to lose. "Did you know Webster Two?" she asked.

"Of course. Didn't you?"

"No."

"Now isn't that surprising, you and Pete being in business the way you are. Seems everyone on Nashtoba used either him or his father to keep the books. His father was an accountant, too, you know. Quite the family profession. This one—I mean the dead one, I mean to say the most recently dead one—and his father, and his son was to come in with him soon. What a shame. Although I suppose the son could still come in. Wouldn't he inherit the family half of it now? Or the widow, surely. Makes you wonder what Abby Fitch will say about it, doesn't it?"

"Abby Fitch?"

"The partner. The Fitch in the Sutton-Fitch Financial Services. Now there. They won't have to change the name, will they? If the son, or the widow, gets half, it's still Sutton-Fitch, just the same."

If the son or the widow gets half. The old *who benefits,* thought Connie. But this wasn't a *who benefits* kind of crime. Webster Sutton had tried to sexually assault a young girl, and Sarah Abrew had shot him.

Or so they'd been told.

* * *

"I'm in Bradford on business," said Dennis Willoughby. "I thought I'd run down."

"Now?" said Sarah.

"Now. If you don't mind. I thought I could take you out to dinner, stay overnight—"

"Oh, dear," said Sarah glibly. "I'm afraid there's no room at the inn."

She explained.

Dennis listened. "I see," he said finally. "In that case . . . well, I do have some papers to sign at the bank, so I'll be in town anyway. We'll leave it at dinner, then."

"Joanna's with you?"

A pause. "No, Mother, I'm on my own."

Odd to feel her innards plummet so. She should be grateful that this time, at least, her son-in-law was alone. All right. Buck up, you old goat. Dinner she could manage, she was sure. "Very well," she said. "You come on down."

Dennis said his usual polite good-byes and they hung up the phone.

And when Pete finally returned from his tiptoe through the tulips with the police chief, he, too, was alone.

"Chief packed up and gone home?"

"Yes," said Pete.

One word, but it made Sarah narrow her eyes at him. What had gone on out there that made him sound like he'd swallowed a fish bone? She didn't much care for the way he avoided her eye, either. Best to move on to the subject at hand. She wasted no time telling him about the arrangement with Carrie. She caught the quick flash of surprise in Carrie's direction. Well, the best defense was an offense, or so she'd always been told.

"You talked to Dennis," she accused him. "Business in town, my foot. I swear, if one of the two of us was younger I'd take a belt to you right now."

No good. He still seemed to be focused on the cleaning woman. Was there some secret eye language going on?

"Carrie, why don't you run along now and fetch the rest of your things?"

Sarah watched the woman hesitate, but finally she did what she was told and left the room.

"Poor thing," said Sarah once Carrie was gone. "I didn't want to mention it in front of her, but she's run into a bad patch just now. Can't pay rent. About to be evicted. Things worked out well enough the last two nights, I said why not pack up Lucy and make this your official home for a spell? That way nobody has to worry about me. You can go your merry way, enjoy what's left of that honeymoon."

"I'll be by in the morning, as usual, to read you the paper."

"You think that woman can't read? You come here in the morning and you'll find nothing but a locked door. Now will you go? I'm going to have a houseful soon. I could use some peace and quiet."

And still he stood there.

Sarah dug deep and hauled out every ounce of ornery she owned. "Blast you, will you get gone?"

And he got, too.

6

They are both in either's powers . . .

Pete drove home with the beginnings of a good-sized headache coming on. First, there was what the chief had told him. There was some big piece missing to this puzzle, and the one who had it was Sarah. But she was coming up with some damned fancy footwork in order not to let it go and Pete knew perfectly well she wasn't going to let it go until she was good and ready. Sooner or later, he assumed, she'd start to wear down. Actually, it had seemed to him early this morning that she'd already begun to wear down. For a while there she hadn't looked too good. Later she'd perked up, right after she'd dropped that Suggs bomb. Well, maybe it was a good thing. Who knew? All Pete knew was he'd be having a long talk with Carrie Suggs real soon. And honeymoon or no honeymoon, he'd be checking in on Sarah tomorrow, too.

Honeymoon.

On impulse Pete turned off Shore Road and past Betty's Bud Boutique. As it pulled into view Pete thought, as he had before, how the name was all wrong. The boutique, or florist's shop, was really the smaller part of the operation. Betty ran a good-sized nursery and greenhouse, too. That's where Pete saw them, out back in the nursery, two tall women, one coltish, one plain old horsey, hustling the long rows of plants and shrubs into the shed and out of the tentative storm. The urge to stop was strong. Instead, Pete tooted the horn and drove on. The colt whipped around, raised an arm. The gesture seemed wistful, like a woman who'd been plucked out of her almost-brand-new-husband's arms too soon. Was he reading into things? Probably, but the relief at the sight of her was too strong. He made a quick U-turn.

She met him at the truck window. "Hi. How are things?"

Pete related the status at Sarah's, leaving out a few key things Willy had told him, the ones that had been hardest for him to get down. Once he'd digested it, he'd regurgitate it, hopefully in more palatable form. Instead he zeroed in on the part of the problem as it affected Pete most directly. "Willy thinks Sarah's going to suddenly open up and tell me the whole story. He obviously doesn't know her the way we do. The minute I set foot in the room I could see her working up to a permanent case of lockjaw."

"Sounds like what we need is a fly on the wall."

Pete nodded. "How are things here?"

"You should have married someone younger. Or

hired someone younger. Can you check out Phelps? It's slow going here."

"I'll check out Phelps." He looked behind her for Betty, saw a privacy-inducing rear view, pulled Connie's head through the window, and kissed her. After all, he owed her one.

He must have taken longer than he'd planned. Suddenly, from somewhere behind Connie, came a deep, throaty voice. "Is that how you got this job? Fooling around with the boss?"

"That's how I got it," said Pete.

Betty laughed, straight from the beer belly. "Feel free to apply here anytime. Well, just came to offer my congratulations. Carry on, you two." She began to walk away, but Pete called her back.

"Whoa, Betty. Did you know this Webster Sutton?"

"I take it you're talking about the late departed? Webster Two? Sure I knew him. Even used him to keep my books till he forgot where to keep his hands." She laughed again. "After that he didn't walk so straight for an hour or two. I keep my own books now."

Pete watched her saunter away. She'd take him two rounds out of three any day.

Who did this Webster Sutton think he was, anyway?

Avery Phelps was one of those gentle, brittle men who seemed constantly surrounded by problems. When they didn't come to him naturally, he invented them, but this time, unfortunately for Factotum, he had them naturally. He walked Pete around his house, pointing to a half dozen tall, dead pine trees that angled precariously houseward. "I think they'd better come down, don't you? No sense leaving them for Charlotte to throw through my windows, is there?"

No, there wasn't, but neither did it make any sense to tackle a job like that alone. Without a rope man to guide them, any trees Pete cut would follow their natural path to the ground, and straight into Avery Phelps's windows.

Pete returned home to collect his chain saw and Andy.

Andy wasn't there, but Dennis Willoughby was. Andy was, as usual, late, but Dennis was early. Hadn't he said *noon* on Monday? And there he was, pacing back and forth just inside the office door. Rita sat behind her desk along the wall, on the phone as usual, rolling her eyes as usual, as Dennis wore out the floor.

Dennis must have been deep into his fifties by now, but the changes since Pete had last seen him were minimal—he had sandy hair that absorbed the gray, a blocky body that absorbed the extra pounds, and a round, soft face that absorbed the wrinkles. The only thing that seemed different was the pacing—Dennis was usually the sedentary sort. Pete herded him through the kitchen and out to the screened porch. It looked like a porch rocker might do Dennis some good right about now.

It seemed to. He sank into the chair with a sigh and looked out over the marsh toward the Sound. "I've always envied you this view."

"And I've always envied you your mother-in-law." Dennis shot him an amused glance. "Until now?"

Pete grinned.

"What do you think's gotten into her?"

"Damned if I know. She keeps changing her story. Is Joanna over there now?"

"Joanna couldn't break free just now. That's why I thought I should hurry down. I'm not sure why. I think you know her as well as I do. Better, in fact. I would have said she wasn't a person who would trouble herself to lie. The truth and nothing but the truth and to hell with you if you can't take it neat. What's happened since I spoke to you?"

"Another version, still a lie. At least that's what the chief says." Pete filled Dennis in, but as he had with Connie, he left out a few things. Webster Sutton cringing against the wall when he was shot. That gleaming, polished belt buckle. "When do you expect Joanna?"

"I don't."

Pete looked up, surprised. Joanna Willoughby was a hands-on, or at least a mouth-on, kind of daughter. Any little ripple in Sarah's life and she was right there, at least via phone. "She didn't want to come?"

"I'm sure she would have, if she knew. She's away on business right now."

Joanna's business was as manager of an apartment co-op in Baltimore. As far as Pete knew, it wasn't the kind of job that had ever required travel. Dennis, on the other hand, sold alarm systems and was on the road quite often. But all Pete said was, "Oh."

"The task at hand seems to be to get Sarah to come to her senses," said Dennis now. "With all due modesty, over the years I've been a bit better at that than Joanna. There are a few too many sparks between those two. I thought if I hopped on down and had a nice long talk with her, the whole thing might sort itself out. The only thing that concerns me is that you haven't seemed to be able to accomplish this on your own. You're usually our ace in the hole."

"Maybe I used to be. I guess now we've developed our own sparks. I'm afraid the harder I push, the quieter she'll grow. How long are you staying?"

"I'd planned to stay overnight, but there appears to be no room."

Pete briefly weighed a few things, such as past differences of opinion that had arisen between himself and his then-ex-wife over the matter of suddenly sprung houseguests. He factored in the present extenuating circumstances and further concluded that this houseguest would be more along the lines of some much-needed auxiliary troops. "We have a fold-out couch that you're welcome to if you want to stick around."

"Why, yes, thank you. It would simplify things for tonight, certainly. If all goes well I'll be leaving early in the morning."

Oh, don't worry, thought Pete, it won't go well. But as Dennis stood he said only, "Tally-ho."

Sarah watched with amusement as her ever chivalrous son-in-law lugged Carrie's boxes and bags up the stairs. If these were all Carrie's worldly possessions she had precious few of them, which was just as well. There wasn't much in the way of extra space up there. The old islanders tucked their children under the eaves and punched in a few windows wherever it looked like they needed a little air. The one room in the upper story with its odd nooks and crannies had once been all Joanna's, but now Carrie and her daughter would have to share. Whatever the wisdom of inviting the two veritable strangers into her home, it had already served one useful purpose—Dennis was far too busy right now to pay her much mind.

But the time soon came. The last sorry parcel went up the stairs. Carrie left to fetch Lucy at the bus stop. And Dennis sat down across from her. Strangely, neither of them seemed prepared to speak first.

"I suppose you want to know what happened," she said finally. Best to get on with it. She only hoped it came out the same way twice. For once. Sarah almost chuckled until she looked at her son-in-law again. Even through her murky lenses she thought she could see the signs of some fraying around the edges, and Dennis wasn't the type who visibly frayed. It wasn't until she'd finished her tale and noticed that it didn't seem to phase him as much as it might that she began to wonder about Joanna, wanted to ask about Joanna. But as she unclamped her jaw and worked her throat around her daughter's name it stuck, making her drag in the next breath harshly. This wouldn't do. This wouldn't do at all. She had to stay collected. She tried again. "How is Joanna?"

"Much the same."

Perhaps Sarah would have done better from the first if she'd taken lessons from her son-in-law on how not to answer a question at all.

Pete adjusted his goggles and ripped the cord on the chain saw. Connie leaned on the rope. When Andy had finally trudged through Factotum's door telling tales of woe that included exploding hot water heaters and run-over squirrels, Pete had rethought his original plan, dropped Andy Oatley at Betty's Buds, and collected Connie. One reason for the switch was that he needed to talk to Connie alone. He had things to report, like their unexpected houseguest, her reaction to which might be best observed in private. Another reason was that it was beginning to look like their time alone was going to get scarce. Better to finagle it where they could, even if it wasn't exactly what you'd call quality time. The last reason was Andy. Pete wasn't about to risk one of his own limbs just to give

Andy a chance to further prove himself. Even Pete didn't much like working with chain saws. He checked everything twice—relation of tree to ground, relation of Connie to tree, relation of his own appendages to spinning blade—before he bore down. The triangular wedge on the underside. The final cut on the upper. The teeth-grinding, ripping sound as the dead pine gave up and crashed to earth. He didn't mind taking down dead trees, but whenever he had to take down a live one he felt like a murderer.

Murderer.

Sarah.

And there he was again, stomach lurching away. If Pete cut through the lies, which way would that particular tree fall? He'd told the chief she couldn't have gunned down Webster Sutton in cold blood. And he'd believed it. He was sure he believed it. But why all the lies? What had happened out there? The chief had been able to more accurately reconstruct only the final minutes in that tower, not whatever had led up to them. If he could only track down that girl . . .

"Is this some sort of Zen thing?" asked Connie at his elbow. "You stare at the tree and it rots away on its own?"

"You know, my first wife was a nag, too."

Connie planted a playful fist in his belly. When he could breathe again he moved off down the tree trunk, hacking it into manageable pieces, while Connie tossed the branches into the flatbed. Pete heaved the logs on top to weigh down the branches, and as he worked he went over the facts once more in his head. Fact number one—Webster Sutton was murdered. Fact number two—

But that was the problem. After that there were no more facts.

At least not of the reliable kind.

When Avery Phelps came out to survey their handiwork, Pete asked him the question of the day.

"Did you know Webster Sutton?"

"Not very well," said Avery. "Occasionally our paths would cross, but for the most part I managed to stay out of his way."

"What made you stay out of his way?"

"He was a frightening man."

"Why?"

Avery looked puzzled. "Do you know, I'm not sure. Not sure at all."

The next time Dennis Willoughby appeared, Pete and Connie were at the tail end of some take-out fish and chips for two, but the minute Dennis started talking Pete cleared away the soggy paper plates, sat the man down, and tried to make sense out of him.

"It's Sarah," said Dennis. "Of course it's Sarah, you knew it would be, didn't you? Another lie. A worse one. I don't know what to think anymore. It's just not like her to . . ." He stopped and looked back and forth at them, unraveling before their eyes.

"Not like her to what?" asked Connie.

"Well, lie, I suppose. I don't even know anymore. She's . . . she's different. This evening was different. Did I tell you? We went out to dinner. I did tell you that. What you don't know is . . . She was tired, I could see that, of course, but she seemed to want to go out anyway. And she had a glass of sherry. I think that might have been the final straw. I'd been trying to get her to open up all afternoon and got nothing. It was much as you said, Pete, the old lockjaw. But tonight, her being so tired, and the sherry, when I asked her if she had any idea who that redhead was she said something. I don't know, maybe I've read into this. No, no, I don't think so. No, not at all. I asked about the redhead."

Dennis stopped again, and whereas Pete was just as glad of the breather, Connie was never too good at waiting through a pause. "And?" she demanded.

"This is what Sarah said when I asked about the redhead. She said she had an idea the chief was finally getting around to doubting her existence. That was exactly as she phrased it. *Getting around to doubting her existence.* Then she said that it didn't matter because—and this is where I finally grew concerned—she said it didn't matter because, and I quote, "That redhead is just like God. If she didn't exist . . .'"

Again, Dennis stopped.

"If she didn't exist, what?" said Connie.

"Nothing. That's all she said. That's the point. She said the redhead was just like God, because if she didn't exist . . . And she stopped there. She collected herself. She stopped herself before she could say the rest."

"The rest of what?"

"The rest of the quote. You know it, don't you, Pete? It's in that little book she used to read so often, she lent it to Joanna, I'm sure you've seen it."

"I don't know any quote," said Pete.

"Oh." Dennis looked back and forth between them, perplexed. "Then you don't see my point, do you? I thought you would know the quote. I know Joanna knew it. I remember her mentioning it. She didn't like it."

"What's the quote, Dennis?" Connie again.

"I can only give you the general gist. It says, if I

remember correctly, that if there weren't a God, it would be necessary to invent one. You see?"

It took Pete a minute. But added to the belt buckle, added to the look on Willy's face when Pete had urged him to find the redhead, added to all the rest of it that Sarah had obviously made up, Pete finally saw.

There was no redhead at all. Sarah had invented her. It was necessary to invent her. Because if there were no redhead, if Webster Sutton hadn't been about to assault an innocent schoolgirl, there would have been no excuse for Sarah to gun him down.

7

Do not infest your mind with beating on the strangeness of this business.

Later that night, after Connie had shown Dennis to the fold-out couch in the spare room, she heard him speaking succinctly into the phone, even through the tightly closed door.

"For Joanna, please. Message number three. I am in hopes that you'll be calling soon. Under the circumstances I think you can see why we should chat. For tonight I'm staying at Pete's. The number here is . . ."

Connie listened to her own number being read into the phone. Strange, but not as strange as the rest of it. What she knew of it. And there was more that Pete knew and she didn't, she was sure. One thing she did know was Pete. When he climbed between the sheets she said, "Okay, what?"

"What, what?"

"I don't know. Whatever it is that's making you look like you sat on a lit candle. If I had to guess I'd say it's something about Sarah that you think I don't need to know, but I think you think you need to tell me."

"On a better day I might be able to think those thinks through, but since I can't . . ." and he told her. In plain language. The plain facts. The fact that Webster Sutton had been trying to claw his way out, straight through a two-foot stone wall, when the bullet had caught him in the temple. The fact that his belt buckle had been wiped off, which meant any fingerprints on it probably weren't Sutton's at all. And now they could add to those facts the additional one that Willy had been unable to find the redhead because she probably didn't exist.

"I don't understand," said Connie finally. "Why? Why would Sarah . . ." she stopped.

"That's where I keep stopping," said Pete.

"There has to be some sort of Sarah-Sutton connection. No matter what did or didn't happen."

"True."

"So maybe we should attack from there."

"Find the connection?"

Connie nodded. "But where?"

"I know where I'd like to start. Sutton-Fitch. What do you say? First thing in the morning?"

"All right." At least it was a plan. She rolled into him, groaning as the stiff ligaments twanged. She hadn't done this much physical work in a while and she was sore and tired. She felt warm, callused hands running down her spine, picking out the sore spots, and the next thing she felt was the morning sun in her eyes.

* * *

Either the Sutton-Fitch office building was one of the ugliest on the island or it was the association of ideas. Whichever it was, there was a moment, standing on the doorstep, when Connie was sorry she'd come. She could have said no when Pete had asked the night before, of course. It wasn't like she needed more things to do. But the truth of the matter was, she felt like hanging out with Pete. She supposed she'd gotten into a certain mind-set on Saturday, the two of them alone for a couple of weeks, and now she couldn't let go. But no, it was more than that. It was more like she'd finally come to feel they were a team. They were in things together now. Funny what a simple little pledge made in a ten-by-ten office under a glaring overhead light could do.

So here she was, in front of a garish green lawn that could be claimed by none of Nashtoba's more modest native grasses and a building that looked like it had been beamed down from the nearest strip mall— cement walk, aluminum siding, plate glass, venetian blinds.

When Connie saw that sign on the door that said CLOSED, she perked up, but when she realized she could see shapes moving around behind the blinds like fish in a cloudy aquarium, she knew she was doomed.

"What's the plan?" asked Connie.

"Plan?"

"Ah. So it's up to me again." She hopped out of the truck, marched up to the door, and knocked.

Pete had just caught up to her when an upper-register voice called, "Closed!"

Connie knocked again, harder.

The woman who opened the door was tall, even taller than Connie, which put her over five feet nine, and big-boned, but thin. "Sorry, we're closed." This voice came from the deeper registers, more in the category of hoarse. Smoker's hoarse, guessed Connie, judging by those ropy white clouds in the air.

"This won't take long," said Connie. "You're Abby Fitch?"

Whoever she was, she seemed to dislike looking up. As far as Connie could tell, she hadn't looked at Pete once.

"Yes, I'm Abby Fitch."

Pete stretched a hand across the doorjamb. "Pete Bartholomew. This is Connie. We're friends of Sarah Abrew."

The eyes finally blinked in acknowledgment, not at Pete, but at Sarah's name. The hand that stretched reluctantly to meet Pete's had a slight tremor. The other hand had a cigarette. "I'm sorry," said Abby Fitch again. "But obviously you know what's been going on around here, and equally obviously, I'm sure you can understand why we're closed."

"Understood," said Pete. "Come on, Connie, let's go." He reached for Connie's elbow.

She shook it off. "No. You can't fob off the IRS just because somebody died, you know."

The look on Pete's face was almost too good to miss. The only trouble was, he was going to blow the whole thing if he didn't change it soon. There. He did. Washington-over-cherry-tree was replaced with something more like it's-not-my-fault-I-just-met-her-in-the-street. Not great, but it would do.

"It's Sarah Abrew's quarterly taxes," Connie went on. "They got screwed up somewhere and she thinks it's here. If you could check your records . . ."

A cloud of something other than smoke filmed Abby Fitch's eyes. "Sarah Abrew's records? Here? I don't think so. She must be confused. We don't handle Sarah Abrew's taxes. As far as I know we don't handle anything for her at all." The woman turned and called over her shoulder. "Melissa, will you check to be sure? Sarah Abrew."

A younger woman appeared through the mist. The first thing Connie noticed was the cigarette in *her* hand. The second thing she noticed was that she looked like she was made of smoke herself—white skin, white-blond hair, white sweater, beige jeans. Behind her boss's back she sat on the metal desk, flipped her legs over it, and slid ungracefully into a chair in front of a computer screen. She punched keys, sucked in smoke, exhaled. "Nope. No Abrew."

Connie turned to Pete. "Okay, go ahead. Say I told you so." She turned back to Abby. "He said the account wasn't here. But I said it was too much of a coincidence. A tax problem surfaces two days after she blows the guy's head off—"

"Connie," said Pete sharply.

But Connie kept her eye on Abby Fitch. Pete may have flinched, but the woman certainly hadn't. Connie decided to apologize anyway. "I'm sorry. This thing has got us all crazy. I didn't mean to speak like that about your other half. Or what used to be your other half. So what happens now, you take over the whole enchilada, or does Webster Three come in?"

And there it was.

The flinch at last.

After that, Pete insisted they split up. His nerves couldn't take any more of Connie's creative approaches. While Connie headed for Sarah's, Pete headed for the widow Sutton's, and right up until the

woman opened the door, Pete had actually thought
he'd gotten the better of the deal.

The widow seemed to have glued herself together
with too much of everything—makeup, jewelry,
clothes. She was at least fifty, Pete decided, partly
because if she wasn't, he was getting old.

"Bidwell's?" she asked.

"I don't think so," said Pete. He told her who he
was, and that was as far as he got.

"You take care of that woman, don't you? I've
heard about you. I know why you're here. All right,
come in if you have to."

Pete hesitated. Even he didn't know why he was here.

An eyebrow rose. "Or don't you want to? That's
why you're here, isn't it, to tell me how sorry you are?
You were away, weren't you? You left her all alone.
And she went crazy and shot him. Or is there something else on your mind?"

"Well, no." Pete stepped over the threshold.

"I suppose you'd like me to tell you it's okay. That I
shouldn't mind that she made me a widow."

"Of course not. We're trying to make sense of it,
that's all."

"Make sense of it." The woman's eyes filled with
tears. She pivoted unsteadily on a pair of high heels
and dropped onto an ugly plaid sofa. She motioned to
Pete to sit beside her.

Pete opted instead for an ugly, matching chair. "I'm
sorry," he began again. "It's just that Sarah hasn't
been too clear and we thought it would help if we
could figure out just what happened. Have you known
her long, Mrs. Sutton?"

The woman blotted under each eye with a much-
used tissue. "Mrs. Sutton. Every time I hear that I feel
so old. Please call me Fern."

Fern? Pete mentally added a few more years to her age.

"I didn't know the Abrew woman at all. I didn't know Webster knew her, either, but I'm not surprised. He knew everyone."

"But aren't you surprised that someone like Sarah . . . that an eighty-eight-year-old woman—"

"Why not? They're the looniest of all. I did wonder what he was doing there, but if she was that old, I suppose she couldn't get out, so he'd have to make a house call."

"He didn't exactly call at the house. His car was parked at the old Indian tower. Sarah was out walking when she . . . ran into him."

"And thought he was a burglar? Or a rapist? Isn't that what they do when they start to go odd? I suppose I can't blame her. Or you. All right. There you are. Does that satisfy you, Mr. Bartholomew? Or should I call you Peter?" Fern gave him one of those coy looks that seemed to come automatically to some women, even while the widow's tears flowed.

"Either will do," said Pete. He stood up and was unprepared for the sudden look in her face, like fear, or panic. It wasn't working, all the paint and spray and bows. It wasn't holding her together. It wasn't even camouflaging anything. All it was doing was making him feel uneasy at the idea of leaving her alone.

"Do you live here by yourself?"

Wrong question. If she didn't before, she did now. More tears flowed.

Pete waited miserably and uselessly while Fern mopped up. "My son is staying here temporarily. He should be home soon. He's at the Natural History Museum. He's the new director, did you know? They offered him the job once before, but he was forced to turn it down. He'd gone back to school to get his Ph.D. I was surprised, really, that he took the job this time."

She rambled on.

Pete lingered, and finally he heard the sound of the car in the drive, the quick step on the walk, the door blowing open, and there was Webster Three, his age somewhat obscured for Pete by the fact that he wore a suit and tie. Pete wasn't used to that around here.

"Web, this is Peter Bartholomew," said Fern.

Either the name didn't ring the same bells as it had with the mother or Web didn't much care. He shook Pete's hand and continued through the room. "Got to run. I have a meeting with the wolf man at noon."

He made the announcement with the same eager anticipation Pete might have used to announce a meeting with Ted Williams. Hell, if the kid wasn't going to hold his grieving mother's hand, Pete wasn't about to. He stood up and made his excuses.

It took six of them to get him out the door.

8

~∾~

*No more yet of this; for 't is a chronicle of day
by day, not a relation for a breakfast nor befitting
this first meeting.*

Connie's assignment was to tackle Sarah over the theory of the fabled redhead. She considered several approaches on the ride over, but in the end she decided on the only one she had any hope of pulling off, which was head-on.

She walked into Sarah's house to noise like she'd never heard there before. A vacuum roared from the vicinity of Sarah's bedroom. The television, cranked up to compete, blared with children's voices raised in something that was probably supposed to be song. Connie rounded the corner and stopped cold.

She'd forgotten about the kid. It sat on Sarah's couch curled in a ball, thumb in mouth, huge dark eyes pinned on the TV screen.

"Hello," said Connie.

The kid's thumb came down. Its eyes swung around. "Mommy!" it shrieked, and ran out of the room.

The vacuum shut off.

The child returned with mother in hand.

"Hello," said Connie. "I guess I haven't met your . . ." she stopped. Son? Daughter? Who knew? The jersey and jeans were nonindicative and so was the hair, a cowlick its predominant feature. Something deep inside Connie twisted and turned. Pete's cowlick had probably looked just like that when he was a kid. She could only hope Pete had never looked this pale and forlorn.

Carrie Suggs drew the child from behind her left leg. "Say hello, Lucy. This is Mrs. Abrew's friend, Mrs. Bartholomew."

Lucy. A girl. "Connie," said Connie. "Nice to meet you, Lucy." She held out her hand.

Lucy crept farther behind her mother.

Carrie crossed the room and turned the TV off. "Mrs. Abrew is sitting out back, in the yard. I'll get her for you. Lucy, why don't you go up to your room?"

"No," said Connie hastily. "Don't shuffle yourselves around. I'll find Sarah."

She headed gratefully for the door, turning the TV back on as she went through the room. By the time she found Sarah, sitting in an Adirondack chair in the sun, the vacuuming had resumed. Connie thought of all the things that could happen to the little girl while her mother was lost behind that wall of sound in the other room. There were scissors in Sarah's sewing box on the table. There were matches on the shelf next to the fireplace. There were electrical cords, or she could choke, or fall, or . . . Connie stopped herself. Obviously, she wasn't cut out to be a mother. Sometimes, most times, when she thought about her miscarriage, she was sure that was why it had happened. She hadn't even wanted the baby. Not at first, anyway. Then, almost as soon as she had wanted it, desperately wanted it, it was gone. And if that could happen while you were supposedly safe inside the womb, how did any of them ever survive in the outside world?

Connie kissed Sarah's cheek and sat down on the woodpile.

"What are you doing here?" demanded Sarah. "You think what I tell Pete doesn't go for you? I don't want to see either of you. Or are you inventing something new—the honeymoon for one?"

"That's what I love about coming here, Sarah. I always feel so nice and wanted."

"You should be feeling nice and wanted elsewhere." The eyes narrowed. "Don't you?"

"Yes, as a matter of fact I do. I only came to see you because I was curious what new fable you could cook up now that the sexual assault hasn't flown."

Silence.

"I'm sure I don't know what you mean."

"I'm sure you do. There was no redhead, was there?"

For a minute the old eyes betrayed her by shifting, going dull. Then the spark was back. "Take this message down so you can share it with the others. The police chief. Your husband. My son-in-law, too. I've said all I have to say on this subject. My days of talking are done."

As Connie watched Sarah's jaw set like dock pilings in concrete, she decided this was probably the truest thing the old woman had said so far. So where to now?

Connie didn't have a clue.

Until she crossed back through the living room and heard Carrie Suggs and her vacuum. Hadn't she said it to Pete just yesterday?

It was just what they needed.

A fly on the wall.

Pete spent the rest of the day just missing Connie at every turn. He boarded up cottages, repaired rotten bulkheads, replaced a few boat cleats, checked a few bilge pumps. At the same time, according to Rita's status reports, Connie was taking down summer umbrellas, stowing picnic tables, unclogging drain spouts. Most of it was work they'd have had to do sooner or later for their seasonal customers, Charlotte or no Charlotte, but Pete found the antsy boat owners tiresome. The Clausens, for example, wanted him to haul out their Boston Whaler today, but insisted they'd be back next weekend, weather permitting, for a last bluefish run. If Pete hauled the boat today and Charlotte never showed, he'd have to put it back in on Friday.

Pete finished up at the dock, hopped into the truck, and switched on the radio. ". . . east-southeast of Miami and eight hundred thirty miles south-southeast of Hatteras. It's moving at about fifteen miles an hour now."

"So you'd say it's looking pretty good for the Carolinas?"

"Well, Bob, we can't say for sure, but my money's going on a Hatteras touchdown."

Pete switched it off. Anybody who knew anything would put his money on a Hatteras touchdown. Cape Hatteras was the hurricane goalpost of the East Coast. The question was, after Hatteras, what then? Whatever it did, it wouldn't make it to Nashtoba by tomorrow. Pete decided to leave the Clausens' Whaler till then.

He swung by Factotum on his way to Sarah's, having it in the back of his mind that Connie might be there by now, that she just might want to come along. He found her and Dennis on the porch, drinking Ballantines. His first unreasonable thought was to wonder just exactly how long this had been going on. His second was to get a beer of his own. His third, once he returned to the porch, was to notice how tired and out of sorts they both looked and at that very minute he realized he was, too.

"She's not talking at all now," said Dennis, even before Pete had managed to sink onto the slider. "I don't know what to do with her. We both told her, in effect, that her story didn't hold water and she said, in effect—"

"F you," Connie finished for him.

"But Connie, here, has a thought. About that cleaning woman. That we might enlist her as a spy. If Sarah was off her guard, if none of us were in the room, she might say something to that Suggs woman. If we could get her to lead Sarah subtly onto the subject now and then—"

"Assuming Carrie Suggs does subtle," said Connie. "And we've elected you to talk to her, Pete, you being the most subtle person around."

Pete might have launched into some sort of if-elected-I-will-not-serve routine, but any speechmaking was cut short by the crunch of gravel in the drive.

Nobody moved.

They could hear, all the way around the side of the house, the sound of the knocker they had somewhat optimistically hung on the door. As far as Pete could recall, it was the first time anyone had ever used it. Usually they walked in and yelled.

"Your turn," said Connie.

Pete didn't know how it could possibly be his turn, since it was the first time anyone had ever knocked, but before he could argue the point Connie got up. "Never mind. I need another beer."

Connie returned without the beer but with a woman in tow. She was medium height and maybe ten pounds overweight. She wore some sort of free-flowing printed pants that reminded Pete of an old bedspread and a white embroidered tunic. A wave of blond hair dipped over one side of her face and a pair of sunglasses camouflaged enough of the other side so that Pete had no idea who she was. For a minute Dennis didn't seem to, either. Finally he stood stiffly and moved forward.

"Joanna," he said, and kissed her cheek.

Well, no wonder Pete hadn't recognized her. The last time he'd seen Joanna she'd been in high heels and a suit.

And brunette.

She surveyed the view first, her husband second, lingering over the beer in his hand. "And here I've been feeling sorry for you. All right, much as I'd like to sit down and join you, I suppose I might as well get this over with. Where is she, at home? Or has the chief finally wised up and tossed her in a cell?"

"She's at home," said Dennis. "I'll drive you."

Sarah was caught unprepared. First of all, she was upstairs, which was bad enough. Joanna had forbidden her to use those steep, uneven stairs several years ago. *What if you slipped and fell? You'd* ... Joanna hadn't finished the sentence, but Sarah knew what she'd meant plain enough. *You'd croak.* But Joanna had never been good at saying what she meant. She was good at saying a lot of other things, though.

Like now.

"Who are those people downstairs, Mother?"

"My new boarders. I did it on your advice. You've been after me long enough about living alone."

That took the wind out of her sails. While Joanna swallowed that one, Sarah kept moving. Best to hang on to the momentum once you had it in hand. "You've gone blond this time."

"And you, I hear, have gone completely out of your mind."

Touché. Sarah almost chuckled, but as she reached out for her daughter's hand she felt it pulled away.

"I'll say this one time and one time only, Mother. You'll call the police chief. You'll tell him the truth. Do you understand? I don't know what game it is you're playing, but it is going to end. Now."

Sarah peered at her daughter. Odd that she could look at her own reflection in the mirror and still feel no age at all. It was looking at her daughter that made her feel old. Joanna was fifty-four. *Fifty-four.* "Dennis doesn't look so well," said Sarah now. "Neither do you. Although I must say I like the blond better than that mud you had last time. What is it really, now? Gray, I suppose."

Joanna didn't answer.

Sarah laid the fresh towels she'd brought on the dresser and looked around. She'd tucked the little girl's bed in under the eaves just the way Joanna had liked it when she was a child. Many years ago her husband had built a bookcase in the southwest corner and Sarah was pleased to see that either mother or daughter had already filled the shelves: a few books, a doll, a mangled stuffed dog. Or was it a rabbit?

Sarah pointed around her. "I'm sorry I have no room for you, but I'm sure you understand. It's working out rather well, so far. Carrie cooks and cleans and makes sure I haven't missed any buttons. I know that always aggravates you, when I miss any buttons. And I pay her next to nothing. Just the room and board and a little pocket change, nothing more."

"Do you even know the woman, Mother? Where did you dig her up? She could be robbing you blind for all you know. And that child looks like something out of Oliver Twist. She probably has rickets. If you didn't want to live alone, you know you only had to say so."

And be scooped up and hauled off to Baltimore? No, thank you. "I've known Carrie a long time," Sarah lied. She noticed with some dismay how much easier lying became once you'd practiced it some. "The child will look better once I'm through with her. All she needs is a little stability, maybe a good big bowl of ice cream now and then."

"Ice cream. That's so like you, Mother. You think ice cream fixes everything, don't you?"

"It fixes more than it harms. Which is more than can be said for most of us, wouldn't you say so?"

Joanna crossed the few steps to her old childhood bed and sat down. "I know what you're trying to do, Mother." She was almost whispering now. "You're trying to go back, to do it over. To erase the past. To make it come out better. To have a less defective daughter. Maybe even the grandchild you always wanted. That's it, isn't it, Mother?"

For a minute Sarah thought she might be having a

stroke. First the room seemed small and close and then it seemed to upend itself. She reached out to touch the bureau and things steadied down. "There is nothing defective about my daughter. You're the only one who ever thought so. And you were wrong."

"So that's it, is it? Business as usual. You right, me wrong." Joanna stood. "I'm going to the police station now. Would you like to know what I'm going to tell the chief when I see him?"

Oh, yes, I'd be more than interested in that, thought Sarah, but what she said was, "Not particularly, no."

"I'm going to tell him that if you don't stop this foolishness he has my permission to lock you up." She walked to the door.

"I've got news for you," said Sarah. "The chief doesn't need your permission. And neither do I."

But she added the last part only after she was sure Joanna was gone.

9

How cam'st thou in this pickle?

It was one of those situations—Pete and Connie trapped in the hall while their houseguests argued in the kitchen. While the Willoughbys had gone to see Sarah, Pete and Connie had run out to buy steaks, their usual emergency-company-standby-meal. They hadn't expected to find them back so soon. Neither had they expected to find them arguing. Joanna and Sarah, yes, but Joanna and the ever-phlegmatic Dennis? No.

But there was a definite chill to his tone when he said, "I think it would be extremely ill-advised for you to drive back this evening."

"Oh? In the mood, are you?"

"As a matter of fact, no."

Forget chill, thought Pete. Try frost.

"Then I don't see where this concerns you."

"I'm thinking of you, Joanna. And your mother. The woman is—"

"Crazy. And they're letting her get away with it. What kind of a nitwit is this police chief? And I'd like to know what Pete thinks he's going to accomplish by—"

That was enough for Pete. He reached behind him, opening and shutting the door loudly.

"I don't know about you, but I'm starving," he shouted at Connie.

"Starving," she shouted back.

If that didn't do it, neither would a typhoon. They pushed through the kitchen doorway at the same time, like two of the three stooges, getting caught up in each other's elbows and bags.

Connie finally burst through and giggled idiotically. "Oh, hi! Anyone for steak?"

Dennis rallied quickest. He even almost smiled. "You could talk me into it."

Joanna's back was to them while he spoke. Now she turned. "You might as well know . . ." She stopped, looked at her husband. "Thank you," she said finally. "Steak would be nice. And I do appreciate the room."

At first Pete had naively assumed that if Dennis was the auxiliary troops, Joanna was the long-awaited cavalry. Finally the full complement of aid at hand. He delivered steak and bread and salad to the table along with the background detail on the situation with Sarah. He pulled out his chair and sat, expecting to get some good ideas, or some useful information, or at the very least a little insight into the situation. What he got was one of those silences that was a few Mississippis too long, followed by a soliloquy from Dennis on the possibly pending storm. Pete decided to try a direct question. Did Joanna know of any connection that might have existed between her mother and Webster Sutton Two?

Joanna's answer: What she knew about her mother's relationships could be contained in the bowl of her spoon. To demonstrate, she waved her teaspoon and dropped it on the floor. While Dennis retrieved the spoon, Connie took a turn. Did Joanna have any idea why her mother might have constructed her particular version of the events in the tower?

Joanna shook her head and did some serious mining for olives in her salad. Pete decided it was time to move on. The only trouble was, he couldn't seem to find anything that seemed to interest Joanna. When he asked about her business trip, he got a blank stare from Joanna and a long analysis from Dennis on the companies he was planning to visit on the mainland. When Connie asked about Baltimore, Dennis again took the floor, this time with a detailed description of the new baseball stadium. Joanna's main contribution seemed to be to drink most of the wine and to drop on the floor, in order after the spoon, her napkin, her glasses, two olives, and a red onion ring.

But it was the wine that made Pete most nervous. When she expressed a desire for a beach walk and Dennis didn't appear to have any immediate plans for joining her, Pete got reluctantly to his feet. It was dark out. There was a marsh and a creek to navigate before she ever got as far as the beach. The last thing Pete needed was to wake up tomorrow morning with a half-drowned houseguest on his hands.

Pete followed Joanna out of the room and threaded her silently along the marsh. The sky was starless, moonless, the air restless. He could hear the tattoo of mild surf against the sand. He could also hear in the silence that his presence wasn't much wanted, but he didn't much care. Twice on the way through the marsh he had to catch Joanna's elbow and guide her onto high ground. But once they reached sand she surprised him by sitting down.

"Do you mind?" she asked.

Pete didn't mind. He sat with her. "Sorry there are no stars."

She laughed. "You take responsibility for everything, don't you? Even my mother."

"She's an old friend."

"Ah. Old friends. What would we do without old friends?" She groped around, found Pete's hand, and to Pete's acute embarrassment, gave it a squeeze and didn't let go. "I want you to know that I'm well aware of the long list of things my mother and I owe you. If something happened to me . . ." She stopped, restarted. "I've always known I could count on you for almost anything. But this is above and beyond the call. You don't have to involve yourself in this, Pete."

Tell it to the police chief, thought Pete. "I'm just trying to find out what happened. I can't believe Sarah could have shot that guy. At least not without a good reason. And the reason she gave doesn't add up."

The hand in his began to tremble. She started to let go, hesitated, probed what she'd found. The ring on his third finger.

"Pete. You didn't! When?"

He pulled his hand away, more embarrassed than before. "Saturday."

"Saturday. Really. Pretty casual, aren't you?"

"Well, no." Pete told her where they'd been, why they'd come home.

When he finished, Joanna sighed, loud and long. "I don't know why I bother saying this, because I know you won't listen. But here goes. If I were you I'd get back in that car and get out of here. Leave it alone, Pete. You won't get anywhere with my mother. She lives by her own rules. The gospel according to Sarah. You of all people should know that by now."

"I know." And he did. Sort of. At least sometimes. But he couldn't stop himself from adding, "We've been thinking about drafting that cleaning woman. Using her as a sort of a mole."

Joanna laughed.

After that there didn't seem to be much else to say.

They walked back the way they had come—silently. But this time Pete didn't have to grab Joanna's arm once. She clung to his all the way home.

It had been a late dinner and when Dennis had helped Connie clean up, he excused himself and went upstairs. Connie went up soon after, but lay awake listening for sounds of Pete and their houseguest. After a while she heard them come in, heard Pete show Joanna the bathroom, fish out the towels, point to the closed door of the spare room. She heard them separate—one set of feet going back downstairs, one set into the bathroom. She hoped the bathroom feet were Pete's. Yes, they were. A minute later he slipped into the room, but hovered, listening through a crack in the door.

"What are you doing?"

He shushed her. Connie tossed back the covers and joined him.

"I want to make sure she doesn't go back out," whispered Pete. "She's sloshed."

Connie listened, but heard nothing.

Pete pushed open the door and crept down the stairs. Connie followed. Halfway down Pete flattened against the wall, motioning Connie into the shadows.

She could hear the sound of a phone being dialed, heard Joanna's voice say, "Sam?" Then at regular intervals, "Yes. No. Awful. Yes. Asleep upstairs. Yes. I'll see you tomorrow. No. First thing. Yes. Good-bye." She heard the phone go down.

They scurried back upstairs, into their room, under the sheets.

"You know—" Connie began, but Pete shushed her again.

"What was that?"

"It's just Dennis walking around in the next room."

"Oh." Pete subsided into the pillows. Connie slid into his arms, or she started to slide into them, but he bolted upright again. "What was *that?*"

"The radio. Joanna must be in the kitchen, still. Come on, will you?" But even Connie couldn't help it now. They lay there listening to the noises that meant they weren't alone anymore. First kitchen noises. Then door-across-the-hall noises. Then feet-on-stairs noises. Finally, two low voices coming from down-stairs.

"He's down there," Pete whispered. "Good." He rolled toward Connie and they had just interlocked flesh with flesh when they heard the crash, followed by tears.

They debated, and waited, and in the end remained in their room, listening to more sounds. Muffled tears on the stairwell. Bathroom noises. The spare room door opening, closing. The second tier of sounds came from below. The squeaky closet door, which meant the dustpan and broom had been found. The tinkle of glass, the bang of dustpan against trash can, and finally more feet on stairs. The spare room door opened and closed again, but the low murmur of voices with an occasional anguished high note went on and on. Pete fell asleep first. Connie felt him go limp next to her. Sometime long after that, but not so long before dawn, she drifted off.

Rita Peck surveyed the list in front of her with dismay. It seemed to grow by two items every time she crossed one off. And that was only the list on paper. The one inside her head wasn't getting any lighter, either. True, she'd finally managed to reach Maxine the night before during a rare lull in what seemed to be a nonstop social whirl. The conversation had run true to form. Rita: *How are those courses coming?* Maxine: *Mom. Come on.* Rita: *Are you coming home this weekend?* Maxine: *Oh, please. Home?*

And then there was the matter of Evan Spender. What were the two of them doing? Rita had no idea. Where was it all going? No clue there, either. And Rita wasn't the type to just drift along. Obviously Evan was, though.

Rita decided to abandon the mental list and return to the paper one in front of her. Honestly, sometimes she felt like the triage nurse in the hospital emergency room. All right, clearly the Wetherells' gutters and the Clausens' boat took priority over the rest of the list, but who to handle which? Considering that Pete and Connie were supposedly on their honeymoon, maybe she should have them do the boat trip. At least that way they'd drive to the Clausens' together, Pete would make the boat run, Connie would meet him at the landing with the trailer, and they'd drive back together. But that left Andy doing gutters. Bad idea. It was usually better to have Andy behind a wheel than on a ladder. And although Rita would never say it out loud, it was her personal opinion that it was always better to have Connie anywhere than behind a wheel. And with Pete in the passenger seat? No, therein did not lie the makings of a happy honeymoon.

When Pete appeared to inform her that he was once again off to Sarah Abrew's and that judging by the pummeling he'd gotten in the night from a restless Connie she might not be appearing anytime soon, Rita adjusted her time frames accordingly and moved on to other, weightier things, such as whether a woman rapidly approaching her fifties could drift forever from affair to affair, and what the odds were on her ever hearing voluntarily from her daughter again.

When Connie struggled downstairs, Pete, Dennis, and Joanna were all gone. On the kitchen table were two antique champagne flutes filled with fresh strawberries and a bottle of Dom Perignon. There were also two notes. The first one was tucked under one of the flutes:

With much love and all our best wishes for future happiness. I've decided to take my own advice and am leaving this morning. Dennis is staying in Bradford a few more days and can be reached at the phone below.

J.W.

P.S. Sorry, but I broke a glass—it must be old age— I've gone all thumbs.

The second note was from Pete:

Gone to recruit our spy. If not back by noon, report to CIA. I love you.

P.

Connie tacked the first note with Dennis's phone number to the bulletin board above the phone. She folded up the second and put it in the pocket of her jeans, to draw on later as needed. The three little words at the end weren't ones Pete was prone to throwing around.

When Pete pulled into Sarah's, Lucy Suggs was perched on the stoop. As he approached the door she made ready to bolt, but when he spoke she paused in midflight. "Do I need a password?"

Big, dark eyes, a mix of several colors, peered back at him, but the mouth stayed closed.

"When I was a kid I used to hide behind a bush outside my front door and make everybody tell me the password or they couldn't go in. Know what it was?"

No response, at least not in words, but Pete felt a peculiar tug from those eyes. "I'll give you a hint. It was something to eat."

They were interrupted by the appearance of Carrie Suggs at the door. She saw Pete and said, "Oh, it's you."

Not exactly the welcome of his dreams. Still, when he asked, "Got a minute?" she stepped outside fast enough. They walked as far as Pete's truck, out of earshot, but still within visual range of the child on the stoop.

"How's Sarah?" Pete asked.

"Her daughter was here again this morning. They argued. Sarah says they always argue. Is that true? They don't get along?"

"They might not always get along," said Pete carefully, "but it's not because they don't care. I think it's more a problem of caring too much. They each seem to think they know what's best for the other one."

"The daughter acts like her mother is doing this to hurt her. She isn't doing this to hurt anybody."

So Carrie wasn't a mindless drudge. So far, so good. Pete decided to run with it. "Any theories on why she is doing all this?"

Carrie looked toward the house. "She must think she's helping somebody."

"Well, it doesn't seem to be helping Sarah any, does it?"

A pause. A nod.

"I'd like to clear this mess up, but the problem is none of us can get her to talk. Maybe you could help."

The large, dark eyes, much like her daughter's, clicked back and forth over Pete's face as he spoke, as if she were looking for a loophole in there somewhere. "How?"

"By looking. By listening. There has to be something to connect Sarah to Webster Sutton. We thought it might be something financial, but we checked at the office and they have no record of her in the computer files. We've been wondering if she might have talked about him to you."

Again Carrie looked off.

"I don't want you to violate any confidences," Pete went on. "I'm only thinking she might say something in front of you without noticing, something you could pass along."

Still no answer. Pete was starting to see where the daughter got it from. "The chief isn't going to hang fire forever," he continued. "He'll have to do something soon and I'm worried about Sarah when he does it. She's . . ." He stopped. He wanted to say something about how special she was to him, but he was afraid it would sound dumb. "She's old," he finished lamely.

"She's old, but she isn't senile. She seems convinced she knows what she's doing."

"Maybe she does. But I'd feel a hell of a lot better if *I* knew what she was doing."

Since Carrie didn't look like she counted that as much of a reason, Pete decided to tell her the rest of it, the part that he hadn't even admitted to himself, at least not completely. "Look, sooner or later the chief's going to get to the bottom of this. I don't know what Sarah did and I don't know why she did it, but whatever she did, it's something that could get her into trouble. I need to find out what it is before the chief does, that's all. I know the two of them better than they know each other. Maybe once I know what went on, I can . . ." He stopped again. What could he do? Maybe Joanna was right. Maybe the best thing he could do was to leave it alone. Pete pushed himself away from the truck. "I guess I'm not making much sense. And I guess I'm not being too fair to you. You work for Sarah, live with her now. You don't owe us anything. Forget it. I'll go bug Sarah and leave you alone."

He walked toward the house. Lucy was nowhere to be seen. He bent down. Sure enough, there was a dusty sneaker protruding from under the yew bush. He lingered on the stoop to do the necessary out-loud wondering where Lucy might have gone. Carrie Suggs passed them without a word and went in.

As Pete reached for the door, a small voice piped out of the bush. "Spaghetti!"

"Sorry," said Pete. "Better luck next time."

Lucy scrambled onto the stoop. It seemed like a major concession, so Pete cast around for something to keep the momentum alive.

"How old are you, Lucy?"

"Five."

"Five. Do you go to school?"

"Kindergarten. In the afternoons."

"Oh."

Apparently the response was less than expected.

"Next year I go all day."

"All day? Wow."

That was more like it. Lucy beamed.

Carrie reappeared. "Lucy, you're covered in dirt. Go inside and change your clothes. Now."

Whatever inroads Pete might have made seemed to disappear. Lucy cast him a baleful look and went inside, banging the door.

"My fault," said Pete. "I—"

"Look," said Carrie so intensely Pete thought for a minute he was about to get sent to his room. "I used to clean those offices at Sutton-Fitch. The computers are new. They kept the files for the older accounts in storage boxes in the back room. I'm not saying you'll find a connection. I'm just saying you might have given up too soon."

She disappeared after her daughter so quickly Pete decided she was going to be a natural at this spy game. The question was, was Pete? What would a good old-fashioned, self-respecting spy do now? Probably go directly to Sutton-Fitch to follow up the lead.

Either that or phone somebody from his shoe.

10

_~~~~_

*. . . the truth you speak doth lack some gentleness
and time to speak it in. You rub the sore, when
you should bring the plaster.*

Pete ducked inside just long enough to make a mad
rush through the newspaper with Sarah. Now that he
had his spy in place he decided to leave all extraneous
conversation alone, but even so, when he checked his
watch as he left he realized there still wasn't enough
time to stop by Sutton-Fitch to check the old files
before his rendezvous with Andy.

When Pete got in the truck he turned on the radio.
Charlotte now boasted a sustained wind of one hundred and four miles per hour, a category-two storm.
Still honed on the East Coast, but plenty of time to
turn. Pete checked his watch again, decided to swing
by the Wetherells' on the way home.

Or sort of on the way home.

He found Connie where he'd expected to find her—

eight feet in the air. Her face lit up when she saw him, but she didn't stop what she was doing—she must have heard the radio, too. She continued to shower the ground with soggy black oak leaves and pine needles as Pete told her about the old files in the Sutton-Fitch back room.

"And great ideas on how to get a look at them?"

"Sure. Walk in and ask."

"Good," said Pete. "Let me know how you do."

Ten o'clock and Sarah Abrew had already had a good, long day. First it was Joanna. Short but sweet. Or not so sweet, but short enough, a kind of reprise of the day before. Then it was one of her more ludicrous conversations to date with Carrie. Honestly, that woman was beginning to try her some. Next, Pete. She'd been about to throw him out until she noticed he seemed to be in some sort of rush all his own. But he insisted on reading her the paper—two paragraphs of news and six pages on the weather—before he tore off. She hardly had time to wonder what he was up to when Dennis strolled into the room. What in the blue blazes? From what Joanna had said she'd expected him to be long gone.

But Dennis was the worst of the lot and then some. He sat on the couch and crossed his legs at the knees, like he planned to sit there some time. Not a good sign. Where the devil was that young woman when she needed her? Even the child might do. "Did you see Carrie on your way in?" she asked.

"Yes, as a matter of fact, I did. She said she had to give her daughter a bath before school."

Blast and damn. Well, if he thought she was going to say one more word about Webster Sutton he was wrong.

But what he said was, "We need to talk about Joanna, Mother."

Which was worse. Far worse. "Joanna and I had a nice long visit this morning," said Sarah hurriedly. "Don't you worry, everything's fine."

"She was here this morning?"

And why in tarnation should that surprise him? Didn't they even talk anymore?

"She was here for a good long while. Everything's fine. She's fine. I'm fine, too. I have Carrie to attend to things now. Why don't you two run along home?"

"Everything isn't fine, Mother. You aren't, and Joanna isn't. As I think you know."

Sarah closed her eyes. Of course Joanna was fine. She'd always been fine. And if she wasn't fine right at this particular point in time, she would be soon.

"I've tried to talk to you about this before," said Dennis. "You know how I feel. You know I would do, have done, whatever I could do. It's just not enough anymore. It hasn't been for some time."

Sarah opened her eyes. "Every life has its rough spots. We ride them out. We move on."

"And what about those who can't?"

"We help them."

"Do we, Mother?"

Sarah closed her eyes again. "We try." Then a funny thing happened. She heard Dennis's voice speaking to her as if from a distance. She heard the sounds of other strangers in her house—the protests of a small child not wanting her hair washed, the answering admonishments of a diligent young mother—and Sarah seemed to lose track of time. Or, more accurately, she seemed to mix up the usual direction in which it traveled. She was going back and back. She was getting younger and younger. Joanna was getting younger and younger. Sarah's husband Arthur was still alive. Her house was full again, not with strangers but with her family. None of the ugliness had ever happened. There was no murder in the Indian tower. There were no evil men in their lives. There was, in fact, no Dennis Willoughby.

And when Sarah opened her eyes, Dennis was gone.

Pete collected Andy at Factotum, swung onto Shore Road and off it again soon after, between the painted white pillars that marked the driveway to the Clausen house. He kept going until the scrub pines shrank from a lofty forty feet down to twenty. He turned left off tar and onto gravel, and when the scrub disappeared entirely and Pete could see nothing ahead but beach plum, bayberry, blue sky, and bluer water, he turned right off gravel onto dirt. He pulled to a stop in back of the Clausens' boat barn, a weathered saltbox-shaped structure that sat on pilings twenty feet from the sand. He opened the side doors and pulled the trailer out first, hitching it to the truck himself. That way he could be sure it would arrive at the landing still attached. He handed Andy the keys to his truck with only a mild sense of foreboding, and watched him rattle out of sight.

Pete returned to the boat barn. He found the dinghy where he'd left it last spring. As a matter of fact, it looked to be exactly where he'd left it last spring. Had they even used the boat all summer? Probably not. He collected the gas can, set the oarlocks, tossed in the oars. He hauled the boat over the sand path, across the beach, and down to the edge of the water, wishing he'd thought to throw in his fishing rod. There was no greater crime on the island of Nashtoba than to happen rodless on a bunch of birds working.

Pete took off his sneakers and tossed them in the dinghy. He cuffed his jeans, pushed the dinghy out and hopped in. The water was dead calm and September warm. It was the air that was off. Muggy. Oppressive. If it hadn't been for that bunch of edgy geese off to the east it might have been early August, not late September. Pete put his back into the oars and the little boat skipped over the motionless water. He pulled up on the lee side of the Clausens' Boston Whaler, tied off, and climbed aboard. First pull and the engine roared. Pete pointed the bow due north, turned, and saw the dinghy bobbing along just fine in his wake. He swung in a gentle arc north-northwest, toward Andy and the landing. He wasn't five minutes out when the first tern took a dive and rose with sand eel in beak.

Pete groaned. Birds working baitfish and the blues couldn't be far behind.

The Wetherells' gutters hadn't been cleaned in twenty-three years. The reason Connie knew that was because the bird's nest that filled the top of the drainpipe contained a piece of the sports page describing the pain and agony of the '75 World Series. It also contained three feet of string, a bushel of twigs, and the same mud that must have been used to build the pueblos. First Connie tried to dig it out. Then she tried to knock it through. Then she broke her trowel. She threw the broken tool on the ground in disgust, climbed down from the ladder, got in her car, and headed for Beston's Hardware Store.

Beston's may have started out as a hardware store, but these days it seemed to specialize more in Coke, candy, newspapers, and Nashtoba's more unambitious residents. Three of them greeted Connie from the porch bench as she trudged up the steps covered in sweat and grime.

"Well, well, well," said Bert Barker. "Mud-wrestling again? Wish you'd call me next time."

"I would if you weren't so overworked," said Connie.

Ed Healey seemed to think that was pretty funny, even though the only thing overworked on Ed was his belt buckle. Worse yet, Connie's encouragement seemed to have sent Bert's imagination into overtime. His eyes snaked over Connie's flesh—first up, then down. He was on his way back up again by the time she pushed past them and went inside.

She found the trowels right where she'd have expected George Beston to put them—in the middle of the tulip bulbs. She selected one with a long, thin blade and a good thick handle and turned just in time to almost castrate Evan Spender.

Evan was, at sixty, the youngest and only working member of the porch brigade, the word *working,* of course, being a relative term. Whenever there was nobody or nothing to talk about on the bench in front of the store, Evan strolled off for an hour or two. First he'd pay a visit to his lady friend, Rita Peck. Second, he'd stop off at Mable's Donut Shop for a cup of coffee. Third, and only as a last resort, he'd do what the phone company paid him to do—repair a few phone lines. Right now he seemed bent on cornering Connie among the tulip bulbs, away from the prying eyes and ears of his fellow porch sitters. "How's she faring?" he asked.

"Who?"

"Sarah. Sarah Abrew. Not surprised he got it. Just a mite surprised Sarah did it, is all."

"Why aren't you surprised he got it?"

"No particular reason. Heard a few things, is all."

Connie settled in more comfortably against the bin of bulbs. She was used to pulling teeth with Evan by now. "Like what have you heard?"

"Oh, the wife, for one. Thought he spent too much time at the office."

"Are you saying Webster Sutton had an affair with one of his co-workers?"

Evan raised his hands. If it weren't for the steel-blue twinkle in his eye, Connie might have thought she'd shocked his socks off. "That was the wife's idea, not mine. Fixed her phone about a month ago, talked a minute or two."

Or an hour or two. And why did Connie suddenly find herself wondering, not about the murdered Sutton, but about the Widow Sutton and Evan? She'd always thought there was something about Evan, a hint of having been around the block and then some. And there was also something about his physical cragginess, all weathered sinew and bone. . . .

It was as if he'd read her mind. "By the way, aren't some congratulations due?" He leaned toward her, but slowly, so she could back off if she had a mind. Strictly out of curiosity, Connie decided to stand her ground. Gentle lips brushed expertly and were gone, filling Connie with some interesting new ideas about Rita's evenings at home. But it also reinforced her previously held notion about Evan and the widow. What the hell? Why not take the leap and see where she'd land?

"Were you and Fern Sutton friendly?" she asked.

She'd never been any good at feigning things, especially not innocence, and she was no good now.

Evan's eyes glittered with amusement. "Not in the way you mean. Could be you're forgetting my interest lies elsewhere now."

"No, I'm not forgetting," said Connie, duly chastened. "I guess I was just thinking about Fern. Sometimes the suspicious one is the one with something to hide."

"True. But I'd say no. Not her. What she's looking for is more like reassurance."

"Reassurance?"

"Making sure we stray men still take notice. If you ask me, what that means is the fellow who should be taking notice isn't, that's all."

Pete had just pulled around the point when he happened to look behind him to check on the dinghy. That was when he saw the big Chris-Craft trailing smoke. Or was that smoke? No, not smoke, ashes. Webster Sutton's ashes. That was Web Three at the rail with the box in his hand. Pete scanned the Chris-Craft looking for Fern, but just then Web Three's eyes swung his way and Pete turned around. He was fairly well obscured behind the point, but now that he'd determined there was no need to launch a rescue, there was no need to invade anyone's privacy, that was for sure.

Pete and the Whaler puttered toward shore. Sure enough, there was Andy in Pete's truck, backing the Clausens' trailer neatly onto the landing ramp. No, wait. *There* was Andy, standing on the rocks, not sitting in the truck; there was no mistaking that shock of surfer-blond hair. Pete hollered. Andy waved back. Pete hollered again, pointing frantically at the truck as it descended slowly down the boat ramp on its own. Finally Andy caught on. He broke into a sprint and reached the truck just as the tailgate went under.

Maybe it was the sight of his truck getting deep-sixed. Maybe it was the ominous stillness in the air. Maybe it was the specter of Sutton's ashes wafting over the water. Whatever the reason, that bodiless sense of foreboding that had hounded Pete since the chief's first phone call suddenly took form.

11

Work you, then.

After what Evan Spender had told her, Connie didn't mind so much Pete sticking her with the second trip to Sutton's office. Not that she'd much minded in the first place. Connie had been working for Pete long before she'd ever married the guy. Either time. As a matter of fact, he'd hired her back before he'd taken her back. Working together had never been one of their myriad problems, then or now. Maybe it was because they'd always had Rita in between. But probably the main reason the whole thing worked out was because Pete was . . . well, Pete. Over the years Connie had found little enough to complain about in her boss. There was usually method to Pete's madness, and if he asked her to do something not fun, it usually meant he'd kept something even less fun for himself.

But Connie found herself struggling to remember that now as she headed for the Sutton-Fitch offices, hastily scrubbed and changed, and caught a glimpse of Pete skimming over the mirrored surface of the Sound with the throttle of Clausens' Whaler wide open.

She had to struggle again when the door to the Sutton-Fitch office was opened and she gagged on cigarette smoke. And again when the woman who answered the door raked her up and down the way Bert Barker had done and shot her a much less appreciative look—more like, *So whose bimbo are you?*

Naturally, Connie didn't take to her right off. It wasn't Connie's fault that she'd been born a couple of decades after the woman in the door, or that she had these breasts, or that she went streaky-blond in September from the months in the sun.

The two women glared.

Finally Abby Fitch saw them and rushed across the room. "I'll handle this, Fern."

So that was the widow Sutton. Connie watched the two women together, Evan's words fresh in her mind, but she saw nothing like the knee-jerk resentment Connie had undergone the moment before. Maybe that was how Sutton got away with it, thought Connie, because Abby Fitch didn't look the part.

Or act it.

"May I help you?" asked Abby, all business.

Connie stepped into the room. "I hope so. It dawned on me yesterday after we left here. You were right, Sarah Abrew's current financial affairs are handled elsewhere. But she seems to think at one time she did some business with you. It must have predated your computer system. Do you keep old records?"

"We keep all our records. What exactly is it she needs to know?"

Good question, thought Connie. "It's hard to say. She's confused, as we said before. Maybe if I could see her old file . . ."

But Abby Fitch was already shaking her head no. "If Mrs. Abrew would like to come in, we'll go over it with her. I'm sure you understand I can't discuss her account with anyone but her."

"You've got a file on her, though? I'd hate to drag her all the way down here if you don't. She's pretty frail. And she doesn't have a clue where things are."

And she'd skewer Connie on that cane of hers if she could hear her now.

Abby Fitch went to the door of the back room and called. "Melissa?"

An unprofessional "What?" wafted back through the air.

"Could I see you, please?"

The smoky waif appeared. "Check the boxes for an old file, would you, please? Abrew. Sarah."

Melissa retreated for the back door and Connie fell in behind her.

No go. Abby Fitch picked her off with a hand on her elbow. "You can wait out here."

Connie didn't have much choice. She turned around. By now Fern Sutton had plopped down behind one of the desks, probably Abby's, judging by the look on Abby's face, and was fiddling with the computer. Abby rushed across the room.

"Is there something I can find for you, Fern?"

"No, thank you. Just poking. I'll have to get familiar with things around here soon. By the way, didn't my husband tell me there was a brand-new no-smoking policy in here?"

Abby Fitch had just grappled a cigarette pack out of her jacket pocket. She let it fall back in. She also let fall one of those looks that kill.

Connie decided to develop a nervous habit of her own. She began to pace, taking a route that brought her across the open door to the back room every minute or so. The first thing she saw was Melissa sitting cross-legged on the floor, upending a box of files, which also upended the files themselves, and spewed printed matter in a wide fan in front of her. The next time Connie cruised by, she saw Melissa shoving papers back in files, without much concern for what belong where. It wasn't long before this lack of virtue was rewarded. Melissa came through the door, file in hand. Connie held out hers. Unbelievably, Melissa dropped the file into it. Connie flipped it open. She had time to see the top sheet, Sarah's name and a short list of assets—treasury notes, insurance policies, a couple of bonds—before it was ripped from her hands.

"Thank you, Melissa," said Abby. She glanced through the file and closed it. "Yes, this is hers, but some years old. If you'd like to make an appointment for Mrs. Abrew to discuss its contents—"

The phone rang. Melissa, who was sitting right in front of it, didn't move.

Abby cast an edgy glance at Fern Sutton. "Melissa? Would you get the phone, please?"

Melissa snatched it up. "Hello."

Fern's head swiveled toward Abby. "Is that how you taught her to answer the phone? *Hello?*"

"She usually does better," said Abby. "She's a bit off this week. I'm sure you know how it's been."

Fern didn't look too happy to hear that, somehow. Connie decided to retreat before the smoke alarm went off, from whatever cause. She walked to the front door, opened it, stepped through, and yelped as a man sprang at her out of the bushes. Okay, maybe he didn't exactly spring, but he did appear suddenly out of the foliage, so suddenly Connie didn't recognize him right off.

"What the hell are you doing?" she said once she'd collected her breath.

"Checking the windows," said the police chief. "And you?"

"Checking the files. Did you know Sarah Abrew had one here?"

She couldn't tell if the squint meant yes or no.

"It's in one of those boxes in the back room, but they won't let me see it. What are you checking the windows for?"

"I've been called to investigate a burglary. You didn't *take* any files, did you?"

"Of course not," said Connie, more indignantly than she might have if the thought hadn't crossed her mind a while ago.

"Or cash?"

"No. What do you think I am?"

"I'm not sure. You and the bridegroom will be home tonight?"

"Yes," said Connie. And there went tonight's plans. She'd been thinking along the lines of an early dinner out, getting to bed while they were still both conscious for once. . . . For the second time that day, some man seemed to read her mind.

"Or maybe you'd prefer I wait till morning."

Connie was mortified to feel herself blush as if she were a . . . well, a bride. "No," she said primly. "Tonight will do."

Sarah Abrew watched absentmindedly as the little girl pushed the checkers willy-nilly around the board. She was having some trouble getting the most recent tell-the-truth chat with Carrie off her mind. The blasted woman just wouldn't let go. Seems Sarah had been right to suspect Pete's sudden disinterest in the subject of Webster Sutton. Seems underneath he was even more fired up and raring to go, determined to get to the bottom of things. And, he was bound to, before long. So Sarah had managed a last-second diverting maneuver, but that wouldn't last him long. Obviously, something more was going to have to be done. Instead of forcing Pete away, giving him nothing to do but fuss and fume, perhaps she'd be best advised to keep him under her thumb. Busy him up. Give him less time to scheme. But what excuse could she use?

As if on cue the music stopped and the radio announcer, Jeff—or was it Bob?—came on, his voice full of that hushed anticipation that cropped up before every piddling little storm. "And what's the current position on Charlotte, Jeff?"

"Still well to the south-southeast of Hatteras, moving northwest at approximately thirty miles an hour, Bob."

Of course, thought Sarah. The storm. "Excuse me, child. I have to use the phone. And what kind of move was that? What color are you on?"

Lucy examined the board. The light dawned. She retreated from red to black. Clever girl. Sarah patted her head as she stood up. "Mind where you go, I'm going to whip you when I return."

"Will not," said Lucy.

Ah, thought Sarah, at last a little spunk. Do her good to get stirred up some. The child was far too quiet. Her Joanna, now . . .

Sarah pushed the thought of Joanna away and moved to the phone. Rita sounded a mite flustered to hear her voice. Sarah played it up some. Confused on what day it was. Worried about this storm. Her roof always leaked when the rain came from the south and she had some boxes in the attic that she needed moved. Heavy ones. Pete should come himself. And soon.

He arrived just as Lucy got home from school. Spent some time in some silliness with the child about food—meatballs, hot dogs, popcorn. Sarah couldn't make hide nor hair of it, but the end result was he got Lucy giggling, and it was the first giggling Sarah had heard since the child had come. She wondered, not for the first time, if Pete and Connie would try again to have one of their own. She'd like to live to see that. At least on good days she thought she might. There were other days when she was convinced it would kill them all.

"What's this about a leaking roof?" asked Pete now. "I thought I fixed that last year."

"I thought so, too. Appears we were both wrong. It's the southwest corner that leaks and that's where it'll come if we do get this storm. I want all those boxes moved down here. Think you can handle it alone?"

"If I can't, I'll call on Lucy, here."

"Peppermint-stick ice cream!" shrieked Lucy.

"Nope," said Pete. "But you're getting warm."

Sarah's attic wasn't much of one—a door in the upstairs bedroom wall that gave access to a triangle of space under the eaves that no human could straighten up in. Directly in front of the door, where the ceiling was highest, were the neatly labeled cardboard boxes. In the far reaches Pete spied a bunch of flower pots, a croquet set with no wickets, paint cans that looked like they'd last been opened before the war, an old badminton set. He should definitely bring the badminton downstairs—Lucy might like a game later on. Or was she too young? Pete knew nothing about five-year-olds. Suddenly his thoughts drifted to Connie and he felt the pucker in his brows. He'd watched her, swallowing birth control pills by the handful, or so it seemed to him. He had his doubts she was going to want to try again anytime soon, if at all. And a funny thing had happened to him back when he'd thought he was going to be a father. He'd gotten used to the idea. But it was an idea that could lose its appeal soon, he knew. He was working with a small window of energy that was already dwindling these days around three or four in the afternoon.

Pete roused himself to the task at hand. The boxes. Downstairs. But again he found himself skipping over the cartons labeled "hooking supplies," "Aida's china," "jelly jars," et cetera, latching on to one that said, "Joanna's books." Lucy could use some children's books, he was sure. He pulled the carton into the middle of the floor.

Wrong era. The box was full of high school textbooks, even Joanna's high school diploma from St.

Mary's School. But here was something of interest to Pete, anyway—a yearbook from his own alma mater, Nashtoba High School, sixteen years before his own not-so-glory days. Pete flipped it open. It seemed only the kids themselves had changed. There was a barely recognizable Joanna Abrew in teased hair and pearls among the seniors on page three.

And Webster Sutton Two among the juniors on page five.

12

—ɷɷɷ—

'T is far off and rather like a dream . . .

Pete brought the box and the badminton downstairs. He was disappointed, and surprised he was disappointed, to find Lucy was nowhere to be seen. He fished out the yearbook, knelt beside Sarah's chair, and flipped it open to Joanna's picture. "Look who I found."

Sarah looked and said nothing. Pete wondered how much of the smiling, vibrant teenager she could actually see. "It's Joanna's yearbook," he said. "I was looking in the box for some books for Lucy and I decided to check out the old school. It's a good picture."

"Yes," said Sarah.

"But what is she doing in here? I thought I saw a diploma from St. Mary's School."

It seemed to take Sarah a while to remember. "She changed schools," she said finally, but her voice was so low Pete could hardly hear.

"She what? She transferred? Then why is she in this yearbook?"

"It was during her senior year. The pictures had already been taken. They forgot to remove hers." After a minute Sarah added, "That's all. Put it away."

Pete turned more pages. "And Webster Sutton was a junior that year."

"Was he?" But she sounded vague, far away.

"Joanna must have known him then. It's a small school."

"Yes, it is." Vaguer still.

Pete looked at the date on the yearbook, even more puzzled now. Joanna's diploma from St. Mary's had been dated a year later than the book in his hand. He decided to try one more rash of questions, raising his voice slightly to try to bring Sarah out of her fog, back to the here and now.

"Why did Joanna switch schools so late? It looks like she had to repeat her whole senior year. And why St. Mary's?" Pete couldn't see Sarah emphasizing religious instruction. She was more from the agnostic school. St. Mary's made no sense. No sense at all.

Neither did Sarah's sudden rage. She reached out and knocked the yearbook closed. "Why in the blue blazes does everyone want to talk about Joanna? Did I call you here to bother me about Joanna?"

Her voice was loud enough to bring the Suggs family into the room. Who knew where the conversation might have gone next if Lucy hadn't spied the badminton.

The next thing Pete knew, he was racing around under Sarah's clothesline, knocking ancient dust and feathers everywhere. Eventually Lucy's squeals brought her mother to the door, but she must have been able to tell a good squeal from a bad one. She watched them for a while, just long enough, Pete figured, to make sure that although Pete was bound to be crippled for life, no harm was likely to come to her child.

First Connie talked Pete into clam fritters eaten in the truck, parked at the dock. Then Pete talked Connie into some impromptu necking. Connie had just begun to feel like she was on a honeymoon, either that or in the middle of a scene from *Beach Blanket Bingo,* when Pete sat up, looked out, and launched straight into a scene from *Jaws.*

"Will you look at that harbor? There's hardly a boat out there. And the hotel. It might as well be closed." He cranked the key in the ignition and turned on the radio. Winds 120 miles per hour, category three now. Jeff was sounding frantic about a low-pressure trough. Bob seemed to think the jet stream might block it after all.

They drove home and had just entered the kitchen when they heard the chief's telltale halloo at the door. He came in and slid into his favorite kitchen chair, the one with the marsh view. He refused beer, which meant he was planning to work, but he also refused coffee, which meant he wasn't planning to work all night.

Thank God.

He tipped the antique Shaker chair back on two legs and folded his hands behind his head so that the khaki shirt strained across his chest, but Connie didn't worry. Despite some extremely questionable judgment in other areas, the Shakers knew how to make furniture.

"Who goes first?" asked Willy.

"You," said Connie. "Did you take a look at that file?"

The chief nodded. "Nothing fishy there. After her husband died, Sarah had Sutton-Fitch go over her assets. They juggled a few things, nothing drastic, all sound. I checked and it's all there."

Connie shot a look at Pete. It didn't shed any light for her. Did it for him? No, there was no light-bulb look there at all. "And the burglary?"

Willy fished around in his back pocket and tossed a small notebook on the table. "The wife found this in the office safe this morning. That's why she called me down there."

The notebook was nothing fancy—the kind you might use for your grocery list or for jotting down the phone number of that old high school friend you happened to run into but don't intend to call. Across the top was written, "Cash Drawer Shortages." Down the left side were dates. After each date was a dollar figure. The figures started small and grew larger, but not by much. The last entry was several weeks old.

"It's Sutton's handwriting. Neither the partner nor the wife admits knowing anything about any thefts, but the wife felt it wasn't unlike her husband to keep something like that to himself."

"And to try to solve it himself?"

"The wife seems to think there's no big mystery about who was doing the stealing. The young woman in the office, Melissa Farentino, has a record of petty theft. She's currently on probation. The wife found out about the woman's record via the usual grapevine and told her husband. She expected him to fire her, but he didn't. He said she was too valuable a worker."

"Melissa Farentino?" asked Connie. "Bleached blond, kind of wasted-looking?"

Willy nodded. After a minute he squinted her way. "You have something on your mind?"

"It's just that I wouldn't exactly call Melissa Farentino a valuable worker." Connie related some of her observances. The mucked-up files. The unprofessional phone demeanor. "But if you ask me . . ." Connie's voice trailed off.

This time it was Pete who said, "What?"

"I don't know. I think, of the two of them, Abby Fitch bothers me more. Nobody smokes that much these days. She'd smoke cow dung if that was all there was. She's a nervous wreck. Why, do you suppose? And I had a talk with Evan Spender. The widow has made a few accusations about her husband dallying with the office staff. And now the widow's hanging around the office just to drive Abby crazy. At least that's how it looked to me."

"Driving people crazy seems to be a specialty of hers," said Willy. "She calls me three times a day. First it was, 'Who did it?' Then it was, 'When do you arrest her?' now it's, 'When do I get the body?' But as to the thefts, I'd say she's on track to suspect the office staff. No sign of forced entry, a good alarm system, the consistent pattern—it smacks of an inside job. And, of the two choices, ordinarily I'd take Farentino over Fitch. The amounts were more Farentino's range. Fitch made a good living off that firm."

"Ordinarily?"

"Fitch had money problems just the same. She wanted to buy Sutton out, but when she applied to the bank for the loan she was turned down."

"You're trying to say she was pilfering . . ." Connie pulled the chief's pad toward her and did the math, "a whopping seven hundred dollars, just to put her over the hump to buy out Sutton?"

"I'm saying she had money problems," said Willy. "That's all. I talked to Del Farber at the bank. He turned down that loan on the basis of a rumor he'd heard. Sutton-Fitch had just lost Milly Blair a neat sum of money and rumor had it she was pulling the rest out of the firm. Number one, news of losses like that have done in small businesses like this one before. Number two, that's a big investment to leave a small firm. Del thought it prudent to sit tight and see how Sutton-Fitch weathered the storm before he put any more money into them."

Which sounded like Del, thought Connie. God forbid he'd actually give money to somebody who needed it. But she didn't waste too much time mulling over Milly Blair, the Blair Pharmaceutical heiress. Willy had dropped too many other bombs at their feet. Melissa Farentino's record. Abby Fitch's thwarted buyout. Fern Sutton's annoying habits. She and Pete would have lots to talk about tonight, that was for sure.

But come to think of it, Pete had been unusually silent through all this. Even now, he was giving the chief one-word answers about his sister, Polly. The chief was more than a little sappy about Polly. Polly, on the other hand, seemed to be trying hard not to get sappy about the chief. Yes. Pete's mind was obviously on something else. Abby, Fern, Melissa, take your pick.

When the chief left, Connie asked him. "All right, which one's sticking in your craw?"

"Joanna," he said.

13

And now, I pray you, sir, for still it is beating in my mind, your reason for raising this sea-storm?

Pete couldn't help it. If he'd been living in the city he'd be roaming around the house checking locks on windows and doors, but since he lived on Nashtoba, he stood on the balcony outside his bedroom and peered into the dark, listening to the night. The trouble was, there was nothing to hear. No wind. No birds. He couldn't even hear the usual wash of water on shore. Nashtoba Sound had never been so still, so motionless, so dead. It was as if nothing lived beneath its surface.

Connie slid a hand under his sweatshirt and a chill crept up his spine that she must have felt. "Okay, what's bugging you?"

Pete found it hard to choose. Sarah lying. Charlotte

coming. Connie evaporating. "I just don't like this Joanna-Sutton thing," he said at last.

"What Joanna-Sutton thing? Anyone in their mid-fifties who grew up on Nashtoba would have gone to school together. It doesn't mean a thing."

"No? Then why was Sarah so antsy when I tried to ask about Joanna?"

"Sarah's always antsy about Joanna. You know how they are."

"This was something more." Pete backed up as far as the wooden bench that hugged the wall of the house, bringing Connie down onto it with him. She stayed close. Was she feeling it now, too? It wasn't cold. They didn't need to huddle together that way because of the temperature.

"I don't know," said Pete glumly after a while. "There's something wrong somewhere. What I should do is talk to Joanna." He look at his watch. It wasn't as late as it felt. He unwound himself from Connie, went inside, and dialed the Baltimore number. For the second time he got the message machine, Dennis's voice droning on and on: . . . *unavailable at present, leave name and number, most important to include time and date of call and which party your message is for.* A tad compulsive, Pete thought, but he complied with instructions, asking Joanna to call.

He was still sitting there staring at the phone when Connie came in and flopped on the bed beside him. "They don't ring when you stare at them, you know. I've been thinking. Maybe we should call Polly."

So she was feeling it. Polly lived in Southport, roughly ninety sea-miles away, in the top corner of an old waterfront warehouse. Not the best place to be in the face of a tropical storm.

"Maybe you could talk her into coming here. We could use the help."

"And our honeymoon?"

"We'll get to it. After Charlotte."

Pete picked up the phone and dialed. It took him exactly thirty-five seconds to convince Polly to come to Nashtoba, help out at Factotum. It took a bit longer to explain about Sarah.

Pete found it significant that her first words were, not "poor Webster" or even, as Rita's had been, "poor Sarah."

Hers were "poor Willy."

And Connie was right—the minute he hung up, the phone rang.

Not Joanna, but Dennis, again, from Bradford this time. What did he do, pick up his messages every five minutes? He informed Pete that Joanna was away on business again. Or still. Was there anything Dennis could pass on?

Pete considered, a new unease forming now, and said no.

By the time he hung up, Connie was asleep on top of the covers. Pete undressed her and slid her between the sheets without her waking beyond a fluttering of the eyelashes. He turned off the light and went back out onto the balcony. Far off to the North Pete heard the clatter of geese, felt—or had he only imagined?— a puff of tropical air like hot breath on his face. He went inside, undressed, slid into bed, collected Connie's hot body against him, and spoke sternly to himself: Will you cut it out? Connie's not going anywhere. Life's okay now. He took a deep breath, closed his eyes, started with his temples and worked down, consciously unknotting his muscles one by one. He got as far as the cords in his neck when the process began to reverse itself. How could he say life was okay when he now had so much to lose?

Connie woke early. She rolled toward Pete, thinking she'd give him a nudge, tell him what had worried her awake, but one look at Pete's contorted pose and mangled covers told her he'd worried enough for now. She tiptoed into the bathroom, showered and dressed quietly, and crept downstairs.

The first thing she noticed was the deathly stillness in the air. It was hot and humid, much too hot and humid for September. Unless, of course . . . She flicked on the radio. Still a hurricane watch, not an actual warning, but Charlotte was picking up speed, with no change in direction so far.

Which meant it was still headed here. Connie pondered. This was no time to waste doing the chief's job. But she couldn't stop thinking about it. Maybe if she hurried she could be back before anyone knew she was gone.

Milly Blair lived inland, which wasn't the usual location for Nashtoba's wealthier residents—usually they congregated along the shore. But apparently Milly Blair didn't want to swim in it or ride over it, all she wanted to do was look at it. She'd bought a bunch of land on top of a hill, mowed down just enough trees so she could see water, and stayed there.

Connie had never been to the Blair house before— Milly Blair had her own, full-time crew of caretakers and didn't need to bother with the likes of Factotum. As Connie wound upward along the drive she found herself pausing at every turn to admire the handiwork. The gardens, even in September, were almost as breathtaking as the sight of Nashtoba Sound beyond—Connie spotted snapdragons, pinks, verbena, phlox, dahlias, and impatiens still in force in the more formal settings, not to mention the wide swaths of chrysanthemums and riots of asters and sea golden-rod springing up in informal clusters along the road.

Connie had expected someone to accost her long before she reached the front doorbell, but although a curious head or two swung her way, she walked up the brick steps to the shiny yellow door alone. The house was big enough to deserve the hill and grounds, but not so flashy as to steal any thunder from the sur-roundings. Connie rang the bell and the door was opened by a slender woman in her sixties with a dirty trowel in her hand. She wore a loose blouse and a pair of blue jeans that looked like they'd once come with a real sailor inside. Maybe this was one of the garden-ers. But what was she doing inside the house?

"I'm here to see Milly Blair," said Connie, without much hope of getting to.

"You're looking at her," said the woman. "And you're . . . ?"

Connie gave herself a flustered introduction and added at the last minute, "I was hoping to talk to you about Sutton-Fitch." To her surprise she was led without further discussion down the hall. The house looked like any other except . . . well, better—the furnishings old, the floor oil new, the paintings the best of the local collection of artists, another touch Connie had to admire. They ended up in a sunny room full of plants, one of which was root-ball-up on a newspaper in the middle of the floor.

"Excuse me for working while you do your talk-ing," said Milly Blair. "These little devils don't do so well on oxygen alone." She poured dirt from three separate bags into a ceramic pot that looked like something the Incas might have tossed together, then waved the trowel at Connie. "Go ahead. Sit down. I know who you are. You're mixed up with that fellow who does all kinds of work. I've seen his advertisement in town. What have you got to do with Sutton-Fitch?"

"Nothing much. We're friends of the woman who's rumored to have shot him."

"Oh? Good for you."

She saw Connie's face and chuckled. "Don't mind me. That's the only fun I get these days, saying outrageous things from time to time. But I do mean it, in a way. I've been preyed upon enough times to recognize them when I see them."

"Recognize what?"

"Predators, dear."

Connie waited.

Nothing came.

The newly potted whatever-it-was got returned to the nearest windowsill and the one beside it was removed. Milly smacked the bottom of the clay pot and another tightly bound mass of roots plopped into her hand. "You may wonder why I let the nasty little man get his mitts on my money. Or do you know my niece?"

"Niece?"

"Abby Fitch. Actually a second cousin once removed. Not that any of it means anything anyway since Abby was adopted, but if we say niece everyone is less confused and much more respectful."

Aha, thought Connie. But a second later she thought: Aha, what? "Your money isn't there now, is it? Since he lost—"

"Of course it's still there. Since he lost what? He never lost any of my money. He wouldn't dare."

"But I heard . . ." Connie stopped. She'd begun to feel like she'd walked through the looking glass ass-end-to. "I guess I got my rumors confused."

"Rumors never get confused. Rumors start out confused. I brought my business to Sutton-Fitch soon after Abby partnered in. But I dealt with Sutton, not Abby. I saw no need to put her through that strain. And he's done well. Or he did well, poor man. I've had no reason to take my business elsewhere. Now where did this nasty little rumor come from?"

"The bank. Which makes no sense, now that I think about it. I guess if Abby wanted to borrow money she'd come to you."

Milly gave the second revitalized plant a satisfied pat. "Obviously you don't know Abby. If she wanted to borrow money, she'd go to the bank. Only if I happened to get wind of it would she come here. Correction. Only if I happened to get wind of it would I go to her. Are you familiar with the expression, 'Chance makes your family, choice makes your friends'? She's one of the few relatives I'd have chosen. Ironic, isn't it, since her parents chose her? But what on earth does Abby need money for?"

"The rumor was that she wanted to buy out Sutton, went to the bank, and got refused."

"That must be one of the most poorly researched rumors I've ever heard. In the first place, why would Webster Sutton want to sell out? I understood he had a son in the wings, ready to step in soon as third man on the team. In the second place, why on earth would Abby get refused? Oh, I see. Hence the first phase of that rumor. I'm supposed to have pulled my investments out of the firm after having been taken to the cleaners. Yes, a rumor like that might make the bank think twice, I suppose. But why . . ." Milly Blair stopped there, obviously as puzzled as Connie by now.

Connie thanked her and said her good-byes. As she left the house on the hill the air felt heavier, the sky looked more queer.

Her thoughts, too.

14

...here have I, thy schoolmaster, made thee
more profit...

Pete bounded downstairs late and confused, but
more rested than he'd dreamed possible at around
two in the morning. Never in either of their married
lives had Connie ever snuck out ahead of him without
waking him either accidentally or with a purposeful
elbow. She wasn't the type who opened drawers
quietly, or, for that matter, moved through space
quietly. So why hadn't he heard her this time? And
what was that he was hearing now? Easy enough to
guess. A throaty old Renault. So Polly had arrived.
Pete set down the Wheaties box and went out to meet
her in the drive. On sudden impulse he greeted her
with a hug. The fact that he didn't always do that was
evident by the way she gaped at him.

"Well, well, well," she said. "Don't you look 'fresh

as a bridegroom; and his chin new reap'd,' too. That's Shakespeare, in case you were wondering. *Henry IV.* I think you're supposed to be 'perfumed like a milliner,' too. You aren't, are you?"

"No."

"Good. Whatever you've done, it appears to agree with you. Despite everything." Polly suddenly drooped. When Polly drooped, she drooped—shoulders fell, amber eyes clouded, dark curls got mashed under fretful hands. "What are you doing about Sarah?"

"Trying to find out what happened. And getting nowhere, I might add."

"Never fear, your sister is here. I can take over at Factotum for as long as you need me."

Pete narrowed his eyes at her. "What happened to the new job?"

"I got laid off. You know how it goes. Last in, first out. So what have you got for me?"

"I'm sure Rita will tell you the minute you walk through the door."

She did, too.

As Polly listened to the list, Pete saw her eyes grow round. "I knew this sudden invitation was too good to be true." She turned to Pete. "So while I traipse hither and yon fending off Charlotte's pending destruction, I suppose you're off on the trail of some obscure lead that you're convinced would never occur to the poor deluded police chief?"

The tone was light, but Pete could tell a major breakthrough when he heard one. Last night she'd actually brought up his name. Today she was even defending him. Sort of.

Pete brought her inside for a cup of coffee while he ate his Wheaties and explained what he was up to. He needed to find Joanna. She'd supposedly left here for someone named Sam, according to her phone conversation of two nights before. But where was Sam? Who was Sam?

"Ask Evan Spender," said Polly. "He still works for the phone company, doesn't he? They have records on everything. See if he can find out who she called from your phone."

"'A ministering angel shall my sister be,'" quoth Pete, collecting their cups. "That's from *Hamlet*. I think."

As Pete approached the steps of Beston's Store the three men on the bench began humming, but Pete couldn't tell if it was supposed to be the wedding march or the funeral march.

"Well, well, well," said Bert. "So we finally lay eyes on the bridegroom. Fine little disappearing act you two pulled. And right in the middle of some weather, too."

"Weather's not here yet," said Pete, and turned to Evan. Every time he saw Evan Spender these days he thought of Rita, and every time he thought of Rita, he had to fight down some vague medieval urge to demand of Evan Spender his intentions. Odd that he didn't feel the same urge when he thought of the police chief and Polly. Maybe it had to do with the fact that Polly had apparently yet to give the chief the time of day. Or maybe it was more that Pete was pretty sure he already knew the chief's intentions.

Pete turned his mind back to the matter at hand. Quickly. "Evan, may I have a word?"

Evan rose and they walked down the street out of earshot. "A phone call was made from my house Tuesday night around eleven. Can it be traced?"

"If it was a toll call."

Pete still owned an ancient black rotary phone that gurgled loudly when dialed. Pete tried to remember the sound of Joanna dialing. Seven numbers or more? Or had she used a credit card? He couldn't be sure. "Could you check?"

"This for a particular reason?"

Pete supposed Evan was entitled to that. "It's for Sarah." At least he hoped it was. But if Pete ended up dragging Joanna into Sutton's murder, Sarah would be none too grateful, he was sure.

Connie was pretty sure she would have gone straight home and straight to work if she hadn't just happened to see Del Farber crossing the bank parking lot. She hung a sharp left and pulled up beside him. After the first few words out of her mouth he backed away from her.

"I'm not talking to anybody about Webster Sutton."

"It's not Webster I want to talk about. It's Milly. Milly Blair."

It looked like in banking circles Milly's name was one to be reckoned with. Del stayed put. Connie skirted the issue of how the rumor about Milly's money had come as far as her ear, but when she got to the part about how the rumor was untrue, Del's reaction was a simple one. He flat-out refused to believe it. He looked pretty damned smug about it, too.

"He didn't lose Milly's money," Connie repeated. "I have it from Milly herself."

"And I have it from Webster Sutton," said Del. "I was in his office when he made the call. It was after hours. He must have been calling his partner at home.

He verified they'd lost a goodly sum for Blair, confirmed her withdrawing the rest from the firm. He said the name three of four times. Milly Blair."

"In front of you?"

Suddenly Del looked a little warm out there in the middle of the parking lot. "I said I didn't want to talk about Web, now didn't I?"

"You did. But I find it hard to believe a financial consultant would discuss a customer's business with someone else in the room. You must have thought you heard—"

"I heard what I heard," blurted Del. "I wasn't *in* the room. We'd had an appointment to discuss . . . we'd had an appointment. After I'd been there awhile Sutton looked at his watch, excused himself, and left the room. I heard him on the phone. He must have assumed he'd shut the door. I heard every word. Sutton-Fitch lost a large sum of Milly Blair's money and she was withdrawing the rest of it from the firm. Sutton was in a panic, let me tell you. He cut our meeting short the minute he returned, and I went home."

"I tell you, Del, I spoke to Milly Blair this morning. She denied every word of it. She said they never lost her any money. She said every cent is still in that firm. Why shouldn't it be? Abby's her niece."

Del didn't answer. So Connie had won that round. Or had she? The puzzlement and confusion on Del's face looked too real.

Pete stuck his head out the window as he drove down Shore Road and looked up. Sky still blue, but still that funk to the air. He should have picked up batteries at Beston's. Lamp oil, too. As he drove by the gas station he noticed a line forming. Damn. Nothing on Nashtoba ever had lines. He should have filled up yesterday. If they lost power, the gas pumps would go, too. He pulled in. He wished he knew where Connie was. Probably out on some wild-goose chase, same as he was. But he needed to know where Joanna was. He needed to know about Webster Sutton and the change of schools.

Schools.

Pete inched forward, topped off his tank, paid up, and continued on down Shore Road. Nashtoba's principal, in Joanna's day and continuing on into Pete's, too, had been a native islander named Elmer Snow. He'd retired, as far as Pete could recall, over a dozen years ago now, but he was easy enough to find if any of his former pupils were foolish enough to want to do so. Pete decided he wanted to do so. He followed the main road as it looped around from harbor side to ocean side and cut inland almost directly across from the Point. After a quarter of a mile Pete passed Shank's Pond, and another hundred feet past the pond he came to the sign: SHANK'S POND KENNEL. In his retirement years Elmer Snow had traded in kids for dogs.

Pete could hear the dogs long before the saw the wire runs or the brick-red roof of Snow's house. No need for a doorbell—the racket escalated as Pete pulled in the drive and Elmer Snow was already standing at the open door by the time Pete's sneakers hit ground. Did Elmer Snow find the sound of dogs a step up or a step down from the noises he'd lived with at the school? Pete wondered.

Elmer Snow recognized Pete right off, which also made Pete wonder. He hadn't been in his office that many times, had he? "Pete, Pete, Pete. Come in, come in, come in." Pete remembered that all right—the principal had always said everything three times.

"Hello, Mr. Snow."

"Hello, hello, hello. What brings you here on this lovely September morn?"

Mr. Snow always said things like that, too. Lovely September morn. And if truth were told, he probably hadn't changed as much as Pete had in other regards, either. He still looked as small and neat and spry as ever. Pete considered trying out that line he'd liked that Polly had tossed him, the one about the chin new reap'd, but decided against it. For all he knew Polly'd gotten it wrong and it was from *The Rocky and Bullwinkle Show*. As it was, Pete almost had to jog to keep up as Elmer Snow led the way down a short hall and into a room full of dogs. Elmer pushed an old greyhound off the couch and waved Pete to it.

Pete sat down. The greyhound eyed him as if he had some nerve. Elmer Snow picked up and sat under a fat dachshund.

"I've got a strange request," said Pete. "I'd like to tap your memory banks. This would go back thirty years or so."

"Oh, I have an excellent memory. Excellent, excellent, excellent. As perhaps you might recall. As *I* seem to recall, you were prone to certain lapses. Feel free to correct me if I'm wrong." The eyes twinkled. Pete was pretty sure the twinkle was new. Or was it? Pete's school years couldn't possibly have been as bleak as he remembered them now.

"Do us both a favor and go back fifteen or sixteen more years. The person I wanted to ask you about is Joanna Abrew. Do you remember her?"

"I do, I do, I do. Joanna Abrew. Joanna Willoughby, she became, am I right?"

"Right," said Pete, surprised. Even for old Blowhard-Snow-hard, as they used to call him, that was going some. "Her mother's run into a little trouble."

"I heard, I heard, I heard. Nasty business. Nasty, nasty, nasty. I take in some strange way you think my memory may help her cause?"

Interesting that he'd assumed the righteous cause was Sarah's, thought Pete. But Elmer Snow probably knew Sarah as well as he knew Pete, or Joanna, or any of the other islanders who'd chanced across his path at any given point in the last fifty or sixty years. Then something else dawned on Pete. "You remember Webster Sutton, too?"

"Of course you're referring to Webster Two? Certainly I remember him. An angry young man. Angry, angry, angry. There were several in those years. Not a good group, as I recall. Not good, not good at all. Of course it's all power, all control. They feel they lack it. Don't know how to get it. That's when they resort to . . ." He slowed down. "I remember one from around your time, too. Jimmy Solene. I seem to recall the two of you engaging in a display of fisticuffs. Never the answer, or course. Never, never, never. Now you were saying?"

Pete's head had gone spinning into the past so crazily it took him a minute to catch up. Jimmy Solene. Christ. "Joanna Abrew transferred out of the Nashtoba late in her senior year. I was wondering if you remembered any of the circumstances surrounding that event."

For once, one of Pete's questions seemed to give the principal pause, not because he couldn't remember, but because he plain old didn't know. "I was never privy to the circumstances," he said finally. "It was a most peculiar thing to do. Most peculiar. Most, most, most. She left school one afternoon as usual and never came back. It was April, I remember vividly. April, with graduation in two months. I spoke to her mother. She'd suddenly decided to transfer to St. Mary's. I got no more explanation than that. Which was no explanation at all, at all, at all. If it was the child's whim I'd say it was shamefully indulgent of her parents, but they'd never struck me as the indulgent type."

No, thought Pete. Not Sarah, at least. "You can't think of any reason why she might have wanted to switch? Grades? Social problems?"

"No, no, no. That was just it. She was a wonderful student. And a lovely girl. Lovely, lovely, lovely. She was seeing a nice young man who was crushed to see her go. I remember speaking with him once, soon after the fact. His schoolwork had gone into a sharp decline as a result of her abrupt departure. We had to effect some emergency repairs. He received the obligatory Dear John note at some point, but it seemed to explain nothing to his satisfaction. Richard Favell. Nice young man. Nice, nice, nice. He moved away after college. Became a veterinarian. I've often thought of him since." Old Blow-hard gave the dachshund dozing in his lap an affectionate pat. "I could have used Richard Favell a time or two. Yes, yes,—"

"Yes," Pete finished for him. "I can see that. Is there anything else you can remember about Joanna Abrew's departure from school?"

Finally it dawned on the principal to ask the question Pete had dreaded from the first. "Why? Do you think Joanna is somehow concerned in this Sutton business?"

"Not really. If I tried to explain, it would take all night."

"I see. I'm sorry. I can think of nothing else pertinent."

Pete stood up and his rear end had barely cleared the seat before the greyhound retrenched. Pete leaned over and gave him a pat, which the dog could now graciously acknowledge with a few good licks. Old Blow-hard held his hand out to Pete. He didn't seem to mind a little dog slobber, so Pete shook, but it didn't feel right. It was something a grown man would do, and Pete didn't feel much like a grown man right now.

What he felt like was a kid who'd just been caught in a display of fisticuffs.

15

I do begin to have bloody thoughts.

By ten o'clock Rita Peck had a splitting headache. By eleven she'd decided to hand Pete an ultimatum—either they hired somebody else, and soon, or she would quit. By noon, when Evan Spender sauntered in looking less than overworked and announced that instead of being there to take her out to lunch he was there to see Pete, she snapped.

"I don't know where Pete is, except that it's not here. Neither do I know where Connie is. I know where Andy is because he just called to say he's broken Jerry Begg's plate-glass window and I know where Polly is because I sent her there. She's at Fergy Potts's, looking for that retarded cat. Again. What else would you like to know? Where Charlotte is?"

The phone rang. Again. Rita reached for it, but

Evan beat her to it. "They're out to lunch. Try again later." He hung up. He picked up her notebook, flipped to a clean page, wrote something, tore it out, folded it in half, wrote PETE across the top, and stuck it under the pencil holder. He returned to the notebook, wrote OUT TO LUNCH in big, strong letters, and propped it up against her work-in-progress rack. He reached across the desk, took Rita's hand, and lifted her out of her seat.

He had come in the telephone truck, but after he collected a large canvas satchel from it he retreated to Rita's Dodge Omni. He slid his package into the back seat, held out his hand for her car keys, and commandeered the driver's seat. As he pulled onto Shore Road, Rita opened her mouth to ask where they were going, but suddenly she decided not to. Knowing Evan, she'd find out soon enough.

Where they went was the Point. What was in the satchel was a small blanket, French bread, chicken salad, cheese, grapes, some unidentifiable but gorgeously gooey thing for dessert, and a frosty jug of iced tea.

"Figured we'll both be busy enough after Charlotte," he said. "Best to take the chance while we've got it."

And didn't that just figure, Rita thought. Here the entire island was running around like chickens with their heads cut off and Evan was going on a picnic. Again she opened her mouth, curious as to what Evan would have done with all the food if she'd refused to come with him, but again she closed it with the words unsaid.

Knowing Evan, he'd have simply saved it for another day or eaten it himself.

* * *

When Connie got back to Factotum there was a sign on Rita's desk, not in Rita's handwriting. OUT TO LUNCH. Odd. There was another message next to it for Pete. Connie didn't read it. She supposed she'd never feel that married. But she did pick up the pile of other messages and flipped through until her own name caught her eye. *Connie—call Abby Fitch.* Connie reached for the phone on Rita's desk, but didn't pick it up. She wouldn't mind taking one more look at the interactions over at Sutton-Fitch.

The no-smoking rule seemed to be back in effect and the air may have improved, but not the moods. Melissa Farentino sat at the corner desk, slamming things back and forth across it, not answering when Abby Fitch asked her a question about something called Blue Star Six. Fern Sutton sat at the computer, alternating her scowls between the computer screen, Abby, and Melissa. Abby Fitch paced and twitched and looked like she was missing a sixth finger.

The sight of Connie's face in the door didn't seem to improve things much. Abby fluttered into high speed, flew out the door, and closed it hard after her.

"I don't want to talk in front of them," she said. "Have you had lunch?"

"No," said Connie, "but . . ." But what? She'd been counting on finding Pete around lunchtime, but the odds of that probably weren't too great. And it seemed to her that Abby had something she wanted to say. So when Abby suggested Martelli's, Connie said, "Great."

She should have known better. It wasn't so much that Abby Fitch had something she wanted to say. It was more like there was something she wanted to find out. She waited till they'd gotten drinks and ordered—a Coke and a sub for Connie, a Perrier and a chef's salad for Abby.

"My aunt told me about your little visit," said Abby finally, by way of explanation. "What exactly is it that you want from her?"

"Nothing, now," said Connie.

Abby lit a cigarette.

No one spoke.

What the hell? thought Connie. She wasn't trying to hide anything; she might as well go first. So she explained how Del Farber's eavesdropping had left Abby loanless and how the two different versions of the state of Milly's money had left her a tad perplexed. "The trouble is," she finished, "I believe both of them. Your aunt and Del Farber. She seemed like the original straight shooter, and he seemed honest-to-God baffled himself. He really thinks he heard what he heard."

"Maybe he did," said Abby, the cigarette already half-gone.

"So your aunt did pull out?"

"Aunt Milly's money is safe and sound with Sutton-Fitch and always was. I'd like to know where you think you're going with all this. Are you out to confuse issues, is that it?"

"I'm out to find out what happened," said Connie with some heat, and to her surprise, Abby Fitch backed off.

"Sorry. All right. Really. But I still don't see what this has to do with Sutton-Fitch."

"I'd say Webster Sutton has something to do with Sutton-Fitch. And Sarah, too. You guys rearranged her assets when her husband died. Did you do that or did Sutton?"

"Sutton must have. I wasn't familiar with the account until you asked. I looked it over after you left. There was nothing out of the ordinary anywhere."

"I know. The chief checked."

"Fine. So if that was all you needed to know—"

"That and whether Fern Sutton's accusations about you and her husband are true."

Abby chose that moment to fuss around firing up another cigarette. When she got through, and after she'd inhaled another six months off her life, she said, "They aren't."

"What about Melissa Farentino?"

Puff, puff, puff. "Maybe I'd better straighten something out for you. Webster Sutton was never as fond of women as his wife may have thought."

The food came.

Connie fell to, but what Abby did to her salad looked more like retossing than eating. Instead, she smoked. And while she smoked, Connie thought up a couple more questions.

"Why did you want to buy out Sutton?"

Puff, toss. "Because he wouldn't buy me out."

"And the reason you wanted out?"

Puff, puff, toss, puff, puff, toss. "I was sick of it, I guess."

"And buying out Sutton, doing all of it instead of half of it, would make you less sick?"

Abby Fitch didn't answer. Obviously, she saw the trap, but only after she'd fallen in. It wasn't that she was sick of the work, Connie guessed, it was that she was sick of Sutton. She wanted out from under Sutton.

In a manner of speaking.

Abby lit another cigarette, but this time she had some trouble doing it. Connie figured what she really needed was a good stiff shot from a tranquilizer gun.

Connie decided to change tack. "What happens to Sutton's part of the business now? I guess the son is out. I'm told he's taken a job at the Natural History Museum."

Aha. Through the haze of smoke, a glimmer of surprise. Pleasant surprise. "He didn't waste any time."

"What do you mean?"

Abby shrugged. Puffed. Pushed away the food for good.

"I keep seeing the widow in the office. Maybe she's planning to jump in?"

"No." Now there was a definitive answer. But was it definitive wishful thinking or definitive actual fact? Whichever it was, it reminded Connie of Melissa again and another good question she might ask.

"Any thoughts on this office thief?"

"None."

"The chief seems to think it's an inside job."

That did it. Abby stamped out her cigarette and stood. "I'm afraid I have to go." She threw some bills on the table.

"Just tell me this," said Connie, fast. "If your aunt's money is safe and sound at Sutton-Fitch, and Del Farber really heard what he thought he heard, what's left?"

"You're forgetting a third possibility."

"What?" said Connie, fumbling her own money onto the table, but when she looked up all she could see through the haze of smoke was Abby's vanishing back.

* * *

Pete was gazing in puzzlement at the foreign printing on the big message, OUT TO LUNCH, when he happened to see the smaller one with his name on it. He unfolded the piece of paper and saw a phone number, followed by: *Samuel P. Oliver, 1225 Newgate East, Boston. Sprung overworked office personnel for lunch. Plan to make it a long one. Call it even, E.S.*

Yes, thought Pete, Rita was overworked. And as soon as Pete and Connie got through squeezing in a honeymoon, he'd send Rita on a long, paid rest. He could handle the desk. He slid behind it, into Rita's chair, just to see what it felt like, and almost immediately fell prey to some weird strain of claustrophobia. He jumped up, circling back to the front, perched on his usual corner, and picked up the phone. There was no time to waste. He dialed the Boston number and an answering machine clicked in, a man's voice reeling out the standard message. *You have reached the Oliver residence. Please leave a message after the tone. Thanks.*

Not good. What message could Pete reasonably leave? *Hello, this Peter Bartholomew from Nashtoba on Cape Hook.* He might as well say, *This is nobody from nowhere.* And then what? *I'm looking for Joanna Willoughby and understood she might be staying with you.* Yeah, that would go over well if the wife picked up. How about, *I'm interested in any information you might have on the murder of Webster Sutton.*

Right.

Pete hung up. Samuel P. Oliver. Samuel P. Oliver. It rang a bell. He was almost sure that somewhere he'd seen that name in print.

The phone rang. Pete picked it up. "Factotum."

"Well, well, well," said Bert Barker. "The big

cheese himself. It's about damned time you did some work around the place. When are you coming to take down these awnings?"

"Soon," said Pete, and hung up. He didn't mean to be rude, even though it was almost impossible to be too rude to Bert. It was just that he'd suddenly remembered where he'd seen Sam Oliver's name.

And his face.

16

It is a sleepy language, and thou speak'st out of thy sleep.

Carrie Suggs and Pete met up where they'd met last time—on the front stoop—one going in, the other going out.

"Were you able to look at those old files?" asked Carrie. No *Hello, hear we're getting some weather, nice to see you,* but Pete was getting used to the lacking social graces by now. Hell, they'd be speaking in code soon if he didn't watch out.

"The police chief looked into things. Nothing out of line, he says. I don't suppose Sarah's said anything to you?"

Carrie hesitated. "She's said nothing to me."

Was it's Pete imagination, or was there extra emphasis on the last two words? He decided a gentle shove in the right direction wouldn't send anybody over any cliffs. "Anything you've overheard might help." He tried to put some subtle emphasis on his own last word, *help,* and it seemed to jar something loose.

"She hasn't been sleeping. I told you that?"

Pete nodded.

"She tosses. And talks." A second hesitation. A deep breath. "She talks about someone."

Maybe one more little push. "Sam Oliver?"

"No." Surprise. Puzzlement. "Someone named Arthur. She doesn't say a last name. And something about a five and dime."

"Oh." Pete tried not to look disappointed. "Arthur was her husband. He ran the Nashtoba Five and Dime."

"She kept talking about 'poor Arthur.' And about someone stealing. And then she mentioned the Five and Dime."

"Nothing about her daughter? Or someone named Sam Oliver?"

Puzzlement again. "No. Just Arthur."

"All right. I appreciate you passing it along."

"Do you think he had something to do with all this?"

"I doubt it. Arthur died years ago."

"Oh." Carrie turned to go and then stopped. "I thought because it suddenly started to bother her . . ."

"We don't know how long it's bothered her. Nobody's been here to hear her, right? For all we know she's been mumbling in her sleep about Arthur and the Five and Dime forever."

"Oh. Yes. Of course."

"Everything else is going okay?"

"Yes."

"Lucy settling in?"

Pete thought he saw the first flicker of a smile, but if it was, it was a pretty sorry excuse. "Yes, she is. Sarah's good to her." She paused. "Sarah's daughter doesn't like us here."

"Maybe not, but Sarah does."

And as Pete watched the colorless Carrie leave without saying good-bye, he found himself wondering why exactly that was.

Sarah wouldn't have admitted it, of course, but she was glad to see Pete waltz in and set himself down on her couch. Part of it was habit. He'd been the highlight of her day for so long it was hard to keep in mind that these days he was apt to be more trouble than he was worth. But part of it was this feeling that the worst was past them.

And then he opened his mouth.

She thought she was hearing things. But when she didn't answer him the first time, he only repeated himself, which was worse.

"I said Joanna mentioned someone named Sam Oliver the other night. Was this a high school friend of hers?"

Sarah didn't dare speak. She didn't dare let go of the arms of her chair. If she did she knew for certain this time her hand would surely shake like a leaf. So this was what it took—not a murder in her precious woods but the name of that boy. Sam Oliver. Oh, dear Lord, what was going to come next?

Pete blabbered on, although it seemed to Sarah through her haze that his voice had gentled up a mite. He saw. He knew what that name had done to her.

"I remembered I'd seen him in Joanna's yearbook. He was in her class, right?"

Sarah nodded. How to not? But the nod was all she had in her. If he didn't leave this minute . . .

It was the child who saved her.

Sarah heard the door, the feet, the small, still tentative voice. Lucy ran into the room, saw Pete, and beamed. Even Sarah could see that much.

"Candy cane!"

Pete clapped his head as if he'd been shot.

Lucy beamed harder. "Guess mine."

"Onions."

"No. Yuck."

What in tarnation were they on about? Not that Sarah should care, just as long as it was something else. She felt as if she'd been sucked out to sea, washed around in the waves, bumped against the rocks, tossed back again, bruised and bleeding, in the very place she'd first washed up.

Lucy grabbed the checkerboard and waved it at Pete. "Do you know this game, checkers?"

Sarah caught the flash of Pete's wristwatch as he checked the time. "I do. And I wish I could play. But I've got to meet someone. Rain check?"

Like the child knew what a rain check was. What was he thinking of? Sarah, obviously. His eyes had barely left her face. And now he stood up, came close. "Sarah?"

Oh, blast, now he was going to see what a state she was in. She made every effort and pulled herself to her feet. "Here, child, where's that coloring book? There it is, on the rug. When I come back I'll be interested to see what you've done with that cat. Good-bye, Peter, don't let us make you late."

* * *

Polly Bartholomew was surprised at how much fun it all was. First she and Andy hauled the sea camp's canoes off the beach. Not only did she work up a good sweat in the strange, hot, humid air, but she and Andy also got a chance to catch up. It seemed he and Rita's daughter, Maxine, had finally called it quits for good. Maxine's going off to school was what apparently made Andy finally realize just how young she was. At least that's what he said. Polly suspected that in actual fact, once Maxine got a look at a few of her options, she'd dropped poor Andy in the dust. Polly, in turn, told him about getting laid off by the newspaper in Southport, told him something she hadn't even mentioned to Pete yet. She'd been thinking she might move back to Nashtoba for a while.

Suddenly and inexplicably she found her thoughts landing on the police chief, felt her skin go all prickly and hot.

"Or maybe I won't," she added quickly. "It was just a thought."

After the sea camp canoes Polly picked the last of the beach plums for the beach plum jelly for the Nashtoba Jam and Jelly Shop. There wouldn't be a beach plum left hanging after, or if, this hurricane hit. As she crawled through the dunes above the Sound, snapping frosted purple plums into her bucket, a flock of neurotic gulls rose en masse from the sandbar below and rattled over her in a cloud of blinding white. A yellow haze crept in, softening the line where sky met water, and a hush descended, making her feel timeless, spaceless. It was nice to be back, she thought, despite everything. Even despite Charlotte, or maybe partly because of. It was fun to watch Nashtoba close up like a tulip at dusk, to feel this odd premonition in the air.

Again, she thought of the chief. What was he doing? she wondered. Webster Sutton things? Prehurricane things? Either way, he was sure to be busy. But later? Tonight? And what would he think if she did move back? That she'd moved back because of him?

No, of course not.

But she couldn't move back.

Not yet.

What *was* he doing? she wondered.

Connie walked into the kitchen to find the table covered with a map of Boston and the counter covered with lamp oil, batteries, matches, crackers, peanut butter, those cans of cooked sausages Pete loved and she hated, a head of lettuce, and a bag of rolls. The counter contents she could understand—the usual prehurricane staples—but the map? When Pete walked in wearing a fresh shirt and told her he was planning to go to Boston to find Joanna, she stared at him in disbelief. When he told her what he wanted *her* to do, it was worse.

"You want me to go to Sarah's and say what?"

"Say you've come to play checkers. The kid'll love it. And while you're doing that, give Sarah a good look. Make sure she's all right. When I left she was pretty rattled. Carrie Suggs was out. I didn't want to go, but Sarah practically tossed me through the door. You know how she gets."

Yes, Connie knew how she got. But Pete obviously didn't know how Connie got. Not these days. Not around kids. Not around Lucy. "Can't Polly—"

But Pete shook his head. "You know Sarah better. If you don't go I'll have to go back myself and that will really get Sarah going. Besides, I've got to get on the road if I want to get back at a decent hour tonight."

Connie tried one more time. "You are paying attention to the forecast?"

"It's way the hell off North Carolina. I'll be back in a few hours. Don't wait to eat, though." He jerked his head toward the refrigerator. "I bought you a present." He grabbed up his map, kissed her unequivocally, got halfway to the door, paused. "Carrie says Sarah's been talking in her sleep. Arthur and the Five and Dime. Someone stealing. Did Sarah ever say anything to you about anything like that?"

Connie shook her head. Pete recrossed the room, kissed her again, looked at her as if he was memorizing her for future use, and finally went out the door. Connie turned in her sudden misery to the refrigerator. A couple of six-packs of Ballantine and a heaping plate of cold, cooked jumbo shrimp. Now *that* she liked.

But, alas, it would have to wait.

The three of them stared at her. Sarah from the chair where she'd apparently been gazing into space, Carrie Suggs from the doorway with a bag of groceries in her arms, the little girl from the rug where she'd been coloring listlessly.

Connie held out the package she'd brought for the little girl. She wasn't above bribery. She supposed, when it came right down to it, she wasn't above much. She could even turn a neat cartwheel if she had to, but so far, the bribery alone seemed to do the trick. Lucy sat up, instantly unlistless. Even Sarah seemed to return from wherever she was. Only Carrie appeared to stared suspiciously at the package. What did she think it was, a box of firecrackers? Oh, well, thought Connie, I wouldn't trust me around my daughter, either. "It's *Winnie-the-Pooh*," she said.

"What do you say, Lucy?" said Carrie.

"Thank you," said Lucy.

Connie moved on, embarrassed. "I'm told there's a famous checkers player somewhere around here."

It was as easy as that.

Lucy dropped the book and scrambled to her feet. She pulled Sarah's battered and scarred checkerboard off the bookshelf, set it on the sea chest that Sarah used as a coffee table, and began to set up the pieces. "You stay on the *black.*"

Connie made the obligatory dumb mistakes and before long Lucy was expounding on her forgetfulness in a cheerfully disgusted state. Connie took a look at Sarah now and then, but she seemed to have rebounded from her initial inertia and listened to the ups and downs of the game with a quiet smile on her face. Carrie poked her head in every so often, still apparently uneasy, but Lucy never once looked up, unless it was to peek at Connie.

Still there?

Still losing?

Good.

Connie tried a smile and immediately Lucy smiled back, her face lighting like a lamp. She's a mirror, Connie thought. If I'm unsure, she's unsure. If I'm withdrawn, she draws back. If Pete and I decide to try again I'll have to remember this. To smile a lot. . . .

Hold it. Who said anything about trying again? As if they'd actually tried the first time. And she wasn't going through any of that again. All those hopes and dreams that had built up so slowly and painfully and were so suddenly and painfully dashed. No chance. No way.

A small hand swooped down, jumped Connie's checker, snatched it up. "You're not *noticing*," said Lucy.

Oh, you'd be surprised, Connie thought.

But inevitably, after a while, her mind began to drift again, and this time, for some strange reason, to her lunch with Abby Fitch. What was this third possibility that Abby thought she'd missed? If Milly Blair's money was safe in Sutton-Fitch, if Del Farber heard what he heard, who did that leave as the liar?

Of course.

Sutton himself.

Maybe he'd set up Del Farber, staged a call from a second phone that he knew damned well was within earshot. But why? Why would Sutton want the bank to think his own business was in trouble? So Abby wouldn't get the loan? What sense did that make? If he didn't want Abby to buy him out he could have just said no. There was no need to go around Robin Hood's barn through the bank. It made no sense.

Connie absentmindedly jumped one of Lucy's checkers and was on her way to jumping a second when she happened to look up. Lucy's face had fallen so fast and so far that it made something in Connie's chest ache. She made a quick survey of the board. Hopped left instead of right. "Drat, that was a mistake. Now I've got to king you."

It didn't take Lucy long to get the hint. Smart for five, Connie thought. Lucy snuck into the space Connie had left for her. "King me!"

But after Connie had piled on the extra checker, Lucy's eyebrows puckered. "Why aren't there any queens?"

"Good question."

"And prince and princesses. There's always prince and princesses."

"I guess they live somewhere else. Moved to another kingdom, something like that."

"Why?"

"Maybe the prince wanted a kingdom of his own. Maybe he didn't want to wait for his father the king to vacate the premises."

"What's vaccinate the purses?"

"Vacate the premises. It means to go somewhere else. Somewhere with no king."

Or at least one who isn't your father. Like the Natural History Museum, for example, if you happened to be Web Three. What had Abby Fitch said when she'd heard about it? *Didn't waste any time.*

"It's your *turn,*" said Lucy.

"For Lord's sake," Sarah called from her chair. "If you're going to play with the child, play with her. If you're going to sit there, move over and give someone else a chance."

Before Pete left the island he gave some thought to a quick stop at the police station. He had it in mind to drop in and get an update on the Sutton situation, but the trouble was, any updating would have to be a two-way street. Better to find Joanna first, talk to her first. But maybe he should at least drop in long enough to mention that Polly had come?

No, again, he decided. He'd learned his lesson. Keep out. Polly was a big girl. If she wanted to see the chief she'd see him. And hadn't the chief himself warned Pete not long ago to stay out?

Pete swung onto the causeway that connected Nashtoba to the mainland peninsula. At low tide there was sand under half the causeway. At high tide there was ten feet of water and a raging current. Pete looked down as he crossed over. Not yet quite high, but also almost full moon time, and therefore already a good ten feet under the planks. Not good. If Charlotte happened to hit at high tide, at a moon tide to boot, good-bye causeway. Pete thought for the millionth time about his own little cottage on the rise above the marsh. He'd seen the marsh nothing but cracked mud and dried grass and he'd seen it nothing but surf. But in the sixty-odd years the cottage had sat on that particular spot, it had never even gotten its cinder-block feet wet.

With Pete's mind on other things he hardly noticed most of Cape Hook fly by, hardly registered as he crossed the bridge. Only as the traffic slowed on the approach to the city did he realize where he was. He turned off the expressway and almost immediately ran into the first of the inevitable detours. The city of Boston hadn't been laid out in neat grids the way the newer cities out West had; it had been laid out along three-hundred-year-old cow paths. Despite the constant efforts to straighten or widen or dig up or smooth out, you'd still get where you wanted to go faster by cow. Last time, Pete had been forced to go over and around where he wanted to go three times. This time he was sent under and around twice. But once he got there he was rewarded with something that was as rare to Boston as piping plovers were to Nashtoba—a free place to park.

He walked up to 1225 Newgate East, a narrow red brick townhouse whose door was opened so fast when he rang it that Pete suspected the man had watched him coming from across the street. Pete could only guess who the man was, but he could see around him into the room beyond to get a good look at the woman curled up on the couch in someone else's bathrobe.

Some man's bathrobe.

The woman got a good look at him, too.

"Hello, Pete," she said.

"Hello, Joanna," said Pete.

17

Good wombs have born bad sons.

As Connie left Sarah's house she was ridiculously pleased to see Lucy look . . . well, not crestfallen, exactly, but certainly not thrilled to see her go, a fact that seemed to surprise Carrie Suggs as much as it surprised Connie. But the game was over and Sarah seemed okay now, and Sarah was the whole point of the visit.

Or was she?

Connie found her mind taking a disturbing turn as she drove away. She had never thought of Pete as the devious type, but the whole thing sounded more far-fetched the longer she thought about it. So she was supposed to check on Sarah. But just so Sarah wouldn't know she was being checked on, she was supposed to say she'd come to play checkers with Lucy.

Right.

So what did he think she was, stupid? He'd brought it up only once since the miscarriage, this subject of children. She'd balked. He'd let it go. Was this his way of bringing it up again? How had he planned to work it when they met up again later? What would he say? *How was Sarah? How was the checker game? Cute kid, isn't she? What do you say we get one for us?*

If that was what he was thinking, he was going to have another think coming damned fast.

Connie flipped onto Shore Road and as she saw the Natural History Museum she forced all thoughts of Pete and Lucy out of her mind. Webster Three worked in that museum now. And what had Abby said about that? *So he didn't waste any time.* Which meant what, exactly? Nothing, probably. But it certainly wouldn't hurt to see what she could learn about the Sarah-Sutton situation from the perspective of the next generation.

The Natural History Museum had begun as an all-volunteer operation in a tent in the woods. It was now a sprawling multilevel structure with a full-time paid staff that not only boasted an excellent collection of Cape Hook flora and fauna, but also well-maintained nature trails and some of the most respected classes, lectures, and research projects in the natural science community.

Connie waltzed in and asked to speak to the director.

The man at the desk shook his head forlornly. "I'm sorry, he's not in today. Funeral. May I help you with something?"

"You're . . . ?"

"Morris Temple. I was the director before him."

"You're filling in while the new director's out?"

Temple chuckled. "Worse than that. I volunteer here now. Full-time. Man the desk, run an occasional marsh tour, even sweep the floor in a pinch."

Connie studied him curiously. "Why did you . . ." She paused. She had planned to ask him why he'd given up the directorship if he was still interested in working at the museum, but the thought occurred to her that maybe he hadn't voluntarily stepped down and for some reason had been asked to resign.

Old Morris seemed to track her thought pattern effortlessly. He chuckled again. "You're wondering why I gave up the paycheck, aren't you? All right, I'll tell you. I gave up one heck of a big headache along with it and my only regret is that I didn't do it sooner. I spent the last five years fighting tooth and nail to get someone who knew what he was doing to run this place. It was too much for me long ago. Nowadays you need someone with some business acumen. I was thrilled when I first latched on to Web, there. Not only did he have the MBA, he had the local background and devotion to the community that I'd been looking for ever since I decided to resign. When he had to back out I nearly had a stroke. I began to think I'd be stuck in over my head forever."

"He's backed out?"

"Not this time, please God, no. But last time. I understand there was some strenuous objection on the home front. This place doesn't pay anywhere near the kind of money someone like Web could command someplace else."

"Like Sutton-Fitch?"

Temple's eye gleamed. "I see I'm not telling you

anything. It was understood around town that he was the heir apparent at Sutton-Fitch. I'm told it should have happened a year or two ago, but young Web decided to go back to school for the Ph.D. He was to finish in June and sign on at Sutton-Fitch. That's why I was so surprised when we readvertised the position this year and Web showed up again. We didn't care whether he had any Ph.D, of course, but it seemed odd he wouldn't want to finish out the program when he was so close."

It didn't seem so odd to Connie, though. She'd had kings and princes on her mind for an hour or two. If Web Two wanted Web Three to join the firm, but Three didn't feel comfortable on Two's turf, the only way he might have stalled his father off was with more school. Come June the jig would have been up. But before that happened, Web Two died. Ergo, son may now give up the unwanted business partnership, quit school, and go after the job he'd wanted from the start.

Which all would have made perfect sense if Web Three had shown up at the museum for the first time this week, after his father had died. The trouble was, Web Three had snatched up the museum job last week.

Which made perfect sense in another way, thought Connie. Job opens that son wants. What stands in son's way? Father. What happens next?

Father gets shot.

Sometimes Pete hated being so smart. He looked back and forth between Joanna's pale face and the obviously embarrassed man standing awkwardly between them. Caught in the act, so to speak. Pete supposed it was easy enough to see the attraction.

Dennis was . . . well, Dennis was Dennis. Sam Oliver
looked more like Superman might have looked when
he first got home after a hard day disguised as Clark
Kent. The eyeglasses were on the coffee table, the suit
jacket was draped on the chair, the tie was pulled
down far enough to loosen the collar button, but even
without a hint of blue jersey underneath, dumb old
Lois herself would have recognized the chiseled jaw
and the impressive physique. Impressive even for
middle age, thought Pete.

"What's happened?" said Joanna. "Why are you
here? It's Mother, isn't it?"

"No," said Pete quickly. "At least not any more
than it was. It's just that a few things came up I
thought we should talk about. I was led to believe you
might be here and I couldn't quite figure out how to
do it over the phone, so I—"

"Dennis told you where I was?"

"No. He . . ." Pete paused in confusion. "You
mean Dennis knows you're here?"

"Of course he does." She reached for a glass of
brown liquid on the coffee table and disposed of a
good half of it. Pete saw Sam Oliver's brow crease.
Then he seemed to remember he was, in theory at
least, the host.

"May I offer you a drink?"

"No," said Pete. "Thanks."

Joanna laughed. "Let's get it over with. Sam Oliver,
this is Peter Bartholomew. Sam's an old friend. Pete
is . . . what are you, this week, Pete? Guardian Angel
or Avenging Conscience? Either will do. Or both. I've
run out and left him to cope with my mother, Sam. Or
I tried to. It seems he's run me to earth."

Now Sam looked in puzzlement between them. "I
thought you said Dennis was—"

"Oh, Dennis is hovering on the outskirts. Pete is the one right smack in the middle of the frying pan. Aren't you, Pete? So what's she done now?"

Pete's turn again to look uncertainly at Sam. He hadn't counted on talking to Joanna in front of him. "Is there someplace we could . . ."

"Certainly," said Sam.

"No," said Joanna. "There aren't any secrets from Sam." The look she gave Sam would have melted Clark Kent. She patted the couch next to her and he sat.

"Go ahead, Pete. Sit. Speak."

The first command was by far the easiest. Pete selected a chair on the Sam side of Joanna. It gave him the best view of Joanna's face, since she kept looking at the man as if she were afraid he'd evaporate. Or fly off the balcony, maybe?

"As you know," Pete began, "your mother's version of events in the Indian tower don't exactly add up. I figured the best thing to do was to find out what really went on. That way we could reach some sensible decision as to—"

"Remove the word *sensible* and I'm with you," said Joanna. "There is nothing about this whole thing that makes *sense.*"

"That's where I'm hoping you can help. It was when your name came up that she seemed to come most unglued. She asked me to do some work up in her attic and I came across your old high school yearbook. I saw Sutton in it." Pete glanced at Sam Oliver. "You, too, in fact. I asked your mother if you knew Sutton, looking for some sort of connection between them, but it was Sam's name, here, that . . ." Pete stopped.

Joanna had rattled her glass onto the coffee table

and groped for Sam's hand. "What did my mother tell you?"

"Nothing, but the conversation obviously upset her." The same way it's upsetting you now, Pete thought. And suddenly a glimmer of light dawned. "I gather you've tried to keep this from her. But I think she knows. Or at least she suspects."

Joanna dropped Sam's hand and sank back onto the couch. Sam's arm came around her. "Of course she knows. Oh, God, Sam. I can't . . . I don't—"

The sound of a key in the lock interrupted them. The door opened and a woman walked in, a shimmery fiftyish blonde in a floating green dress. She looked first at the two on the couch, then at Pete, then back at Sam Oliver. The smile left her face.

"Well, darling?" she said.

Blast and damn, thought Connie, as she pulled out of her driveway. What did she ever do to Rita to deserve this? The list she'd been handed began with the massage-mystic at the Whole Healing Body Shop and ended with Bert Barker. Connie decided to take the worst first and headed straight for Bert's.

Bert's house was close to a hovel. At least that's how it always seemed to Connie ever since she'd seen his other piece of property—a big, sprawling almost-mansion on the waterfront in Naushon he'd inherited through his wife, the rental income from which seemed to keep him from starving without him needing to do much else. That property got kept up nicely by the realty company. This property got kept up only when Bert could talk someone else into doing it cut-rate. Enter Pete. It wouldn't be so bad if Bert would just disappear once they got there, but he never did. He sat on the porch and bitched.

And sure enough, there he was sitting on the porch, staring into space. "'Bout time," he said when Connie got out of her car. "But what'd they send you for? This is man's work."

Right. As long as the man wasn't Bert. Connie marched around the corner to the first awning she saw, examined the screws, went back to the car, and pulled the appropriate screwdriver out of the old rubber tackle box she kept in her trunk. When she straightened up, Bert was gone. Good.

Or not so good. As she rounded the corner of the house a second time, there he was. Worse yet, he was coming at her with a leer on his face.

"Reckon I better kiss the bride, too."

Blast and damn again. He must have seen her and Evan among the tulips at the store. But Bert was no Evan and these were no tulips. There was a hard wall behind her and Bert Barker closing in up front, with no gentlemanly pause where Connie could say, *Oh, all right,* or *Get the hell out of my face if you want to walk right for the rest of your life.* Connie barely had time to raise her screwdriver point outermost.

"You want to take down your awnings yourself?"

Apparently she'd hit Bert where he lived.

He backed off.

Once he was at a safe distance she decided to take advantage of having one of the island's biggest news-hounds all to herself. "You remember Arthur Abrew's Five and Dime?" she asked, and that was all it took.

Bert lounged against the relevant corner of the house as Connie worked on his awnings and dispensed his jaundiced view of bygone Nashtoba life. "Old Arthur's Five and Dime. What a joke. Opened up in 1932. Not four years later it went bust. Some businessman, old Arthur." Bert cackled.

"Why did it go bust?"

"Why do you think? You can't buy something for six cents and sell it for five, can you? And you can't go giving away the kitchen sink just because somebody's on hard times this week. No businessman, that Arthur. Biggest sucker that ever lived. That's why he went bust."

"You never heard anything about anyone stealing from him?"

Bert cackled again. "Stealing what, a spool of thread? Now there's the heist of the century. Where'd you get that little morsel of information?"

"Nowhere. What did Arthur do after the Five and Dime?"

"Ah. Smartened up a mite. Became a tobacconist. Go for people's addictions and you'll never go belly-up, that's what I say. He was sitting pretty with that little shop, not like the Five and Dime. 'Course that was before the surgeon general came along. But old Arthur had some luck that time. He'd just sold out to Percy Cobb. No flies on Percy. He turned the place into a candy store. Same principle, different population. Aren't you done yet? I'm not paying by the hour, I'm paying by the awning."

"So Arthur made out all right on the Percy deal? It wasn't like Percy robbed him blind?"

"Other way around, if anything. That's what Sarah's been living on ever since. And old Percy's been griping about it ever since. But you don't see him standing idle over the cash register much, let me tell you. Stop your bellyaching, that's what I tell him, you made out all right."

And Connie only wished she could say the same thing to Bert. He followed her from awning to awning, bellyaching, more or less in order, about the surgeon general, the Better Business Bureau, the Chamber of Commerce, Factotum, the price of cigarettes, the price of gas, the price of candy.

And the weather, of course.

The Whole Healing Body Shop was run by a couple of sixties leftovers named Jensen and had only just opened at the start of the summer, across Shore Road from the harbor. Connie gave them, tops, another two months. But the male Jensen fluttered up to her when she came in as if he were convinced his building were some sort of local monument.

"It's this Charlotte," he said, twisting his ponytail as he spoke. "We're so close to all that water. We have so many valuables. We have to do something." He waved his free hand behind him. The first thing Connie saw was something that looked like a tub full of mud.

"What's that?"

"Now there. Exactly. Do you have any idea what it costs to replace that mud? I think we should move it out. But how?"

Connie wasn't about to offer to pick up one end, that was for sure. The tub looked like it was made out of cast iron and was easily ten feet long by six wide. She looked further. There was another tub, equally as big, that looked to be full of green water, shelves full of oddly shaped bottles, a gold-colored tent in the corner, and behind a partially open curtain what was either a massage table or an instruments-of-torture rack. She would have kept looking longer if the flap of the tent hadn't opened to expose Fern Sutton.

She must have run here straight from the funeral

meats, Connie thought. She wore a white robe, her hair was wrapped in a white towel, and her face was covered with blue muck. The female Jensen came rushing over and helped her out of the robe. Underneath was a bathing suit. Fern stepped out of the robe and into the mud without hesitation.

Now there's desperation, thought Connie.

18

. . . you cannot tell who's your friend . . .

The tableau before Pete had stayed where it was long enough to sear permanently into his brain—husband on couch with arm around other woman, wife at the door with eyebrow up. Finally Sam Oliver removed his arm from Joanna's shoulders and bounded to his feet. "I'm sorry, love. This is Peter Bartholomew, an old friend of Joanna's. He's just popped up from the Cape. Peter, this is my wife, Ann. There. All introduced. I never can seem to remember to do that. Now. What will everyone have?"

Joanna held up her glass. "Scotch."

Pete watched the Olivers exchange a look, but not the look he'd been expecting. Pete had heard of blasé, but this was a bit much.

Sam looked at his watch. "Actually, Joanna, I'd say

it's almost time to eat. Let me shove along to the kitchen and stir things up." He turned to Pete. "Perhaps you'd join us?"

"No thanks," Pete managed. "I've got to get back."

"Then let me walk you out. Ann, you might make sure I haven't burned up the sauce. Or down the house."

"I'll help," said Joanna. She got up and followed Ann Oliver out of the room, the two women chatting like they were sharing a recipe, not a spouse.

The two men were much quieter. But once on the street Sam Oliver said, "Something tells me this visit hasn't gleaned for you what you'd hoped it would."

"No," said Pete. Here, obviously, was an offer to help do something about it, but Pete was too confused by now to think straight. The best he was able to do was a lame, "You've known Joanna since high school?"

"I have, yes. Ann just met her last year when we ran into her in Baltimore. I was giving a talk on Lyme disease. Joanna read about it and looked me up. We've stayed in intermittent contact since."

So he was a doctor. That figured. But what exactly did this "intermittent contact" mean? An ongoing ménage à trois? Somehow Pete was beginning to think not. "Look," he said, "I don't how much Joanna has told you about this situation with her mother, but I gather she's told you enough. What I need to know is what you've got to do with it."

Sam blinked in surprise. "Me? Not a thing. Joanna's visit is entirely coincidence. She showed up here a few weeks back and . . ." he stopped. "I take it you've talked to Dennis?"

"I've talked to him."

"How is he?"

"How should he be?"

They stood face-to-face and stock-still on the sidewalk. For a good long while Sam studied Pete. "Let me make a few things clear," he said finally. "I think you think I know more about this than I do. All I know is Joanna showed up on our doorstep a few weeks ago in distress. This was long before her mother got involved in this situation of hers, but Joanna has been here more or less ever since. Other than the fact that her marriage appears to be in some disarray, I know nothing else. As to which is cause and which is effect, I can only guess, but neither Ann nor I have been able to come up with anything more constructive than a shoulder to cry on, so to speak. We certainly aren't about to chuck her out on the street, but . . ." He paused. "Dennis always struck me as a reasonable fellow."

"Yes," said Pete. "He is."

"And he's staying around to look after Joanna's mother until this matter sorts itself out, is that it? Or are you doing that?"

Pete considered. Somewhere after the part about Joanna showing up on their doorstep and before the part about chucking her out on the street, Pete had begun to think that whatever Sam Oliver's connection in all this, he was as much in the dark about Pete's half of it as Pete was about Sam's. He'd also begun to think he might as well trust the guy. If he wanted to get something more out of Sam, maybe the best way to do it was to go first. So he did. He told the man about Sarah's confession. He also told him why nobody believed her. He then explained, again and much better this time, the two factors that had driven Pete to Boston in search of Joanna and Oliver—how Sarah had refused to talk about her daughter's high school years, and how she'd become so obviously distraught at the mention of Sam's name.

By the time Pete finished, Sam Oliver was obviously distraught, too. If Pete had to guess, he'd have said that until now the man had known little about the real situation back on Nashtoba. But if Pete had to guess again, he'd say the man knew plenty about something else. What? It had to go back to high school.

What the hell? He might as well cast around before he left. "You knew Webster Sutton in high school?"

"Not really. I'd only moved to Nashtoba my junior year. He was a sophomore, I believe. But I knew who he was."

"I hear he wasn't so nice."

Sam shrugged. "I was too busy trying to get my feet under me with my peers to notice much about the ones coming up behind. And as soon as I graduated my family moved off again. I never really did connect."

"I guess you connected with Joanna well enough."

Pete hadn't meant it to come out the way it did. Sam Oliver's eyes burned into him like Superman doing his damnedest to see through lead. "We're friends," he said evenly.

"I only meant that you must have connected well enough to be the person she ran to twenty-five years later when she needed a shoulder to cry on. It isn't every high school chum who . . ." Pete stopped. Something had happened to Sam's face.

And suddenly he looked at his watch. Remembered that sauce. "I'd better go salvage my culinary efforts before Ann beats them to death with the garlic press. It's an ongoing war between us."

"She seems very nice." Pete hadn't meant anything

by that, either, except that it wasn't everyone who would welcome an old high school chum crying on her husband's shoulder. For three weeks.

And again, Sam Oliver seemed to catch Pete's meaning.

"Love me, love my dog," he said.

Connie managed to calm Jensen down about the state of his art in the face of Charlotte and still managed to leave before Fern came out of the mud. The opportunity seemed too good to waste. She drove straight to the Sutton house. Because she hadn't come up with a single idea on how to present herself, she was thrilled to see a brand-new FOR SALE sign on the lawn. Connie went up to the door and knocked.

There were post-funeral signs all over the place—crumby cake plates on the coffee table, cups and saucers on chair arms, suit pants and shirt on the man who opened the door, long shadows on his face. What had Connie been thinking of? This was bordering on cruel and unusual punishment. She decided to retreat. "I'm sorry," she said. "I saw the FOR SALE sign and knocked. I just noticed it also says BY APPOINTMENT. Wren Realty, is it? I'll give them a call."

"No. It's all right. I'm here by myself just now, and better to . . ." He didn't complete the thought. Better to run the tour when his mother was out? Or better to do something besides sitting here alone in his dead father's house?

They introduced themselves. Connie said she was sorry about his father and the smile went taut.

"A quick once-around," Connie finished lamely.

Without further discussion Web turned right and trotted up the stairs. Connie followed. "Three bedrooms," he said. He led the way to the master bedroom first. Neat as a pin and, other than the masculine air to the dark, heavy furniture, devoid of any sign of male occupancy. She opened a closet. After all, closets were fair game in checking out a new house. This one was full to bursting, but only with women's clothes. It seemed all Webster Two's effects had been speedily cleared out. She peeked into the bathroom. "Full bath," she said approvingly. She gazed at the mirror that almost covered one wall. "No medicine cabinet?"

Web Sutton reached forward and pulled on a corner of the middle panel in the mirror and the entire section swung out. It had everything. Vitamin E. Shark cartilage. Hot pepper cream. Ginkgo. Pumice scrub. Miracle rub. Things that promised to revitalize dead cells. Things that promised to burn fat. Things that would lift the face, reduce the pores, tighten the gut. Connie closed the cupboard and followed Web out. The next room seemed to be more feminine, but also very empty. An older, married sister's, perhaps? Connie dutifully checked the closet, also empty. The next room was obviously Web Three's. Connie could tell by the jacket on the chair that matched the pants on the legs, but not by much else. The decor was as generic as a guest room. There were even two suitcases standing next to the dresser.

"Excuse the mess," said Web. Obviously, the man didn't know what the word meant.

"I've only just moved back in and since it won't be for long I've kind of just piled stuff up."

"Leaving the island?"

"No. No." For the first time the fatigued look left and Web's face lit up. "I'm the director of the Natural History Museum."

"Congratulations," said Connie. "Sounds like a big job."

"I hope to make it bigger. I have plans for that place. More school programs, conservation programs, projects to involve not only the museum's regular visitors but more of the outside population. I want to put on a good push, educate the public about our environment, enlist them to protect it but also to get them to appreciate it. Use it. There are so many . . ." He stopped, flushed. "Once I help my mother settle her affairs I'll be moving into my own place."

"She's selling the house?"

"Yes, she is. She's originally from the South. This was never her favorite weather."

"Tell her to wait a day or two."

Web Three smiled.

"And what will happen to the business?"

The shadows came back. "I'm not sure. I thought we should sell outright, but my mother can't quite. . . . My father would have hated that."

"Are you sure? I've heard that your father had planned to sell out himself."

Web couldn't have looked more surprised if she'd pushed him down the stairs. "My father? Sell the business? I don't think so. He was keeping it for . . ." He stopped.

Keeping it for Web Three. But Web Three didn't want it, that much was clear enough.

They went downstairs and dutifully through the rooms, but the shell-shocked look never left Web's face. There was more to the house than Connie surmised. Kitchen, den, dining room, living room, none of it giving much in the way of hints about the people who lived there. Even the finished basement only added to an already well-established theme—it was a fully equipped, top-of-the-line exercise gym and Web cleared up any small question of whose when he said, "My mother likes to stay in shape." He seemed embarrassed by the room, as well he might. This was well beyond the pale of someone who just wanted to stay in shape. This was certifiable obsession. Yes, old Fern was running scared, all right. But with cause? Connie didn't feel right asking Web if his dead father used to cheat. But where to go to find out? Evan had told her as much as he knew. Abby Fitch had told her as much as she would.

Connie thanked Web and left him, still with that shell-shocked look on his face.

19

~~~

A south-west blow on ye and blister ye all o'er!

Sarah thought he was gone. She thought he was five hundred miles south of here and she wasn't happy to find herself disabused of the notion as he came walking into the room with a miserable smile on his face. Lord, if you were that miserable, best not to try to smile in the first place.

"You're supposed to be in Baltimore," she said.

"Not yet. I've still got a few things to take care of here."

"Like me?"

Dennis pointed into the air behind him. "I'm concerned about this storm. I brought you a generator so at least you won't have to worry if the power goes out. And I thought I might board over the windows for you. Those shutters won't—"

"You will do nothing of the kind. Do you want me to sit here for days in the dark? I'm not alone, you know. Carrie has already spoken to me about the windows and she's shopped and gone to the pharmacy and the bank and right now she's in the kitchen hard-boiling enough eggs for the Easter rabbit. Does that satisfy you? Now will you go home? Do you want poor Joanna to be left all alone in the middle of—"

"Joanna is not all alone, Sarah. Neither is she at home. As I think you know. As I think you could explain if you saw fit. She's still with the Oliver fellow."

Sam Oliver. Sarah listened to that name again, the name she wished with all her might she'd never had occasion to hear in her life. And she listened to her son-in-law's voice. It barely sounded like Dennis. Nothing seemed right. Nothing was as she'd planned.

Sam Oliver. She thought of the day she'd first laid eyes on him. One short day. One long hour. And how unfair that it should haunt them all for life.

"Sarah," said Dennis softly from somewhere close beside her. "I'm sorry. Are you all right?"

For a second time the child saved her. Sarah could hear the *put, put, put* on the stairs of the small, bare feet. Odd how normal it sounded, a child's feet on her stairs. All these years without that sound and in just a few days she'd come used to it, come to expect it. They'd each come to expect certain things of each other, she and the child. Queer little girl. Lonely. Still looking for places to attach. As if her own mother weren't enough. As if the woman didn't worry and pray every day, just trying to do what was right. Trying to make what wasn't right go away. Trying to . . . Sarah drew her thoughts up short, no longer sure just whom she meant. She held out her hand and the child drew closer, but not close enough to touch, as if she were still not completely sure if this was safety or harm.

Wise child, Sarah thought.

Connie stepped off the Sutton doorstep still thinking about Web Three's face. Sure, the news that Web Two had planned to sell his firm might come as a shock, especially if Web Three had killed his father so he could get out from under his thumb, and then found out his father's thumb hadn't really been all that firmly in place. But what about old Fern? Maybe she'd gotten tired of competing every day of her life. Maybe she'd gotten tired of running that futile race against the clock. Maybe she'd wanted to go home to Old Virginny, or wherever it was. Maybe she'd wanted out from under Sutton's thumb herself.

As Connie walked to her car she looked up. The day had gone dark since she'd last looked, the sky turning thick. She'd never felt the air so dead or so dank. In the dozen or so years she'd lived on Nashtoba she'd never witnessed an honest-to-goodness hurricane. She'd sat through many a howling northeaster huddled around the hurricane lamp, but Pete's house sat on the south face of Nashtoba. This would be different.

A sudden twinge in Connie's stomach reminded her of the refrigerator full of shrimp. She looked at her watch. Six-thirty. Pete probably wouldn't be home till eight at the earliest. It seemed like they hadn't seen each other in weeks. She'd at least like to eat dinner with the man, but she'd never hold out without a snack.

The first place she passed, either by accident or by subliminal design, was Cobb's Candy Manor. She supposed she could suffer along with that in a pinch. She walked in and selected her own assortment of saltwater taffy from the open bins, taking care to include a good helping of Polly's favorite flavor—peanut butter. Yuck. But there would be two of them starving to death if they waited for Pete. She took her bag to the counter and old Percy Cobb himself appeared from the dim recesses to ring her up. Connie observed him with interest. Percy was old. Sarah-old. Arthur-old, if Arthur had lived. As she stood there wondering how to bring up the subject of Arthur Abrew's Five and Dime, Percy spoke up. "Getting some weather."

After a decade on Nashtoba Connie had at least got the weather thing down. "Yup," she said.

"Don't care what Charlotte pulls. Won't hold a candle to '38."

"Nope," said Connie. Which brought her neatly to the next obvious remark: "This was the tobacco shop in '38, right?"

Percy must have been a little hard of hearing. Either that or he wasn't about to be railroaded off the subject of the weather one-two-three, just like that. "Nobody knew it was coming, see. That was the trouble with '38. Turned north off Florida and everybody said that was it. Gone out to sea for good. But what she did was feed up on all that warm water and come right back at us here up north. Sixty miles an hour, she moved. Won't see another like that."

"Nope," said Connie. "Wasn't that the year you bought this shop?"

"Bought the shop in '49. This we're talking about, this was '38. Ground was saturated already, see. That was the trouble with '38. Rained for two months straight, before that storm even hit. Nowhere for the water to go but down the street. And the wind. Clocked that wind at one eighty-six on the bluff off the Point."

"Wow," said Connie. "This shop rode it out all right, I guess?"

Percy pointed to a notch in the doorframe behind him. "See that? That's the high-water mark from '38. Won't see the likes of that with Charlotte. Ground's dry as a bone. And plenty of warning. Not like in '38. Water rushed down this street like it was the Mississippi, carrying everything with it. A twenty-three-foot catboat came floating by. Ran out and tied it to a telephone pole across the street. Risked my life. Fellow never even thanked me. Car washed up in the lobby of the bank. Battery shorted, horn blubbed away underwater. Wouldn't believe the stuff floated down this street. Trees, fences, outhouses, saw a dead deer go past the window in—"

Connie tried a visual this time. She pointed to the notch. "So Arthur Abrew made that mark?"

Eureka. "Arthur did, sure. He was the one here in '38. Tobacco shop back then. Lost the Five and Dime down the street, moved up here, set up shop. Shame about the Five and Dime."

"What happened to it?"

"What happened? The Depression happened. Simple as that."

"I heard something about some thievery."

Percy's eyes narrowed. "Where'd you get something like that? Weren't any thieves. Not on Nashtoba. Only thief was the one cooked the books when I went to buy this place."

"Cooked the books?"

"Paid a pretty penny for this place, I did. Couldn't budge that accountant on the price. But this was the only shop front on Main Street available and I wasn't of a mind to wait around for another to crop up. Knew it, too, Web did."

Connie's pulse hopped. "Web?"

"Web One. He was Arthur's accountant. Would have been mine if I'd seen him first."

"And you actually think he cooked the books?"

Percy Cobb dropped his chin, a move that effectively hid any telltale expression when he said, "Don't care what she does, this Charlotte won't hold a candle to '38."

And that was the last thing he said.

But Connie's luck was in on other fronts. As she left the candy shop she looked down the street and saw Melissa Farentino coming out of the drugstore. Connie sprinted down the sidewalk and caught up with her just before she got into her car. She must have recognized Connie right off. Her first words weren't *Who are you?* but "Now what do you want?"

Connie tried to cull down her many questions into some sort of succinct opening remark. What she came up with was, "I want to know what your dead boss was like."

Melissa's eyes narrowed. "Who are you from?"

"The person who shot him."

The eyes unnarrowed. "Then you know what he was like."

"Not really. Can you describe him in one sentence?"

"A fat, frigging son of a bitch."

Connie grinned. "And in two sentences?"

"Fat, frigging asshole."

Now they were getting somewhere. "If he was so bad, why did you take the job?"

There was a dead minute there. Dead face, dead air,

the whole bit. Finally Melissa crossed her arms and cocked a blue-jeaned hip against the car. "Where else was I gonna go work? Know where I learned computers? Hatchet."

Hatchet. Pohachett, to be exact. The halfway house for ex-cons over on the Hook. It was true, there was probably not a long list of businessmen looking to hire Melissa Farentino with a résumé like that. The question was, why was Webster Sutton on the list? From everything Connie had ever heard, he didn't seem the type.

"Anything else you can tell me about him?"

"Like what?"

"Like how did he get along with his partner?"

"How do I know? Ask her, why don't you?"

"How do you get along with her?"

Melissa dropped a few bricks from her defenses. "She's been okay. She told me right off: Keep out of his way and you'll do all right."

"That must have been hard to do."

"Nah. She helped."

"She helped you keep out of his way?"

"Yeah. I had to get there on time. That's one of the things they check off on your sheet. If they've put down you're late, even once, that's it. Like one minute. You're out. So sometimes I'd end up early. Five or ten minutes, even. At first it was just the cleaner there ahead of me. I'd sit outside, have a smoke, it wasn't bad. Then all of a sudden he was there, too. Every morning. Then it really sucked. I'd have to go right in and get busy. Didn't care if I was ten minutes early. Bang. Get to work."

"That was it? That he made you start work a few minutes early?"

The eyes narrowed again. "I told you. He was an asshole."

"Like how?"

"Like shoving me around. Like making me do the cleaning after the old cleaner quit. Like dropping things so I'd have to pick them up. Like screwing up a computer file and blaming me for it. Like . . ." She stopped.

"And how did Abby Fitch help?"

"She'd find me stuff to do out back. He never worked out back. Always had to sit up front in the big office. Mr. Big Shot."

Interesting, Connie thought. While Abby had so neatly tucked Melissa out back, what was she doing with Mr. Big Shot up front? Probably nothing. Too big a risk. All Melissa had to do was to walk out there and . . . and what? Tell old Fern? A young ex-con on her first job, on probation? Fat chance. It began to make sense why someone like Sutton had hired someone like Melissa. But as Connie thought of Abby Fitch she somehow couldn't make the rest of the picture work. Still, that didn't mean Sutton wasn't cheating with someone else.

"Can you tell me anything else about him?" she asked. "Anything about his home life? For example, did you ever pick up on any evidence that he might be cheating on his wife?"

"Not with me, he wasn't." It seemed such a point of pride that Connie wondered what it had taken her to achieve it.

"What about the son? Did you ever meet the son?"

"Yeah. Once or twice. He hated his guts."

"How do you know?"

"Been there," said Melissa.

And that was it. Like Percy, Melissa seemed to hit

some invisible threshold on talk. She got in her car, slammed the door, and drove off into the growing dark.

It's the barometer, Polly thought. She always reacted poorly when it dropped this fast, like she had a giant case of PMS. Her body felt like it would explode. Her sinuses ached. She couldn't sit still, but neither could she do anything. And she couldn't stop looking at the stupid clock. She knew the chief was busy. Still, she'd have to admit to some surprise that he hadn't at least stuck his head in the door, or called, or left a message that said, *Sorry, too busy, see you next trip.* It wasn't like he wouldn't know she was here—Pete would have told him five seconds after she'd hung up.

When Connie got back she made it worse. Banging around the kitchen like a bull in a china shop, also looking at the clock.

Finally, Pete arrived. Connie settled down and Polly got enough of a grip on herself to help set up the table. They ate cold shrimp and salad and rolls and drank Ballantine and kept the radio turned on low and talked. Or more accurately, thought Polly, Pete and Connie talked. Polly listened and watched the door as they ran through everything each of them had learned or thought or suspected about this murder thing. Polly had to admit there was enough stuff. Her head alternately swam and pounded and drowned in names, places, dates. Joanna, Sam, Fern, Sarah, Arthur, Web One, Two, and Three, Melissa. Boston, Bradford, Baltimore. Things that had happened sixty years ago. Things that had happened thirty years ago. Things that had happened yesterday and the day before that and the day before that. Things Pete and

Connie had just found out, or things they'd just had time to share with each other. Right now, for example, it was something about Web One and the old Five and Dime and cooked books.

Polly looked at the clock again. Was that all it was? It seemed like a month since she'd last looked. It seemed like a year since she'd last seen him and it was all of five days ago, standing on the town hall steps, waving off the bride and groom. She'd just been thinking he'd looked a bit envious when he'd turned to her and said, "Lucky son of a bitch." And then, "Lunch?" and then the radio had crackled. He'd gone to the car, come back stone-faced. Said he was sorry, but he was going to be tied up.

Five days ago, that was.

Of course now Polly knew what that radio call had been about. Sarah Abrew, confessing to murder.

Okay, a pretty good excuse.

And on top of all that, Charlotte. No, she couldn't blame him for not showing up.

Much.

Polly helped clear up and the three of them went out to sit on the porch in the dark. Polly took one good whiff of the pregnant air and didn't need the radio after that, but that's when they made it official—the hurricane watch turned into a warning at last.

For some seconds after the big announcement the three of them sat silent. Connie broke it first by turning to Polly and laughing. "Pete's got this divine retribution thing. We have to pay for being happy. Apparently the wrecked honeymoon isn't enough. He's waiting for the other shoe to drop. That's it, isn't it, Pete?"

Pete's voice cut over hers as if he hadn't heard a

word she'd said. "All right. This is the situation. We're a hundred and fifty yards from the Sound and most of it's marsh. I'm going to watch the tide and I'm going to watch the weather, but when I say jump, we jump. We leave here fast, no discussion, no running upstairs for your toothbrush. It's not just the water in front of us, it's the road behind us. I don't want us cut off with no way out. Everyone agreed?"

"Agreed," said Connie.

"Agreed," said Polly.

"Good. So let's get to work. This furniture has to come in, the porch screens have to come out—"

That was when they heard the knock. Nobody moved. Polly didn't know what the other two were waiting for, but she was waiting for the door to open and the usual *halloo* to echo ahead of the chief into the hall.

Nothing.

Pete went inside. The man who returned with him was, in Polly's limited experience, just about as good-looking as middle-aged men got.

The disappointment was shattering, nonetheless.

20

---ᢞᢞᢞ---

The strangeness of your story put heaviness in me.

Pete wouldn't have said he was exactly surprised to see him.

"I'm sorry to bother you so late," said Sam Oliver. "And I wouldn't if Charlotte weren't out there. I knew this might be the last chance for a day or two and I wasn't sure it should wait."

Connie offered him a cup of coffee. The man accepted politely, but added, somewhat pointedly, Pete thought, "I won't stay long. After I have a quiet word with Pete, here, I'll be heading straight back."

Connie and Polly took the hint and left.

Once the kettle began to boil Pete poured them each a cup of instant coffee and pointed Sam to a kitchen chair. Pete sat in silence as the first scalding mouthful went down Sam's throat. Pete was content to wait. By the look on Sam's face he could tell whatever was coming wasn't going to be any day at the beach.

"After you left," said Sam finally, "or I should say after I realized the implications of what you had said, I decided to have a long talk with Joanna. I could see what was going on. You'd derailed in our direction and needed to be put back on track. But I should make one thing clear at the outset. Joanna absolutely did not tell me to come here and in doing so I'm violating every confidentiality rule there is."

"Joanna's your patient?"

"No. Of course not. I'm talking about the rules of common decency. She confided in me as a friend. Or rather, she didn't confide in me so much as she . . ." Sam ran a hand through unthinned and unruffled hair and left it looking only thicker and neater. "The situation is this. I feel I have some information that it's crucial for you to know, but I have no right to tell it to you. And I wouldn't be telling you anything now if I hadn't gotten the feeling from Joanna tonight that she wanted me to. She didn't tell me to come here. I'm not going to give myself that out. The responsibility is mine and mine alone. But I do feel if she were emotionally able to speak to you about this herself, she would. With that understanding, do you wish me to continue or should I go home?"

So much for taking all the responsibility himself, thought Pete. But all right, he could take half his lumps with the best of them. "You've come this far," said Pete. "Go ahead."

Sam made some inroads on the coffee first, apparently not noticing how bad it was. Again, Pete waited.

"Joanna Abrew was raped in her senior year in high school," said Sam finally.

Pete's first thought was of his stomach. Sam Oliver's words had made him feel physically sick. His second thought was: Webster Sutton.

Sam seemed to read the second thought, at least. "Sorry," he said, "this isn't going to be as neat as you think. The charming fellow who raped Joanna was someone named Joe Twicks. Ever heard of him?"

The name was vaguely familiar, but Pete shook his head.

"He's the assistant district attorney for Brixton County."

Pete felt even sicker, the last swallow of coffee hovering just under his chin someplace.

"Twicks was neither charged nor convicted. Since that time I've done some homework on this and I find it's a not uncommon outcome, as a comparatively small percentage of rapes are ever actually reported. But in this case the victim had something you don't get too often—an eyewitness."

"You?"

"Me. I may have told you earlier I was pretty much of a loner in my Nashtoba years. I was new, I didn't know how to fit in, I decided it was easier to keep moving. When I was in school I spent a lot of time walking the halls. When I was outside school I spent it walking in the woods. That's how I happened to stumble onto them. I suppose *stumble* is the wrong word. *Charge* would be more correct. I heard her, first. This gagging, crying, choking sound that I still hear about twice a week in my sleep. When he saw me he got up and ran, but by then it was too late. There was nothing I could do. Nothing." He stopped, sipped his coffee, looked into it as if he were still looking for a pair of faster feet.

"Hard to catch someone who's got a good head start," said Pete.

Sam waved a dismissive hand. "I didn't even try. You wouldn't have, either, not with her lying there. She was a mess. She was . . ." Sam raised his own hand like a traffic cop's and switched tack. "I'd already seen enough of Joe Twicks to have given him a wide berth. From a few things I'd heard I'd gotten the idea Joanna had, too—that he'd tried and gotten rebuffed. I have no idea why she went with him into the woods."

"I'd say that's beside the point."

"Thank you, I'm aware of that."

It was Pete's turn to raise a hand. "Sorry." His anger might be newer, but the other man's was still obviously plenty hot. And he'd been living with it how long? Joanna had been living with it how long? Christ. "What did you do?" asked Pete.

"What I could. Not much. Covered her up, tried to calm her down, asked her if she could walk, but she wouldn't, or couldn't, answer me. Finally I picked her up. I had a car. I wanted to take her to the doctor's, but she became hysterical. I said something about the police and it got worse. She wanted to go home. All she wanted to do was to go home. So I took her home."

When nothing else was said for some time Pete summoned his voice. "Did Sarah—" But that was as far as he got before the rest of it came out in a rush.

"I felt at the time it was the wrong tactic. I suppose that's easy for me to say. I wasn't the one who . . . Just the same, I felt it was a mistake. I was a witness. We could have put him away for a good long time. But what could I say? I hardly knew these people. I'd noticed her, of course, it would have been hard not to, it was like staring into a flame. I don't mean just the red hair. Once you looked at her you couldn't look away. She was captivating. You don't know what it was like to find her after . . ." He stopped. Restarted. "The minute I put Joanna on the couch her mother tried to shoo me out. I didn't blame her. I told her who I was and what had happened and offered to get the doctor, the police. I was sure they'd want me to make a statement. But she said no, thank you, and sent me out. As I walked away I thought, well, of course not, this wasn't the time to get into all that. But when I went back the next day . . ." He stopped again.

"You went back?"

"I thought I should at least make sure they had my name and address. Again, I was thinking of the police. And I wanted to see how she was, of course. But when I went back Joanna was stashed somewhere out of sight and my inquiries were met with 'Joanna is fine, thank you for calling, good night.' I again offered to testify and was told by her mother that they would not be pressing charges. It would be too difficult for Joanna, the mother said. She felt the best thing for everyone was to pretend it had never happened. She said—and I remember it almost word for word, even now—she said the best thing I could do for Joanna was to erase the entire episode as if it didn't exist."

"Easier said than done."

"Yes," said Sam. "And I'm talking on my own account now. I wanted to get Twicks. I wanted to get him more than I've ever wanted to get anyone in my life. But leave me out of it. I imagine what it must have been like for Joanna to try to 'erase' it, so to speak."

"Did you talk to Joanna about it?"

Sam shook his head. "I never saw Joanna again. She never came back to school after that day, and after graduation I moved off island. That was it. Until she ran into me in Baltimore last year."

The two men looked at each other. Coincidence? Pete doubted it. "And now?" he asked finally.

"If you mean what is she doing at my place, I can only offer the theory that my wife Ann gave. She's the house psychologist. Sooner or later an unresolved issue like this will take its toll on the best of marriages and it took its toll on the Willoughbys'. Joanna only ran in my direction because—"

"Because you'd saved her before." After all, he was Superman, right?

But Sam shook his head. "I didn't save anybody and I was of little help afterward. Ann thinks the reason Joanna came to me is because all along she's wanted desperately to talk about what happened. To try to come to some sort of terms with it. When she saw me again last year it forced some sort of crisis, but it also reminded her when the crisis came that there was someone who understood what had happened, someone who would understand her."

"You're trying to tell me Dennis doesn't understand?"

"Dennis doesn't understand because Dennis doesn't know. That was the decision, remember? To pretend it never happened. Joanna tried that. It resulted in what according to Ann is the inevitable result in that situation—relationship problems, bouts of depression, substance abuse. Her mother pulled it off better, until you brought up high school, me, the transfer, the whole ugly mess. Now you see why she reacted the way she did."

And maybe now Pete saw why Sarah and Joanna had always had such a difficult time with each other.

Every time they came together, there was that big old water jump.

"But what about now? Have you and Joanna talked since she arrived?"

Sam shook his head. "Not very effectively, I'm afraid. For the first couple of weeks I sat around waiting for Joanna to bring it up, but she never did. Finally Ann encouraged me to broach the subject. It seemed obvious to her that subconsciously, at least, this was what Joanna had come here for. So I brought it up, but apparently I did it badly. I suggested she get some professional help. She became quite upset. It was as if she viewed that course of action as some sort of personal failure. Finally I told her to at least tell Dennis."

"And what did she say to that?"

"Two words. 'I can't.' Ann thinks there are several forces at work. One is Joanna's misplaced guilt, and possibly related to that, a feeling that she has misrepresented herself to Dennis by marrying him without telling him about the event up front. The other is that Joanna is waiting for permission to speak. Either in some tacit way from Dennis himself, or from the person who, with the best of possible intentions, tied her tongue in the first place."

"Sarah," said Pete.

Connie and Polly got straight to work. They put the Factotum files in the spare room where Polly now slept. They likewise moved any books and anything belonging to the various customers of Factotum—a desk awaiting refinishing, a bike awaiting repair, a fishing reel awaiting cleaning—and, incidentally, a favorite old lamp of Pete's. They also rolled up the braided rug in the downstairs office, lugged it upstairs, and shoved it under Pete and Connie's bed. The rest of the downstairs, full of Factotum detritus and some less-than-desirable old rattan furniture, would have to take its chance. They brought in the tools hanging on the side of the house—rakes, shovels, hoes—but avoided the porch furniture and screens, which were within sight and sound of the two men at the kitchen table.

Finally they heard them in the hall, Pete's voice first. "I appreciate this. I know what it took."

Sam Oliver's voice, less distinct at first: ". . . hope of some help. Good luck."

"And you." Pete again.

The door shut. The car pulled off into the night. Pete's feet taking the stairs in threes, bursting into the spare room where Connie and Polly were piling things around the fold-out couch. He looked around. "Good job. Let's tackle the porch."

Polly gave Connie a shot in the ribs as they followed him downstairs. "Ask him," she whispered.

Connie shook her head. There was a look to him that told her to let it wait.

They stripped the porch, added one or two more items to the hoard in Polly's room, dug out the candles, filled hurricane lamps, loaded flashlights, and went to their respective beds. Pete and Connie left the radio on. Charlotte was moving at thirty-two miles an hour north-northwest, with one-hundred-thirty-mile-an-hour winds, still a category three storm.

Pete clicked the radio off and silence descended. Connie had just decided he must be asleep when the whole story of Joanna's rape and its aftermath came tumbling into the dark.

* * *

"But it wasn't Sutton," said Connie a long time later.

"No," said Pete.

"So it has nothing to do with all this."

"I don't know," said Pete. "He came all the way down here."

"To help about the murder. You said yourself, he saw you heading on the wrong tack."

"I don't know," said Pete again. "Maybe he just wants me to back off from Joanna. It's only natural he'd feel a bit protective, after all that."

"But it wasn't Sutton who raped Joanna. She has nothing to do with Sarah's mess."

"Oh, no? I bet you a week of dinner dishes she was the inspiration behind Sarah's redhead in the tower."

"So what? That and Goldilocks gives you two fairy tales, that's it."

"You don't find it strangely coincidental that Sarah Abrew confesses to the murder of a man she accuses of a sexual assault when her daughter was the victim of one herself?"

"I find a lot of things strangely coincidental. That doesn't mean they aren't just that: coincidence."

Pete lay silent.

After a while Connie said, "She should have told Dennis. He would have helped." She heard in her own voice a note of been-there-done-that, and Pete must have heard it, too. A subtle shift in body parts and she was suddenly much closer, much warmer.

Much happier.

But she couldn't sleep. Thinking of her own situation made her lie awake long into the night trying to come up with the Willoughbys' best shot at a second chance.

21

—◦◦◦—

*Now would I give a thousand furlongs of sea for an
acre of barren ground . . .*

Pete woke to a soft breeze. He slipped out of bed,
tapped the barometer, and the needle plunged. He
opened the door that led out onto the railed-in porch
roof and went through. The sky was sulfurous, the air
like a slap in the face with a wet dish rag. He looked
off toward the Sound, still only washboard rough, tide
only slightly higher than normal. He lowered his eyes
to measure the beach, the marsh, the lawn, if that's
what you could call the mixture of anthills and sand
sprinkled with a few green tufts.

Right now, whatever it was, it wasn't long enough
by a few hundred feet. Pete wasn't worried about the
rain. It had been an extremely dry summer and fall.
The water table was as low as it got and that would
help. It was the storm surge that caused most of the

coastal damage, a dome of water sometimes twenty feet high that hammered any coastline within a hundred miles of the storm's landfall. Come high tide there would be no beach and precious little marsh. If peak surge coincided with high tide they could be in trouble.

Pete stood on the deck like the captain of the *Titanic,* weighing the divine retribution thing Connie had referred to against his intense reluctance to abandon ship. High tide was at two o'clock. He'd have to keep careful watch on the forecast as well as the clock, but Pete's little cottage had ridden out plenty of hurricanes before this. Dammit, he was going to stay put as long as he could. That didn't mean everyone else had to, though.

Pete went back inside, going over his mental checklist as he showered and dressed. When he got to the kitchen he turned on the radio along with the stove. School had been canceled, a shelter set up in the building. All residents in the flood plain fifteen feet or less above sea level were advised to evacuate.

Connie appeared at the door and paused there, listening. "Have they decided when it's supposed to make landfall?"

"Early afternoon, here. It hit North Carolina at dawn."

"Sarah's in a good spot."

"Yes," said Pete. And then he thought: *Yes.* The proverbial two birds.

When Polly appeared and they'd collected around the table, he tossed it out. "Might be a good idea if you two camped out at Sarah's for a while."

It was like two of the three Supremes. "No," they said in unison.

Pete took one more shot from the other direction.

Sarah was worried about a leaky roof. There were a lot of big pines around there. Who knew how the Suggs crowd would do under fire?

Connie retorted, "You fixed that roof last year."

Polly tossed in, "Those pines survived '38."

"And the Suggs crowd has survived Sarah. Charlotte will be nothing compared to that." Connie again.

Pete gave up. They sat around the table and divvied up the remaining preparations. Polly would tackle the home front while Connie went to the bank for emergency cash and checked on the remaining waterfront properties for which they caretook. Pete would make last-minute checks on Rita, Sarah, and the boats at the dock.

Rita Peck woke to a soft breeze. It didn't have her fooled. Time to move. She found herself lingering in the shower, the thought crossing her mind that if they lost power this could well be the last hot water out of her electric tank for a while, but she drank her coffee on the run. She started with the plants—hanging baskets of impatiens and fuchsia and tubs of chrysanthemums. She removed them from the outside deck and brought them indoors. Next she took in her Japanese lanterns, her clothesline, and the bucket of clothespins. She was trailing garden hose and watering can when Evan showed up.

"Need any help?"

"No," said Rita perversely. She was an old hand at being a single woman, wasn't she? She could fend for herself. But she didn't balk when he took an end of the heavy gas grill and helped her wheel it into the garage. The lawn furniture also went faster with two and when Evan suggested boarding up the garage doors she didn't argue. He shifted the heavy boards in place and expertly wielded the hammer. When he finished and moved without comment to the plate-glass window Rita realized there was nothing else outside for her to do. She could go inside and deal with the household things. It gave her an odd sense of déjà vu. There had been a time in her life when it had been like this—whole halves of her existence that someone else had attended to. She supposed in some ways these modern mothers who started out single had it easier—from day one they knew it was all up to them, there was no painful adjustment when they were suddenly left flat.

Rita watched Evan saunter up to Pete's truck when it pulled in, heard him say he had everything under control in this neck of the woods.

If she wasn't careful, thought Rita, she'd get used to this.

As Pete approached Sarah's front steps a small, pale streak dove for the yew bush and a thin voice called out, "Password!"

"Mustard," said Pete, the peculiarly colored sky still on his mind.

Whatever the original password had been, this one seemed to suit the new door-guard better. Round eyes popped out from behind the bush. "Pass. I don't have any school. It's being made into a shelter. We're having a hurry game."

"A hurry game?"

"Hurricane," said a voice behind him. Pete turned to see Carrie Suggs holding open the door. "Come inside, Lucy."

"I thought I'd see about getting Sarah battened down," said Pete. But for the second time that morning he found he was not needed. Carrie reeled off an impressive list of the precautions she'd taken and it left Pete little room for improvement.

Carrie disappeared through the door. Pete followed Carrie, and Lucy followed Pete, but when they went right he went left. As he crossed the threshold to the living room Sarah said, "What in the blue blazes do you mean by going to see Joanna? And don't look so bamboozled. You think I wouldn't find out? My daughter happened to call me. She let slip she'd just seen you. What the devil are you up to?"

"I'm not up to anything."

For a half-second silence fell between them. Finally a weary-sounding Sarah said, "Joanna has nothing to do with this."

"Doesn't she, Sarah?"

It took her a long time to come out with it, and when she did it was only three words, cracked, rasped.

"No, she doesn't."

Connie saw Del Farber behind the pane of glass that was apparently designed to keep his customers from bothering him while at the same time assuring them he hadn't absconded with their money. The sight of him reminded Connie that she had a question for him. She strode past the young woman at the desk and tapped on the glass. Del Farber waved her in.

"Good morning," she said cheerily.

"It was," said Del. "What may I do for you? We're planning to close early and I have a great deal—"

"I'm just wondering. Now that you know there was nothing to that rumor about Sutton-Fitch, have you changed your mind about lending Abby money?"

"If Ms. Fitch wishes to discuss the situation further I would be happy to do so," said Del warily. "I'm afraid that is all I'm at liberty to—"

"Thanks, that'll do." Just then Connie caught sight of Fern Sutton in the teller line. The bank was busy, Christmas-Eve-day kind of busy, and Fern was four back in line, chatting merrily to the woman in front of her. Connie figured Fern would be captive for the next few minutes, anyway. Connie strode past the secretary a second time and lined up behind Fern at the far window.

"Hear we're getting some weather," said the woman in front of Fern.

"I've been a wreck," Fern answered. "We only just got my husband buried yesterday. It was like pulling teeth to get that police chief to return the body to me and here we were, one eye on the weather, one on the clock, one on the . . ." She stopped.

Maybe she realized she was up to three eyes, thought Connie.

"It must have been a strain," said Woman Number One. "And Web busy with that new job, isn't he? I saw him over there, hard at work already. Such a shame, here he was almost fixed to join his father and look what happens. Have they done anything about that Abrew woman?"

"Not a thing. I said when they brought in that new chief that things were going to change around here, and not for the better. Was I right?"

The woman in front of Fern Sutton chose to maintain a judicious silence at that particular moment, a fact that Connie found encouraging. It had taken the island a long time to cut the chief any slack and in Connie's opinion it was long overdue. The line moved forward and when Woman Number One had reestablished herself in the new position she resumed the conversation. "What happens now? I mean about the business. If Web's lost heart for it . . ."

"I know. I suppose I'll sell out, but somehow I hate to do it. I know my husband would never have dreamed of such a thing."

Oh, no? thought Connie. Better talk to old Abby. But suddenly she remembered the confusion that still reigned over the subject of Abby's buying out her partner. Had Sutton, in a moment of weakness, agreed to the sale, and then resorted to underground means to prevent it from coming to fruition? Of all the things Connie had heard about Sutton by now, this scenario seemed unlikely. Easy enough to see him subverting things later on, but to have lost control of them in the first place? Connie thought not.

Woman Number One was now at the window, and Fern, having lost her conversational companion, turned hopefully behind her. She saw Connie, and although it was obvious she'd have preferred Attila the Hun on one of his bad days, her need to commune seemed to overcome her. "We're due for some weather, I hear."

"Yes," said Connie.

"Don't I know you from somewhere? What is your name?"

"Connie Bartholomew," said Connie. "I saw you in your husband's office and I saw you in the mud. I couldn't help overhearing. If you're looking for a buyer for your husband's business, start with his partner. She might still be interested."

Fern's smile was patronizing. "I believe you're confused. She expressed interest in my husband buying her shares, not vice versa."

"That was her first choice, yes. But when he refused, she tried to go the other way. The only stumbling block was a loan problem that may have resolved itself. If I were you, I'd talk to her."

"Believe me, I know my own husband's plans. He lived and breathed that company. In at seven every morning, home at all hours, that was all he talked about at the dinner table. He was not going to *sell* anything. He was going to get rid of the partner when Web finished his degree and joined him."

The line moved. "Excuse me," said Fern. She must have rolled her eyes at Woman Number One as she passed because the woman gave Connie one of those looks that curdled things.

Connie didn't care. She'd learned how to talk to people like this.

"Hear we're getting some weather," she said.

22

I will here shroud till the dregs of the storm be past.

Polly ran around latching windows, hooking screen doors, filling the bathtub. If the power went out the electric pump in the well did, too, and there the water would sit, fifty feet down. She turned up the fridge, too. Best to get things good and cold. She distributed flashlights, lanterns, and candles in strategic locations and it was as she swung a little too fast through the kitchen doorway that she cracked a lantern against the doorjamb and broke the globe. She knew where to get another one. The question was, was it worth the aggravation? Once she remembered that the police station was three doors down from Beston's Store, she decided it was.

* * *

The first thing Polly did as she arrived at Beston's porch was to take a casual glance down the street. The chief's car wasn't in its usual spot in front of the station. And what would she have done if it was? Nothing, of course. She turned her attention to the porch. She seemed to have interrupted an argument. It wasn't hard to do there, since there was usually one going on, and although this one was less lively than some Polly could recall, the subject matter captured her interest.

"Right back in," said Bert as Polly stepped onto the porch. "She loses the job she's right back in."

"Who?" asked Polly.

"Melissa Farentino," said Ed Healey. "Bert here is trying to tell us it's the condition of her probation. Maintain steady employment or she's back in. I say she has to commit a crime to get tossed back in. What do you say?"

What Polly said was, "Who's Melissa Farentino?"

"That klepto," said Bert. "Alice Houghton's kid."

"Alice Houghton Farentino," said Ed.

"She knows who Alice is. Jemmy Abrew's big blooper."

"Now, Bert, you don't know for a fact—"

"She's what happened when he took Belle Houghton to those fireworks in Boston and didn't come home till daylight, that's what she is."

"It was car trouble," said Ed. "That's what he said."

"So he could refuse to marry her come payday," said Bert. "Denied up and down it was his, and all that red hair staring him in the face. Old Jemmy had balls, I'll give him that."

"Who's Jemmy?" asked Polly. She had a feeling she'd be doing it all day, asking who this was, who that was, but Jemmy's last name was too close to current events for her to let it go at that.

"Jemmy Abrew," said Evan. "Arthur's brother. Sarah's brother-in-law."

"Black Jem, they called him," said Ed.

"So Melissa Farentino is Sarah Abrew's great-niece?"

"Depends who you ask," said Evan at the same time that Ed said, "No," and Bert said, "Yes."

Having cleared that up, Polly went inside and purchased the replacement chimney for Pete's hurricane lamp. There was a line at the register. There was never a line at Beston's register. Polly waited patiently for the hammers, nails, saws, batteries, flashlights, and lanterns ahead of her to get rung up.

When Polly stepped outside again the wind had finally stiffened enough to ruffle the feathers of the men on the bench. They were actually standing now, still arguing, this time over which blow had done more damage on Nashtoba—'54 or '38. She could picture them still there, leaning into the wind, arguing about previous storm damage as Beston's porch blew down around their feet.

Sarah never heard the car. What she did hear was Carrie, speaking to her daughter. "Lucy, go upstairs. I'll be up in a minute. Why don't you look at that new Winnie-the-Pooh?"

"Is it the hurry game?"

"Not yet. Go upstairs. Don't come down till I get you."

Lucy came stomping through the living room. Sarah had to hand it to Carrie—the child did what she was told. But why tell her to go away?

And then she heard his voice in the hallway. She

felt strangely calm. Suddenly it seemed not to matter what he'd come to ask her, or come to say to her. She didn't have to answer him, did she?

Fool.

She'd underestimated him. Something she'd sworn not to do from the beginning. Carrie led him into the room where Sarah sat serene, and as Carrie made to withdraw, he said it.

"Actually, Ms. Suggs, I've come to speak with you, if I may. Preferably somewhere private."

It took most of what Sarah had left to come out with it. "I was just going upstairs. I'm told there's a new book waiting."

"Thank you," said the chief.

Carrie Suggs said nothing.

The question was, of course, what was she going to say once Sarah left her with the chief? Sarah pulled herself slowly up the stairs, straining to listen. Idiots. They were talking about the weather. The chief running through a safety checklist with Carrie, promising to swing by later if it seemed warranted. Oh, blast. Why didn't they get on with it? Any idiot knew old ladies couldn't hear worth a damn.

But not these two. They were drifting backward, out of the living room, into the dining room, probably. By the time Sarah reached the landing at the top of the stairs she could hear nothing but a low rumble. What the devil would Carrie say to him? Sarah tried to look at it from the carefully constructed perspective that was by now the most familiar. What could Carrie say? She didn't know anything. She'd found Sarah at the tower. She'd fetched her home. Later she'd sniffed around and uncovered the failure of a few falsehoods. That was all. That was *all,* blast you, Carrie, and you'd do well to remember it.

Sarah was still lingering on the landing when an elfin form appeared in the bedroom doorway. "Watchyou doing?"

Sarah took a dogged step forward. "Come to see about this new book of yours."

"It's got tigers," Lucy warned her.

"Mercy. Tigers?"

Lucy seemed to take pity on her. "Well, only one. Sort of small. But he *bounces.*"

For the first time in a long time Sarah felt an honest-to-goodness regulation-size smile stretch her cheeks.

I'm going to miss this child, she thought.

The rain had begun to smack into the back of Pete's neck by the time he left the dock. He'd done everything he could to Factotum's marine charges—shut off the fuel tanks, removed spare gear, backed cleats, checked bilge pumps and drains, set out extra lines and chafing gear. As he walked away he paused and looked behind him. The dock was rimmed with boats packed against the bulkhead, a spiderweb of lines running between boat and piling. As he got into the truck he noticed the deciduous trees behind the Whiteaker Hotel were showing the white sides of their leaves, and as he drove along Shore Road, all he could hear were the sounds of hammers. The radio bleated frenetic warnings. The landfall in North Carolina had knocked Charlotte's force back a hair, but not enough so you'd notice it if you were in the middle of it. Winds a hundred twenty miles per hour, forward speed twenty-six miles per hour. Predicted landfall on Cape Hook—two P.M.

Smack in the middle of high tide.

Moon tide.

Evacuation areas were announced, the available shelters were listed. Other ominous announcements followed—all beaches were now closed, all bus, ferry, and plane trips canceled, the airport was closed, the post office was closed, patients were being discharged early from the hospital, a moratorium on insurance coverage was now in effect. That figured. There followed a list of hurricane pointers: Contain your pets. Stay indoors on the downwind side of your house, away from the windows. Use the phone only in an emergency.

All right, thought Pete, time to hole up.

When he got home the first thing he did was go upstairs and check the barometer. It was falling like the second hand on his watch. He pounded downstairs and called, "Connie? Polly?"

"Out here!"

They were sitting on transplanted kitchen chairs on the stripped porch, waiting, watching. There was a smell of raw wood in the wind, a preview of things to come, an indicator of what Charlotte had done to the trees to the south. The rain was coming at a good angle now, the water on the Sound already buckling in rebellion. There was still time to leave. Pete considered, and finally recognized a fact he wasn't too proud of. Whatever logic might demand, he was constitutionally unable to leave his cottage on the marsh.

Once more Pete asked Connie and Polly if they would go to Sarah's. Once more he got the Supremes act. Once more Pete went over the plan of escape.

Finally, there was nothing left to do but wait.

Rita didn't know why she kept redialing Maxine's dorm. Maxine was far enough inland. Safe. And the call would not be appreciated, she knew that much. She could almost hear Maxine's voice right now—a groan, probably, followed by something like, *Mom. Will you cut loose?* Couched, of course, in those tones of total disgust, as if Rita were a large wart she couldn't quite shed.

But the phone rang and rang unanswered.

Rita hung up. Now what? She hated to admit it, but she felt . . . well . . . on edge. It was the odd dark to the noon sky that had started it, and the uncharacteristically constant whine to the wind hadn't helped. Only forty-eight miles per hour here on Nashtoba, according to the radio, and already the noise of it was getting to her. It never backed off. It never ebbed. It only flowed ever onward.

Closer.

Faster.

Louder.

Rita picked up the phone again, contemplating calling Evan, but slammed it down in disgust. It was such a female thing to do. She even thought of calling Pete, just to see how things were over there on the marsh, but decided he'd see through that. He'd only start to worry about her and he had enough to worry about without adding her to the list.

Rita decided to make herself a cup of tea. A good cup of tea had gotten her through worse things than this. She went into the kitchen and the first thing she noticed was the inverted leaves on the wild cherry, streaming out over the branch ends like a woman's long hair as she washed it in the sink. She was so engrossed in watching the tree disembowel itself that she didn't hear the knock. He was already in the kitchen, standing behind her, when she finally heard him. It was only that, really, the fright, the shock of seeing him, that caused her to jump, not away, so much, but toward.

He kept her there, folded up against him.

"Oh, Evan," she said.

23

Shall we give o'er and drown?

The little girl stood wide-eyed at the unshuttered dining room window while the two women spoke in hushed tones behind her. Sarah was almost glad the shutter had splintered early on—even Carrie seemed as fascinated by the view as her daughter. The rain was coming at them sideways, rat-a-tatting against the glass. The pines had a certain oriental look to them as they flattened and extended leeward. Soon they'd be well advised to move to the other room, but not yet. Best to keep the child occupied.

"I saw a bird!" she shrieked now. "It blowed right past us!"

Carrie raised her voice to say, "Yes, Lucy," and then dropped it again. "He didn't ask about you at all," said Carrie for, Sarah realized, at least the third time now. Curious how none of those times had eased her mind as yet.

"He'd been looking at all the bank accounts," said Carrie. "He looked at everyone's who'd ever worked there. Not just the regular people in the office, but repairmen, people like that. And me, because I'd cleaned there. You see? He came straight to me, nothing to do with you at all. He saw deposits to my account similar to some missing cash from the office. I explained them, and he left. That was all."

So there. It was childish of her, Sarah knew, to feel miffed. The police chief had been here a good long time and not one word about Sarah? She supposed she should feel grateful. She should also, she supposed, ask a few questions about the money. This was how she'd gotten by so far, by trying to feel what she should feel, by trying to do what a woman in her situation would do normally. So she'd ask about the money.

"Apparently your explanation, whatever it was, seemed to satisfy him."

Sarah thought she saw a ghost of a smile. It was, she thought, one of the few, possibly the first, she'd ever seen on Carrie. "I explained how Sutton had paid me under the table, in cash, for the office cleaning. He knew I was only squeaking by financially. This way I wouldn't have to declare the income on my taxes. I guessed Sutton compensated for the lost expense deduction on his end by recording the money as stolen. You can write off things like that."

"I see," said Sarah. "Very neat."

"I thought so," said Carrie. "Until it occurred to me that it was illegal. But when I asked the chief if I would have to pay some penalty he said he wasn't the IRS. He seemed nice. But he didn't ask me anything about you at all. Don't worry."

Curiouser and curiouser, thought Sarah. Carrie, sounding like she was trying to protect Sarah. What convoluted route had *her* mind been taking these days? Whence had gone those self-righteous speeches about telling the truth?

Something thumped gently against the window and Carrie leaped to her feet. "All right, Lucy, let's go to the other room."

They all three moved in unison to the downwind side of the house. It was quieter in the living room, but not by much. Sarah got down the checkerboard while Carrie went to the kitchen to make popcorn and cocoa, and after a few minutes Sarah felt a goodly portion of the uneasiness the police chief's visit had caused begin to leave her.

"Is this the hurry game?" asked Lucy.

Sarah smiled. "When the popcorn gets here it is."

By one o'clock the porch was slick with rain and they'd lost all visual on the beach, not to mention the horizon. They retreated to the kitchen and hunkered down around the table. Polly sat facing north. Connie sat facing east. Pete, of course, faced southeast, straight into the storm, his eyes flicking alternately above Polly's head out to sea, then down at his watch, his forehead apparently buckled for the duration.

Polly had long ago given up on hearing any friendly sort of *halloo* when it finally reached them tinnily over the wind and the police chief blew into the kitchen.

He'd seemed about to say something else until he

saw her sitting there. "You're here." Not a *"you're here,"* or a "you're *here,"* but each word evenly weighted, and he stared so fiercely she grew hot.

"Pete needed some help," she said. There was, of course, no reason to explain. And there was absolutely no reason to feel so flustered.

The chief's gaze swung to Pete. "I guess you're planning to sit tight. In the middle of the flood plain."

Pete's eyes barely left the sea. "At the moment. How is it out there?"

"Okay so far. But I'd guess it won't peak for a couple of hours. The state police are gathering in the Cape barracks." His eyes returned to Polly. "I've been calling you."

"Oh?" said Polly.

"We figured the odds were better on this place than on that old warehouse she lives in," said Pete.

"Barely," said Willy. "But I can't make you leave. I guess you know that. In the Carolinas they hand out dog tags."

"Dog tags?" asked Polly.

"To help identify the bodies."

Polly watched Pete cast a doubtful eye to Connie, give it up as hopeless, fix on her. "Polly—"

"No," said Polly.

The chief gave up, too. He went over a few key points that they'd already covered and changed the subject to something about the discovery of some so-called stolen money. Pete first, then Connie, countered with news of their own, and more names rolled by Polly. Abby, Del, Milly, Fern, Arthur, Percy, Melissa, Sam, Joanna, Dennis, Webs One, Two, and Three, and, through it all, Sarah, Sarah, Sarah.

* * *

By one-thirty, according to the radio, the winds on Nashtoba had finally reached seventy-four miles per hour, official hurricane strength. Sarah didn't need the radio to tell her that—the thumps of dislodged branches against the house would have been enough. She went into the dining room and peeked out the one clear window. The lawn was already littered with leaves, sticks, a few good-sized branches.

No long after, the first big pine came down. They heard it even over the wind, a crack like lightning that wasn't lightning, and the ripping, wrenching, tortuous descent as the massive trunk cut a swath through its neighboring branches and crashed to earth.

Lucy hopped and shrieked and jabbered.

Carrie ran into the dining room and gaped through the window.

And for Sarah, the first nagging doubt descended with the old tree. What was she trying to do? Who did she think she was? What could she possibly fix? Maybe, after all, she was too old for this.

"Carrie," she said, and reached out blindly. The hand that caught hers trembled. Again. And it was that trembling hand that infused Sarah with new strength, the same way it had on Saturday in the woods. The devil take them all. She was still standing. And she was a long way from dead yet. She raised her chin. "We'll get through this."

"Of course we will," said Carrie.

But were they talking about the same thing?

Sarah doubted it.

Less than thirty minutes to high tide and the marsh was now filled with waves. Pete kept one eye on the edge of his lawn and another on his watch as Connie and Polly took occasional tours of the house to check on windows and doors. The lawn was already littered with things that had blown off the marsh—dry seaweed, dead plant stalks, salt hay. Even a few pine branches had succumbed early to the torsion—the prevailing wind on Nashtoba was northeast and the pines had learned to bend away from it; now they were being asked to reverse the trend and they didn't like it one bit. Most of the trees around Pete's cottage were stunted from living so close to the water, but there was a big oak that had managed to get majestic, sheltered as it was on the south side of the house. It was the very tree Rita had suggested he hang a swing from for the child that had never happened. Pete worried about that oak. He worried about his house. Mostly, of course, he worried about his wife and his sister and the other regulars on his worry list.

Sarah, he noticed, had now moved up.

Maybe the chief hadn't lingered, but his topic of conversation had. It had belatedly dawned on Pete and Connie that pieces of news they'd shared with the chief were also news to each other, and as they brought each other up to speed, Polly came along with them. The first point of conflict was the funeral. Connie had heard Fern talk about burying her husband on Thursday. If that was the case, what had Pete seen Web Three toss into the water from the boat on Wednesday?

Not his father, apparently.

"Evidence," said Polly.

"Evidence of what?"

"You expect me to do everything?"

The lights flickered.

Held.

"What's bugging me," said Connie, "isn't so much whose ashes Web Three deep-sixed on Wednesday, but why Abby Fitch's loan was deep-sixed. Fern Sutton was adamant her husband would never have sold out. And it begins to look like Sutton sabotaged Abby's loan himself. Why?"

"Control issues," said Polly.

Pete had to count Polly as somewhat of an expert on men who were controlling. She would have married one if he hadn't gotten murdered first. And since then she'd put some effort into learning to identify the profile.

"I heard about the other woman who worked for Sutton," she was saying now. "Melissa Farentino. The man is a type. Hires someone whose condition of probation is steady employment. She can't quit or she goes back to jail. So he has a built-in wedge. Then he realizes his partner wants to break with him, but he's not ready to let her go. So he pretends he's willing to sell to keep her around, then makes sure it won't happen soon by letting Del Farber overhear the business is in trouble. I bet you anything he'd have gotten rid of her as soon as the son came in."

"She's right," said Connie. "That's what Fern said. And that's what Milly Blair called him. A predator. He seeks out the weak and attacks. Look what he made his wife into. She's so insecure she runs from her own wrinkles."

"And I heard something else interesting at the store. There's a rumor Sarah Abrew's brother-in-law knocked up Melissa Farentino's grandmother and refused to marry her."

"Which has nothing to do with anything," said Pete. "We're getting way off track here. The focus has to be on Sarah. She's the one who's lying. Both about the attack and about her role in the killing."

"About her role in the killing, maybe. But about the

attack? The type of person I've described is just the type to do what Sarah says he did. Sexual attacks aren't about sex. They're about power and control. And anger."

The words rang true enough to Pete, and partly, he realized, because he'd heard them before, from Elmer Snow. Power and control and angry young men like Webster Sutton. But there was still something wrong with the picture, and Pete elaborated for Polly. The absence of the redhead. The fact that Sarah had practically admitted to Dennis she'd invented her. The additional fact of Webster Sutton's neatly-wiped-off belt buckle.

But Polly was undaunted. "So there was no red-head. Sutton still threatened somebody. And whoever it was, maybe it was somebody Sarah decided to protect by taking the brunt."

"Melissa Farentino," said Connie. "Melissa hated Sutton. He pushed her around just as you said, Polly. And if Sarah felt guilty on account of her brother and decided to protect Melissa by saying she shot Sutton—"

The lights flickered again, and this time died completely. That was when it dawned on Pete how dark it was for midafternoon September. He got up and assembled the first of the emergency provisions—cheese and crackers. When he returned to the table he found someone had relieved the refrigerator of three Ballantines.

"Might as well drink it before it warms up," said Polly.

Pete popped the top on his beer, carried it to the window, and saw his back yard awash in roiling, dirty water. There was no lawn, no marsh, no beach. As far as he could see there was nothing but smoke-colored sky and water. He looked at his watch. Two o'clock on the nose. If it turned now they'd be all right. Pete set his beer on the windowsill and left it there. Over the next few hours he was going to need a clear head.

He felt a hand on his shoulder blade and turned. "Listen to it," said Connie.

Pete listened. The wind roared like a train on a too-close track. The gusts whistled and whined and sent a shudder through the cottage. The water drummed like thunder against the ground, making the house seem small and frail, the people in it insignificant.

Why should the sea stop for them? thought Pete. Call it force of nature or act of God or divine retribution if you had to, but if it was going to take them out, it would take them out. Pete turned. The head-count was down by one. "Where's Polly?"

"Making the rounds. Do you think Lucy's scared?"

"Nah. When I was a kid I loved hurricanes."

"And now?"

Pete thought of now. Of what could happen to the people he loved. And he thought of the aftermath, of what he'd have to clean up. "Now, not so much." He put his arm around Connie. "We'll give it ten minutes. If it doesn't back off, we leave. All right?"

"All right."

After one of the ten minutes had passed she said, "I keep thinking about Lucy."

"They'll be fine over there. Sarah's tucked into that nice little hollow."

"I didn't mean that. I meant . . . well . . . seeing you with her. You'd like to try again, wouldn't you?"

And leave it to Connie, thought Pete, to finally bring it up when he had a few other things on his mind.

Like survival.

24

*. . . the strong bas'd promontory have I made shake,
and by the spurs pluck'd up the pine
and cedar . . .*

"A hurry game, a hurry game, a hurry game!"
shouted Lucy.

"Stop shouting," said Carrie. "Come over here and
we'll read something."

"Winnie-the-Pooh!"

An excellent choice, thought Sarah, and the particular episode she chose was most appropriate, too: "In
Which Piglet Is Entirely Surrounded by Water."

Carrie began. The part about it raining and raining.
Ah, yes. It had been a long time, but Sarah still
remembered reading these very words to her own
daughter. It seemed to Sarah now as if the beautiful,
comfortable little stories should have worked as a
charm, or a talisman, should have been able to stay
with Joanna, to guard her, to keep her from harm.

Or to erase it later if it had to come.

Something hit the house. Something big, this time, something big enough to rattle the windows and set the china quivering. Sarah, Lucy, and Carrie tore into the dining room and peered out to find a scrawny old pine cantilevered against the roof, one long branch draped across the window. It was a miracle it hadn't broken the glass.

A miracle.

A charm.

A talisman?

"I would like to try again," said Pete cautiously. "But if you don't, that's okay, too. I don't look at it as a necessary ingredient."

"No," said Connie. "But you want to. And I'm afraid to. Or I was afraid to. I don't know. For some reason all of a sudden I feel braver. Maybe it's the storm. It's just not possible to guard against everything, is it? You just have to go for it, sometimes. Take that chance."

Pete didn't answer right away. He was too busy trying to figure why he suddenly felt so chicken. "If we do this we should do it soon," he said finally.

"All right. Soon. Meaning . . ."

They looked at each other.

"What are you two looking so spooked about?" said Polly behind them.

They both jumped.

"The lawn," said Pete.

Polly snorted. "What lawn? We've got leakage, by the way. A little rainwater under the upstairs balcony door. Nothing alarming. I stopped it up with towels. I've been thinking. Those undone pants must mean something."

It took Pete a mental leap to get there, but he did it, finally. "Webster Sutton's pants?"

"It makes you think somebody wanted it to look like a sexual assault. Somebody who knew what he was like and knew what would be believed."

"Like his wife or his son," said Connie. She added, apropos of nothing that Pete could see, "You know, Abby Fitch was adopted."

"So?" said Polly.

Pete turned his attention back to the ocean in his yard, the watch on his wrist. Two-ten. A long curl of seawater slammed into the stone step and whooshed geyserlike into the air before peppering the kitchen windows.

"Wow," said Polly. She strolled to the table, too casually, thought Pete, and picked up the phone. "Out," she reported. She flicked the switch on the radio from AC to DC. Nothing. She snapped open the battery compartment and popped out the battery. "What is this, ten years old?"

"I bought it yesterday."

"Well, it doesn't work."

"I think we know what the weather is," said Connie.

"There's more to the world than this island, you know. I'd kind of like to find out if my home's still there, for one thing."

"Like you can do something about it right now if it's not?"

Pete reached for the radio. "Let me see that thing."

Connie shot him a traitorous look.

It's the barometer, Pete thought. Strange things happen whenever it drops. It squeezes people, forces things out. Emotions. Babies. The birth rate in low-pressure moments was abnormally high, he knew. Also the conception rate. Look at the two of them.

Theoretically, at least.

There followed a moment when Pete had to wonder if these low-pressure decisions should count.

Polly sat down at the table and picked at the cheese. Connie stayed at the window.

"How about this one?" she said finally. "Abby Fitch killed him because he wanted to make the office nonsmoking."

A surge of seawater brought a tree trunk with it and rammed the porch piling. The whole house quivered, but the piling held.

Just.

The lantern turned his blue eyes gold and carved the gashes deeper that ran from cheek to jaw. He tipped some more crisp wine into Rita's glass. Either the wind had definitely subsided or Rita was definitely drunk. Just the howling, raging *sound* of it would have driven her mad if she'd been by herself, she knew it, and she found the thought troubling. Don't get used to this, she warned herself. You were on your own before, you'll be on your own again. Evan Spender had gone through life alone for almost sixty years. He wasn't going to suddenly decide to . . .

"What do you say we get married?" said Evan.

"Enough of this gloom and doom," said Polly. "You've got enough lamp oil on that shelf to reconstruct a whale. Let's light the lantern." She removed the globe, fished the matches out of the tin, and put flame to wick. It did seem to help, thought Connie. It actually made her believe she could hear the wind

Sally Gunning

subsiding. It seemed to have the same effect on Pete, too.

"I think it's backing off," he said. "See? There's the step again."

He left the window to check on the upstairs water damage.

Connie returned to Polly at the table. "See how this sounds. Abby Fitch is adopted. Sarah's her natural mother. Abby killed Sutton either because he was such a pig or because it was the only way to get control of the company, told Sarah, and Sarah covered for her. What do you think?"

"I think it's the barometer," said Polly.

Yeah, thought Connie. They were getting crazier and crazier, just because none of them wanted to discuss the one possibility they hadn't yet discussed. When Pete came back downstairs, looked out the window, and actually sat down at the table, she cleared her throat and came out with it.

"Maybe we should consider this. That Sarah, for whatever reason of her own, did pretty much just what she said she did. Went out into the Indian tower and cold-bloodedly gunned down Webster Sutton. We have Arthur's bankrupt Five and Dime, the question raised of some cooked books by Webster One. What if she recently found out about it? What if she—"

"No," said Pete suddenly. "It's finally dawned on me what's not right about all this. It's Sarah herself. She's having too much fun. At first, anyway, when she was telling us what happened. She was actually enjoying it. It was like she was telling a story about things that had happened to someone else. If she'd really done what she said she'd done, she wouldn't have gotten a kick out of it."

"So if she didn't do it—"

"She's covering for someone who did. As you said before, Polly. It's the only explanation that works. Sarah was just too damned pleased with herself. She thought she was pulling one off. She thought someone was going to get away with something."

"Who?"

"I don't know. Obviously it has to be someone she cares a lot about. I guess that's why I keep coming back to Joanna—that and the coincidence. And that makes you right, too, Polly. Maybe Sutton got killed because of the type of person he was. He sounds too much like this fellow Sam described. It doesn't have to be Sutton who raped Joanna, it just has to be the type, in order to have triggered this reaction in Sarah."

"Joanna was in Boston," reminded Connie.

"Was she?"

The three of them looked at each other.

"It's the barometer," said Polly.

"And what brought this on?" asked Rita.

"Dunno. Seeing you by lantern light, maybe. But seems to me there's no sense in us holing up alone. Now that Maxine's away at school—"

"I am perfectly capable of looking out for myself," said Rita primly, and immediately hated herself, not for her answer, but for the primness. That was one thing she'd thought Evan had successfully knocked out of her. She could actually get undressed with the light on now. Amazing, when you thought about it. But now that it was finally here, she wondered. She'd been on her own all this time. Was it wise, after all, to give in to this sudden urge toward dependency? Did she really want to take all this on again at this stage in life?

"Never figured someone like you would drift my way," Evan went on. "Sure would hate to have you drift off again. So what do you say?"

Oh, Rita knew just what to say. That she was grateful and flattered. That she would certainly give it some considerable thought for the future, but that it was important for her to learn to fend for herself.

The wind, subdued or not, gave a fierce shriek and rattled the windowpanes. Rita trembled. Evan drew her closer and ran a rough thumb gently across her cheek. "Well?"

"Yes, please," said Rita.

When Pete called down the stairs for Connie, Connie left her spot by the window and Polly took her place. She could see grass, again. Or, not grass, exactly, but thready-looking sludge, a good ten feet of it stretching back from Pete's porch step. And wasn't the wind a hair less deafening? She listened.

Yes.

And then she listened harder. Was that a *halloo?*

Yes again.

The chief blasted into the kitchen in a dripping slicker, hood tossed back, hair spiky with wet.

"You're all right?"

"All right. One leaky door upstairs, that's it. So far, anyway."

"You're lucky."

"Bad?"

The chief nodded. He looked tired and harried. "I can't stay. I've been to your friend Sarah's. She lost a few trees, one onto the roof, but no damage. Not yet."

"I'll tell Pete. He'll want to get over there."

"Tell him to wait till morning. It's a mess out there. Trees, wires everywhere. Sarah's all right. She's got a generator."

"Okay."

The chief continued to stand there. To look at her.

"I didn't know you were here," he said finally.

"I know. I thought Pete would have told you."

"You could call me yourself next time. I promise I won't think you're proposing."

Polly flushed ridiculously. She couldn't think of a thing to say next.

Neither, apparently, could Willy. "I have to go. As I said." He looked cross. He turned around. He looked bigger from the back but at the same time much farther away. Polly didn't want him to go feeling cross. She didn't want him to go at all, as a matter of fact. It was the storm. It had to be.

"I'm glad you came by," she said.

Willy about-faced. "Me, too."

"Maybe you could try again, later. If you find an hour someplace."

He looked doubtful.

But definitely less cross.

"I'll try," he said.

Pete checked the barometer. It had started to rise. Finally. He pushed around the soggy towels under the balcony door and looked out. It had also stopped raining.

"He's leaving," said Connie from the window on the other side. "You're a sneaky little devil, you know that? Getting me up here the minute you saw him pull in. And you said you were going to stay out of it."

"That's why we're hiding up here. We're staying out of it." He crossed the room and stood beside her, looking out with her. It took him a minute to see the old oak tree, another one to register. "I don't believe it. Still here."

"You'd better be talking about that tree," said Connie.

25

∽∾∽

He receives comfort like cold porridge.

Pete woke next morning to one of those perfect post-hurricane days—crisp air, bright sun, and cornflower-blue sky. He raced up and down stairs and out and all around the house, but no matter how hard he looked, the worst he could find were a few absent shingles and a lot of debris on the lawn. He was standing there scratching his head in disbelief when Connie and Polly joined him.

"Don't look so disappointed," said Connie. "God will get you next time. And you still haven't checked the beach."

"True." They scrambled over the scoured marsh and drastically reduced dune to see what Charlotte had left them. The gifts were scattered across beach and marsh—a fiberglass hull stripped by the waves of all movable parts, a dock piling, several uprooted trees, an optimistic lobsterman's pot, a dirty tarp, some mangled line, a NO PARKING sign, three battered fish boxes, four buoys, assorted boots, shoes, and clothes remnants, and, kilted crazily against the remains of the dune, the Clausens' boat barn.

They walked around it, like Pooh and Piglet, twice. It was essentially intact.

"Now what?" asked Polly.

"I'll have to get in touch with Clausen," said Pete.

"No phone," said Connie.

"Maybe the chief could reach him," said Polly.

Pete raised an eyebrow at Connie. So now suddenly everything was the chief?

The three of them stood there, hypnotized by the sea swells lunging across the beach, until Polly finally galvanized them into action.

Polly and Connie would stay behind to clean up the home turf, Pete would collect his chain saw and head out to check on the other women in his life.

Pete soon discovered the rest of Nashtoba had not been as fortunate as they had been. Shore Road looked like a giant had walked along it, flattening everything each time his foot hit ground. The air whined, not with the sound of the wind now, but with the sound of the chain saws, the sour smell of fresh-cut wood burning Pete's nostrils. The Department of Public Works had been out early and cleared the road of obstructing trees, but the detritus was piled high along both shoulders.

One of the biggest post-hurricane problems was the sightseers. They slowed Pete to a crawl the minute he hit the shore route. They gawked at the boats piled up on the beach like cordwood, the small cottage lying collapsed on its side, the masts strewn along the road, somebody's roof on somebody else's lawn, the car snapped in half by a thick pine; they even gawked at the line at Rudy's ice house.

When Pete pulled into Rita's he expected the worst and found that even here, this strange new lucky streak of theirs had held out. Evan was in the yard with a rake, but the worst that Charlotte had dealt them was a bunch of leaves and sticks.

That was according to Evan.

According to Rita, there was a crisis and it was big. Pete found her in the kitchen, frowning over a can of Sterno.

She heard him and looked up. "I'm getting married," she wailed.

"Oh," said Pete.

"Oh, fine. I know. You think I'm crazy. Don't say anything, I can see it in your face. And you're right. Of course you're right. What was I thinking of? I don't want to get married again. I've done everything for myself this long, haven't I? I can do everything for myself from here on out. Well? Can't I?"

"Sure you can. But there's more to getting married than—"

"What? I'd like you to tell me. What am I doing this for?"

"Well, maybe because you love the guy."

Rita looked up at Pete with anguished eyes. "Do I?"

Pete put his arm around her. "Why don't you think about it for a while?"

The sound of someone's squealing brakes made Pete whip around. Through the window he saw a bright red Porsche rock to a halt in Rita's drive, saw a shadowy young man in the driver's seat, saw Rita's daughter Maxine bolt out of the passenger's side and tear into the house.

"Mom! Mom! Where are you? Are you all right?"

She streaked into the kitchen. "Mom!"

Pete let go of Rita just in time to avoid getting squashed between them in Maxine's grizzly-sized bear hug.

"I've been going *crazy,*" said Maxine. "Why didn't you *call* me?"

Pete was almost relieved to see that at Sarah's, at least, his muscle was required. He picked his way across the lawn, dodging the crazed, displaced bees, drunk on sap, and surveyed the damage. Several pines had come down, one of them kilting precariously against the dining room. So that was the first order of business. Pete walked around it. Not so big as the others. Angled just right. As a matter of fact, one good, hard yank on this branch and . . .

The sound of splintering glass echoed into the crisp blue air around him.

So his luck had finally run out.

Pete ran inside. Glass was everywhere, a mix of big shards and fine dust. And here was Lucy running toward it, or him, in bare feet.

"Mustard!" she shouted. "Did you say it? Did you say the password?"

"Mustard," said Pete, scooping her up. It was the fastest, safest thing. He carried her into the living room and handed her to her mother, but before Lucy let go she surprised him by tightening her arms in a quick hug.

It was hard to say who looked more surprised, Pete or Carrie. She settled Lucy on the couch next to Sarah and followed Pete into the dining room. "I'll take care of this." She went to the kitchen and returned with the vacuum. Just what Dennis must have had in mind when he brought the generator, thought Pete, a little emergency vacuuming.

Pete bent down and began to collect the larger shards. He could hear Lucy in the other room, chirping away to Sarah. Now was as good a chance as any to pump Carrie, he supposed. "Anyone mention anyone else in her sleep lately?"

"No," said Carrie.

But Pete had learned to be specific. "Or any other time?"

"No," said Carrie.

Pete sighed. So much for the double-oh-seven stuff. But there was still a resource here as yet to be fully tapped. "You mentioned the other day you used to clean the Sutton-Fitch offices."

"Yes," said Carrie.

"I'd be interested in your impression of the man. I get the idea he wasn't on anyone's Philanthropist of the Year list."

Carrie's head twisted quickly in the direction of her daughter in the other room, her maternal ears apparently having picked up some sound not heard by the usual mortal membranes. "I wouldn't know. I hardly knew him. I wasn't there very long."

"When did you leave?"

"Early this month. There were scheduling problems. My daughter started school. I had to get her to the bus."

So nothing useful on that front. Pete went to the kitchen and deposited the glass he'd collected in the garbage can. In the other room the vacuum roared to life as Carrie sucked up the smaller fragments. Pete had had enough noise yesterday. He headed toward the door and the relative peace of the chain saw, but the sound of the vacuum followed him.

Pete had once heard about something called white noise—a background sound that camouflaged distracting noises. White noise was used to induce sleep, to aid relaxation, to clear the brain of extraneous thoughts.

Maybe that's what Carrie Suggs's vacuum cleaner did. At least at first. Whatever the reason, that was when it dawned on Pete what had—or, more accurately, what hadn't—happened last Saturday morning in Sarah's woods.

26

∽⧼∾

Look, he's winding up the watch of his wit;
by and by it will strike.

They spent the rest of the day inventorying the damage to Factotum's various clientele, but that night, after dinner, the three of them sat and talked around the lantern for a long time. They compared notes. Again. They took each puzzle piece, looked at it from both sides, made sure it didn't fit in any other likely place, then tried it in some other place anyway. By eleven P.M. there was no way around it. There was only one way they could make the picture whole. The trouble was, they had no motive. Not for sure. The only other trouble was, they couldn't figure out how to prove it.

That was when Pete began to perk up. *They couldn't prove it.* Maybe it would end up all right after all. But could the status quo be called all right? Pete wasn't sure, but even as he pondered the imperfect bubble it got burst with one vicious stroke of Polly's pin.

"I've got it! A reenactment!"

Pete tried not to let his face fall, but knew by looking at Connie that he'd failed. Connie tried a discouraging snort in Polly's direction, and failed, too.

"It'll never work," said Pete finally, feebly.

But it might.

He knew that.

Polly was suddenly in one of those Unsinkable-Molly-Brown moods. She didn't know these people the way they did. She was caught up in solving a puzzle and that was all. Or was it all?

"We have to tell Willy," she said, jumping up.

Pete looked at his watch. "It's closing in on midnight."

"He'll be up. He'll want to know."

And she was suddenly the big expert on the police chief? She picked up the phone. Obviously, she'd forgotten how Evan Spender worked.

Polly listened to the absence of dial tone and clanked down the receiver. "So we'll walk down the beach. If there's no sign of life, we'll go home."

Pete waited for Connie to tell Polly she was crazy, but Connie must have been waiting for Pete to do it. Either that or both of them knew they weren't going to have any peace of mind until they'd gotten it over with. They stood up. Connie picked up the flashlight. Pete blew out the lantern.

We should definitely have stayed in Maine, he thought.

Or New Hampshire.

* * *

Polly followed them and the beam of light around the flotsam and jetsam toward Willy's house. They found the path through the storm-stripped beach plum and bayberry and soon the flashlight picked out the remains of the ravaged garden the chief had been at pains to maintain since he'd first rented the house from the green-thumbed Connie. Polly felt a stab of pain of the sort that might accompany a small wound. Curious. Next she saw the house, and, thank God, candlelight flickering through the glass panes in the kitchen door.

Pete stepped up to the door and knocked. Polly saw the chief's long face squint in the flashlight glare and the door swing open. She saw him spot her at the back of the line and for a second the guarded, on-duty look left his face, but not for long. The look didn't go with the outfit—he was in plaid flannel pajama bottoms, a long-sleeved Henley jersey pushed up to the elbows, and the bare, browned feet of a perennial beach-walker. The kitchen table was littered with paper, official-looking paper. The kitchen itself had been cleared of most of the clutter that had originally belonged to the two old ladies who'd left the house to Connie, but Polly recognized a few things—a blue willow teapot, a pot holder shaped like a lobster, an egg cup shaped like a cat.

"What now?" said Willy. "You found Jimmy Hoffa in Sarah's basement?"

Polly giggled.

Pete and Connie didn't. They didn't say anything, either, so Polly felt it was up to her to speak. "We think we know what happened in the Indian tower," she said. "And we think we know how we can get the perp to cough."

Willy turned to Pete. "You encourage this kind of

talk?" But at the same time he pusned the papers into a pile and with his usual Old World charm he pulled out the two kitchen chairs on either side of him for the ladies to sit. Pete sat at the end of the table opposite Willy. He didn't look like he was going to rush into speech anytime soon, so Polly reached out and touched his elbow. "Go ahead."

Pete went. Reluctantly, she could tell, but he went, and for the first time since her brainstorm had struck it occurred to Polly that there might be something more at stake here than she'd first thought. But it was too late now. Even Pete seemed to realize that. He plodded onward. At several points Willy halted him to thumb through the papers in the pile beside him. When he found what he was looking for he would read, nod, motion Pete to resume. At several other points Willy asked questions. Connie added her two cents, and finally Polly explained her theory on how they could reenact the crime and set the trap. At first Willy wouldn't buy it. He had various objections based on things like the laws of probability and accepted police procedure. Meaningless details, thought Polly. And eventually Willy rubbed a large hand across his face and said, "All right. Sarah's. Tomorrow. Ten o'clock."

And that was it.

They filed out the way they had come, the chief holding the door for the ladies, of course. He said something to Pete about making the necessary calls first thing in the morning. He said something to Connie about needing her advice on the garden. When Polly drew abreast of him he said only, "Good night."

Polly paused. "Maybe after tomorrow it will be easier to find that hour somewhere."

Willy looked at his watch. "Easy enough right now. Unless it's past your bedtime?" He raised his eyes.

The heat rushed from her feet to her face. All right. So yesterday it was the storm. So how did you explain this? And what did she want to do about it, fish or cut bait?

"Hey," said Pete from out of the dark someplace. "Either get moving or borrow a flashlight."

Polly couldn't seem to find enough saliva for speech.

"I'll see she gets home," said the chief.

Polly stepped back inside the candlelight and the chief closed the door.

"Coffee?" he asked. "Or . . . ?" He reached into the cupboard above the refrigerator and withdrew a crusty-looking bottle, on whose label Polly could only make out the word *vintage* and a year close to the one in which she was born.

"Or," said Polly.

27

Hell is empty, and all the devils are here.

The weather continued to hold, about as good as it ever got, and Sarah was in the garden with Carrie and Lucy surveying the damage to her plants when Pete and Connie came into view. They started out hand in hand, Sarah noticed, then dropped hands awkwardly and came on side by side, but separated. And what was it in those matching strides that set Sarah's alarm bells clanging? It was altogether too much the condemned-man-on-way-to-gallows kind of thing. And who was the condemned man?

Oh, Sarah could make a good, wild guess.

When they reached the group in the garden they divided—Connie cutting Lucy from the herd and engaging her in quiet conversation, Pete chatting inanely to Sarah and Carrie. He started with the weather, of course. He then moved the subject on to Polly. Apparently the chief had gotten through to Southport and learned Polly's warehouse was still standing, but barely. She was wanted back pronto to clean out what she could before it got demolished and she'd left early that morning for Southport. Right about there Sarah stopped listening. Her good ears had just picked up what was going on with Connie and Lucy. She heard Connie ask how Lucy had spent the hurricane, heard the child launch into a mix of fact and fiction that would have put Dr. Seuss to shame. Trees falling out of the sky. Birds flying upside down. Rain made of arrows. Connie then told her own version, about the marsh and the beach and the barn that had washed up on it. She finished with, "Would you like to see it?"

Lucy's yes was loud and clear. Connie crossed to the child's mother to get the necessary permission and in the space of five seconds, Connie and Lucy were gone.

The alarm bells chimed louder.

Left alone with the two remaining women, Pete seemed ill at ease, but they weren't left alone long. First came Dennis, which was not a surprise, since he'd been hovering constantly, neatly stacking the wood Pete had cut, hauling the brush, raking up the mess of leaves and twigs Charlotte had deposited on the lawn. Sarah supposed Joanna shouldn't have been much of a surprise, either. About time she appeared to see if her mother had made it through in one piece. Sarah could feel the tension between husband and wife loud and clear.

Sarah had just herded them all inside and settled them in the living room when her last two uninvited guests arrived—that nincompoop Ted Ball and the police chief.

The chief began to speak, a pretty little speech, all told. He hoped those present would indulge the forces of law and order for a moment, there were one or two points of confusion concerning logistics. He had brought with him the statements of the involved parties. Using them as a guide, he would like to walk through the events of last Saturday morning.

Logistics. So he was off on another wild goose chase. There was no problem with the logistics. Hadn't Sarah run through the entire scenario herself? Still and all, no sense rushing in where even a fool might fear to tread. "I'm not traipsing through any woods," said Sarah crossly.

"No need," said Willy. "Mrs. Willoughby, perhaps you could stand in for your mother."

Oh, Lordy Lord, thought Sarah. But it was Dennis, darling Dennis, who rose to his feet. "I'll stand in for my mother-in-law if you don't mind."

A pause. "Very well. Ted, here, will be Webster Sutton. Ted, you have the gun?"

"You're letting us sit in the same room with that boy and a loaded gun?" Sarah snapped.

"Loaded with blanks," said Willy. "Which he will fire at exactly ten-fifteen, the approximate time, according to the various statements, here, that Webster Sutton was shot. All right, Ted, why don't you take up your position in the tower?"

Ted Ball left the room, looking important, Webster Sutton's gun in hand.

Willy looked around him. "Now, who else was on hand? Ah, Ms. Suggs. "Let's see." The chief rustled his papers. "According to both Mrs. Abrew's and your accounts, you were vacuuming in this room at the time. We might as well be as accurate as we can. Would you be good enough to collect the vacuum?"

Carrie left the room.

"And Mrs. Abrew—"

"So formal today."

Willy ignored her, chasing paper again. "Let's see. I don't believe you say exactly where you were before you took your walk."

"And I don't believe I recall." But as Carrie returned with the vacuum she knew where she would have been. As far away as possible from that noise. "I believe I was in the dining room. Out of harm's way. But if you don't mind, I'll stay put."

"I don't mind. Since you leave the house soon anyway. So other than your presence in this room, everything is approximately as it was on Saturday? Wait, no. The windows are closed. I seem to recall they were open on Saturday."

Pete jumped up and opened a couple of windows.

"Now, Mrs. Abrew? Ms. Suggs? Would you say this is as close to the scenario Saturday as we're likely to come?"

"Yes," said Sarah. "And if we're paying you by the hour I see what's happened to our tax rate."

Again, Willy ignored her. Too bad she couldn't do the same to him. "All right. Mrs. Abrew, this is approximately when you went out for your walk, correct?"

"Approximately." She might as well cooperate. She was on safe ground. After all, she'd taken the walk, just as he said. There was no danger here. Not yet.

"Mr. Willoughby, then, if you would be so kind?"

Dennis followed Ted's path out the back door.

"Pete?" said Willy. "If you'd plug in the vacuum?"

Pete disappeared around the corner with the vacuum cleaner cord.

"All right, Ms. Suggs. You were vacuuming. Go ahead."

The machine roared to life.

Willy raised a finger, looking at his watch.

But there was no need for the silly pantomime.

Sarah saw it, but too late.

Too late.

The damage had been done the minute Carrie had switched on that infernal machine. *Blast* Dennis and that generator. The vacuum cleaner roared like a jet plane.

No matter how many shots Ted Ball, or Webster Sutton, or Sarah, or anyone might have fired from the Indian tower, it was obvious that no one in that room could have heard a thing.

28

⚙️

Is it so brave a lass?

Pete watched the terrible light dawn across Sarah's face and thought glumly; Okay, that's it.

But the old woman just wouldn't go down.

"Carrie," she said, "I think one or the both of us got confused. Didn't you tell me you'd stopped vacuuming by the time you heard the shot? That's right, you were dusting the bookshelves. I recollect you saying when you pulled the car around—"

"Mother," said Joanna, "whatever you think you're doing, it's time to stop."

"Yes," said Carrie.

"No," said Sarah. "You tell him the way you told me. You were dusting. You heard the shot. I had told you I was walking to the tower, you knew enough to run straight there. Tell him. It's only a silly mistake about the vacuum. Go on."

Carrie stood in the middle of the room, frozen under the multiple glares.

Willy shot Pete a look.

"Maybe this would be a good time to straighten out something else, Carrie," said Pete. "You told me you left Sutton-Fitch because the cleaning schedule interfered with your getting Lucy to the bus."

"Carrie, did you hear that?" said Sarah. "We're talking about Lucy now."

"Yes," said Carrie. "I had to get Lucy to the bus."

"The offices got cleaned early in the morning," said Pete quietly. "But Lucy's in afternoon kindergarten. I was here the other day when she caught the bus. She doesn't leave till noon. Isn't that right?"

"And who wants to rush hither and yon all morning?" snapped Sarah.

"And there's that money Sutton supposedly fed you under the table. At some inconvenience to himself. We talked about this before. Of all the people who knew Webster Sutton, you're the only one who gave him credit for being that nice. And why would he go out of his way to help you, of all people? You told me yourself. You hadn't worked there long. You hardly knew him."

"Carrie, you stick to your guns," said Sarah, but there was desperation in the voice.

Carrie crossed to Sarah's chair. She took the old woman's hand. "No, Sarah. You did what you could. Now it's time to let it go." She turned to the chief. "Webster Sutton blackmailed me."

Willy looked around the room. "Perhaps you'll excuse us."

But the old woman wouldn't let go of Carrie's hand,

and Pete didn't want to leave the old woman. And Joanna sat on the couch as if she'd been nailed there.

Willy looked around again, seemed to decide he was dealing with essentials, proceeded to read Carrie her rights.

She listened politely and then continued.

"Webster Sutton put that money in my account. He stole the deposit slips from my bag and dropped them in the night box. He made a false record so he could prove the money was stolen the same days the deposits were made."

"And why would he do that?"

"To blackmail me into sex. It hadn't worked the other way. First he began to show up in the mornings when I was alone in the office, cleaning. He made . . . unwelcome advances."

"You call it unwelcome advances," said Sarah. "I call it attempted rape."

On the couch, Joanna closed her eyes.

"I should have quit right then, but I needed the job and there aren't that many around here. I decided to go to Abby Fitch and tell her what was going on. She didn't seem to want to make waves, but she did start to show up early in the mornings. That worked for a while. Or I thought it did. I guess he only backed off long enough to set up his blackmail scheme. When Abby Fitch didn't come one morning and he walked in, I walked out. I quit the job cold." Carrie paused. "I would like you to understand what that meant. I have a daughter. I . . . That one job paid more than the rest of the week's cleaning jobs combined. The minute I quit I was unable to keep up on the rent. There was no one to . . . I have no family. Lucy's father disappeared before she was born. I was on my own. But I decided I couldn't stay at that job no matter what else it meant I had to do. After I quit it seemed to be all over. Then, out of the blue, he called me. He told me what he'd done. He said when he got through exposing me as a thief, I'd never get a job again. I asked him what he wanted from me."

Sarah snorted.

"He didn't answer me. He hung up. The next morning I went to the bank and asked for an interim statement. The deposits were all there just the way he'd described."

And that's when she should have gone straight to Willy, thought Pete, but suddenly he remembered the conversation he'd had with Rita the day before. Like Rita, maybe Carrie had fended for herself for so long she'd forgotten how to do it any other way. Obviously, she truly felt as if she were on her own.

"And then what did you do?" asked Willy, a key point, Pete knew. Had she premeditated this crime?

"Nothing. I waited. And he came."

"To your apartment?"

Carrie nodded.

"Lucy was asleep. I was terrified she'd wake up. After that one time I knew I couldn't let it go on. And it would have. On and on and on. I went to the office. I spoke with Abby Fitch first. I told her I needed to speak with Webster Sutton privately, but that I was afraid to be alone with him in his office too long. I asked her to call him into the other room five minutes after I'd gone in. She agreed. As soon as Sutton shut the door I told him I would not let him into my apartment again. I explained I had a small child at home. But I told him I would arrange for a sitter and I would meet him the next morning at the old Indian tower." Carrie stopped.

Joanna's eyes were now wide open.

Sarah's eyes were closed.

"I'm sorry, Sarah," said Carrie. "I should never have brought him so close to your home. It was just that it was the only place I could think of where no one would see or hear us."

Sarah opened her eyes, patted Carrie's knee. "It's all right, dear. You're a brave girl."

Joanna stared at her mother.

"And the gun?" asked Willy.

"I knew he kept it in his desk drawer. When Abby Fitch called him out of the room I slipped it into my bag. When he came back, I left. I suppose you can figure out the rest."

The chief didn't answer. He turned to Sarah now. "Would you care to give us an . . . adjusted version of your movements from here?"

Sarah, eyes wide open, jaw set firm, said, "No."

Everyone was looking at the old woman now. Pete thought he and the chief might be the only ones who saw Dennis Willoughby and Ted Ball slip back into the room.

"Please, Sarah," said Carrie. "You wanted to help me before. This is what would help me now. I didn't want that to go on and on. I can't have this go on and on, either."

"I was walking in the woods by the Indian tower," said Sarah. "I heard voices. I looked in, and there was Webster Sutton with a young girl. Plump. Red hair."

The only sound was Joanna's half-sob, half-moan.

29

What! An advocate for an imposter? Hush!

But it was Joanna who finally broke through. The sob was cut off. She got up and crossed the room. She knelt down.

"Mother, listen to me. Please. I see what you're trying to do, but you have to believe me when I tell you it's not only wrong, it doesn't work. You can't make things go away. You couldn't before and you can't now. Don't you see what it's done to me, pretending what happened to me never happened to me? I was *raped,* Mother. I can only barely even say it now. Don't you see what it made me feel like to be hushed up while he went free? It's like it's been *my* crime all these years, Mother. Not his, *mine.* You've always expected me to have been able to do something

I couldn't. Something to stop it, something to get over it."

"No," said Sarah.

"Yes, Mother. *Yes.* And I kept trying. But I couldn't. I couldn't move past it. It's gone on and on. You wanted me to be like Carrie, but it's Carrie who's going to be like me. Did you hear what she said? She doesn't want it to go on and on. Did you hear it, Mother?"

Joanna fell silent. The room stayed silent. Pete snuck a look at Dennis's face and quickly away. Joanna stood up and turned, exposing a face sheeted with tears. The tears seemed to jump-start Dennis. He met her in the middle of the room, led her out the back door.

"I shot Webster Sutton," Carrie went on. "I lured him here and shot him before he could lay one finger on my flesh again. It's *my* flesh and he had no right to it and I'm not sorry, except for one thing. That after I shot him I ran here, to this house. I should have gone somewhere else, but I knew this house, I knew you, Sarah. So I came here."

Pete wouldn't have believed it if he hadn't been sitting right there. He watched, stunned, as with superhuman effort, Sarah collected herself for a final charge.

She addressed the chief first. "All right. You want my corroboration, here it is. I was sitting here Saturday morning listening to the radio when Carrie came tearing in. She was shaking from head to foot." She turned to Carrie now. "Never you mind you trying to sound like you were all cool and calm. You were near hysterical is what you were. 'I shot Webster Sutton in your tower,' you said. 'I need to call the police.' Did you hear that part, Chief? She was going to turn herself in. And she said something else you'd be well advised to take note of. She said, 'I didn't mean to. It was an accident. The gun went off of its own accord.' So I sat her down and made her tell me from top to bottom what had gone on."

Sarah paused and looked sheepishly at the chief, but Pete, for one, wasn't fooled.

"I suppose we should have called you right then and there, Chief, I see that now. But at the time it seemed a darned shame. A young woman who through no fault of her own gets put upon by this despicable man, a young child who needs her mother, no other family in the whole wide world. And here I was, my life as good as gone anyhow. What could it hurt, even if I did get locked up? But I told Carrie, and I was right, too, that you'd never cart an old woman like me off to jail."

The chief opened his mouth, closed it without speaking.

Smart man.

"But first things first," Sarah continued. "Once Carrie could collect herself we went back to the tower, made sure the man was truly dead. You make note of that, too, Chief. We weren't about to let him bleed his life away if he hadn't already done so. But he was as dead as they come. So we came back here and I came up with the plan."

And the plan, as Sarah told it, sounded just about as devious as plans like that got. Pete had to admit he was impressed at the workings of Sarah's criminal mind. As soon as Sarah had convinced Carrie, by preying on her concern for Lucy, to let Sarah take the blame, she set in thinking what to do with the contradictory evidence on hand. Carrie's prints, Carrie's tire tracks, were all over the scene. They'd be asking for trouble if they tried to wipe off every place her fingers might have touched down and they could never erase the tire marks. Better to offer an innocent explanation for Carrie's presence at the scene. So Sarah had invented the rescue plan. Next was the matter of Sarah's motive. Pete supposed that a combination of Carrie's real story plus Joanna's past woes brought the sexual assault on the young redhead readily enough to mind. That a plump young redhead was almost the morphological opposite of the dark, lean Carrie was a plus of either ingenious design or convenient accident. But there was one small problem with Sarah's scheme. Although the intent was clear enough, Carrie had never given Sutton the chance to disrobe. It was Carrie who had thought of adding the undone pants, Carrie who had unfastened and then cleaned off the belt buckle. And once Sarah learned it was Sutton's own gun that had done him in, the self-inflicted wound theory came right behind.

Then came what seemed to be Sarah's proudest moment—she knew the entire masquerade was going to hinge on their testimonies fitting like a pair of matched gloves. How better to set the details firmly in mind than to reenact the entire scene as they had constructed it?

And that's just what they had done.

Carrie had pretended she'd arrived at Sarah's that Saturday morning, as usual, to clean. Sarah had walked yet again to the tower, had planted Sutton's gun in Sutton's hand and waited for Carrie to come to her rescue as they had scripted it. Oh, they had recreated it all, right down to the last little flourish, never imagining that it was one of those flourishes, the vacuum cleaner, that would do them in.

"We reenacted every last little thing," Sarah said now. "Except for one. I didn't want to shoot the gun a second time. So we couldn't know Carrie wouldn't have heard it over the vacuum. Oh, well, better luck next time."

Sarah looked like she might almost smile, but as she looked away to the window, she seemed to see something that made her change her mind. Pete looked, too. He wasn't sure Sarah could see what he saw—Joanna and Dennis were sitting on the woodpile. Dennis had pulled Joanna's hand into his lap and held it tight between his own.

Behind Pete, official and unofficial conversations were going on. Willy and Carrie. Willy and Sarah. Sarah and Carrie. Pete stood up, intending to leave the room, but Carrie Suggs called out to him to please wait. She spoke quietly to the chief at length a second time and the next thing Pete knew, he and Carrie were alone in the room, Ted Ball and the chief standing guard at the doors.

"I'm sorry about this," said Pete. "I didn't know now else to cut Sarah loose."

Carrie waved his words aside. "Your wife has Lucy."

"Yeah. We didn't think she should—"

"I want you to keep her."

Pete was stunned. "There must be somebody else you—"

"There's nobody. Please. Sarah can't do it alone. I don't want her with strangers. It might be till Monday, it might be a little longer. They'll lock me up until I'm arraigned Monday morning, but the chief seems convinced I'll get bail. Sarah has offered . . ." Carrie's eyes filled. "If the amount is reasonable, I'll be out on Monday. I'm told it's sometimes high at first, but in ten days, after bail review, it should be lowered."

So in other words, maybe till Monday, maybe for ten days. And after that? Pete figured the odds were good that Carrie Suggs would be going back to jail eventually. Even a best-case scenario like voluntary manslaughter would get her a few years. Still, she'd have plenty of time before the trial to make more permanent arrangements. Until Monday, ten days, even, they could manage, couldn't they?

"I'll have to talk to Connie."

"Of course," said Carrie. "The chief will bring me by when we're through at the station . . ." She stopped, but Pete could follow the thread easily enough.

No matter where Lucy ended up, the chief would bring Carrie to say good-bye to her daughter.

30

. . . for my part, the sea cannot drown me . . .

Connie squatted on the sand, watching Lucy race the mammoth swells, ready to leap if called upon. The kid had already lost a few close calls—her sneakers and jeans were soaked and in another minute the sweatshirt would probably go, too. Oh, well, thought Connie, she'd take her home wrapped in a blanket if she had to. That much she could handle, she knew. Already these few hours with the little girl had set Connie off into the old panic. Never mind decisions half-made in the middle of the storm. She hadn't stopped the pills yet. It wasn't too late. Nothing was cast in stone. When Pete got back she would talk to him It was too much risk. Too much pain. She wasn't ready to take it on. She never would be, she supposed. But Pete would understand. It was not a necessary ingredient, he'd said so himself. They were happy at last. Why rock the boat, after all?

Connie looked at her watch. So where was he? It seemed like it should have been over, one way or another, by now. And after it was really over, after their lives returned to normal, they were going to pick up where they'd left off on that honeymoon.

Lucy took a hop that carried her a foot too far away for Connie's comfort. She scrambled to her feet, captured the kid by a flapping wrist, and led her back within range. When she turned around, there was Pete, just topping the dune.

Connie met him halfway across the sand.

"Having fun?" he asked.

"Something tells me more fun than you. How did it go?"

They sat down side by side and he told her.

When he was through, Connie looked across the sand at the little girl. "And what happens to her now?"

"Ah," said Pete. "Funny you should ask. Carrie goes to jail till Monday, at which time, or soon thereafter, with a little help from Sarah, she makes bail. She's asked us to look after Lucy till then."

Connie looked at Pete. She hoped she didn't look as wild-eyed as she felt. "Till Monday?"

"Till Monday, for ten days, depends what they do on bail. Sarah's ready to cash in some bonds, but there's a limit—"

"There are other people who might want to help," said Connie, thinking of Abby Fitch, Milly Blair. Between them all, they should be able to make Carrie's bail.

"And after Monday we'll get back in that car and—"

They heard the halloo from behind them. They

turned together and saw the police chief and Carrie Suggs crossing the marsh. Carrie's eyes never left her daughter, even when she came within speaking distance of the couple on the sand, even when she said to them, with all the urgency Connie had ever heard in a voice, "You'll keep her?"

Pete looked at Connie.

And what could she say? It was only till Monday, after all. "We'll keep her. Sure."

That was all Carrie needed. She kept going, down to the water's edge where Lucy still hopped, soggily but happily. The chief sank onto the sand next to Pete and Connie.

"I guess she's got a few things to explain," said Connie finally.

"Yeah," said Willy. "I told her to take her time."

They watched the mother and daughter walk hand in hand along the wrack line toward the eerily kilted boat barn, Lucy pointing and jabbering the whole time.

Connie turned to the chief. "I don't see why you have to lock her up."

The chief didn't answer. Connie supposed she wouldn't have, either. Pete coughed, one of those time-to-change-the-subject coughs that were his specialty. He handled the new subject with tact, too. "I didn't get a chance to talk to Polly before she left this morning. Did she tell you her plans?"

"She's supposed to leave a message at the station. She'll probably be in Southport for a couple of days, anyway."

"Good," said Connie, "considering we just gave away her room."

"But, as a matter of fact, she's thinking of moving back here, looking for a place of her own."

"Oh?" Connie cast a curious eye at the chief, but he looked away and all she got was a view of one pink ear.

When his eyes swung her way again they narrowed, focused beyond her. He exploded out of the sand.

Connie looked behind her, but she didn't see anything.

It took a second for it to dawn on her.

She didn't see anything.

Or anyone.

Anywhere.

31

<hr/>

*This blue-eyed hag was hither brought with child
and here was left by th' sailors.*

Pete had never seen the chief so angry. His face was mottled, his respirations ragged, his pants soaked to the knees with marsh mud when he finally ran them to earth not twenty yards from the highway. But the minute he spied them he sprinted after them so fast it left Pete flat-footed in the bull-briers. Carrie Suggs, though, seemed to have anticipated the chief's moves. She set Lucy on the ground and cried out something that was so twisted with anguish Pete caught only his own name and Lucy's. But Lucy began to run.

Toward Pete.

And when Carrie cried out again, Pete caught those two words all right: *Keep her.*

After that, it got confusing. As Pete ran to meet the little girl he saw Carrie running away from them, toward the road. He scooped up Lucy and turned, thinking only to get the frightened little girl away before her mother got collared. He didn't see how it happened. He heard only the chief's roar, heard the brakes scream. An eerie, subterranean instinct made him push Lucy's face into his shoulder as he turned again, and there was Carrie Suggs lying motionless in the road, the chief and the DPW truck driver racing toward her.

Keep Lucy.

Two little words with a whole new big meaning. They tucked her between clean sheets in the spare room and took turns dredging up childhood bedtime stories. It took everything they had between them before the little girl finally began to breathe the breath of the unconscious.

And their night was just beginning. They had to come up with a way to tell her in the morning that her mother was dead.

And they had to make a very big decision.

Pete and Connie huddled across the hall in their own room, listening for any sounds from the spare room, talking softly, determined to think it through to the most rational end.

"So what would happen to her if we didn't keep her?" asked Connie finally.

"I'm sure they'll find a foster family somewhere."

"And if we did keep her?"

"It won't be easy. Think what that kid will have to get used to."

"Us," said Connie, which wasn't exactly what Pete meant, but now that he thought about it, that alone was a daunting enough prospect. What did they know about five-year-olds?

Nothing.

That was as far as they'd gotten when Lucy woke, crying.

The first time Pete settled her.

The second time Connie did.

In between they talked. Forward, backward, sideways. They even made a list of pros and cons.

That was when Connie started to laugh and woke Lucy.

When Pete came back from calming her, he said, "Just out of curiosity. You find something funny?"

"Yes. We are. Making lists. Using reason. There's no decision here."

"There isn't?"

"Pete. It's too late. Lucy's *here*. Are you trying to tell me you could send her away?"

After a minute, Pete laughed, too. "No," he said. "I guess I couldn't."

The next time Lucy woke, they went together.

32

~~~

I have done nothing but in care of thee, of thee
my dear one, thee my daughter . . .

Sarah Abrew sat in her chair and listened to the
silence around her. She'd lived like this before, she
reminded herself. Enjoyed it, too. And she was still
seeing people, wasn't she? For example, she'd only
just got home from a picnic in the white pine forest
with Pete and Connie and Lucy. They seemed to
think it helped the child to have Sarah around. Lord
knew the little girl was going to need all the help she
could get. Not that she hadn't landed as best she
could, considering. And it seemed to Sarah the little
girl had already settled in some. Leastways she'd
come up with enough spunk today to give Connie a
good argument about that airplane Pete bought her.
Lord, she'd never in all her born days heard so much
fuss about poking eyes out. How many children ever

poked their eyes out? Leave her be, Sarah had said finally. She gets poked, she'll learn to duck quick enough. Besides, she's got two eyes, hasn't she? That was all it had taken. Connie had snatched the plane away altogether and then the ruckus had begun.

But all in all, the afternoon had served as a nice, healthy distraction. Sarah had gone forward and back and round and round over it all so many times she was near sick with it. Pete had told her what the chief had said—that Carrie had run out in front of the truck, looking straight at it the whole time. What had she been thinking? That a mother in jail was worse than no mother at all? Was there something else Sarah should have done? She'd gone over it so many times there was no seeing it clear anymore. To have it end like this. After all those silly little details she and Carrie had sweated out together. Even Arthur's Five and Dime. They'd cooked up the business about the old account at Sutton-Fitch, even the business about her talking in her sleep. It was all to give Pete a bone to worry on, to keep him off the Carrie scent. Nobody had stolen anything from Arthur. The poor man's Five and Dime had been the victim of the Depression and the man's good heart, nothing more.

And what had Carrie been victim of, Sarah wondered now, Sutton or Sarah? And what would Arthur have said about this if he'd known what she had done? Would he have approved?

Suddenly Sarah's old ears picked up the sound of tires in the drive. A visitor. Wouldn't be Pete and Connie. Who? she wondered.

But she didn't wonder much.

Not really.

She was overdue, after all.

She came in alone. She sat on the hearth next to her

mother's chair. Sarah rested a hand on the awful blond hair and saw so many things, all of a sudden, that should have been clearer sooner. Would her daughter ever stop trying to reinvent herself? she wondered. Would Sarah ever find the right words to help her child without stirring up all those old, painful embers? In the end she decided to keep it simple.

"I was wrong," she said. "I'm sorry. For everything I did and didn't do."

"You don't need to apologize to me, Mother. Deep down I never doubted your good intentions."

"No? You might as well pave hell with them. I've spent some time wondering over all this, and I've got myself unsure of that, even. Was I thinking of you? Was it you I couldn't bear to see dragged in front of those policemen, stood up in a public courtroom? I don't think so. I think it was my own foolish mortified self I was protecting. I don't think I could have borne it, Joanna, to have heard what he did to you spoken out loud."

But Joanna smiled and shushed her. "We can do anything we set our mind to, Mother. That's what you've taught me. That's what I'm shooting for. After what you tried to do for Carrie—" She paused, almost whispered. "It was for me, too, a little, wasn't it, Mother?"

Sarah closed her eyes. They got so tired these days. She got so tired. "Dennis told me. One day when I called to speak to you. He told me you'd moved out, were staying with your old friend Sam Oliver. I only had to hear the name and I knew. Dennis could tell I knew something I wasn't telling. He knew you needed help. But I didn't tell him. I didn't see. Not then. But it was all I ever wanted. To help you."

Sarah felt dry lips on her forehead, heard another whisper. "I know, Mother. And I'm getting help. I'm seeing someone. And Dennis is helping me. Now it's our turn to help you. Come back with us to Baltimore."

Sarah opened her eyes. "Thank you, child, but no. I'm not blind yet. I think I can hang on here a little longer. And besides, I'm needed here just now. But I'll tell you what you can do."

Sarah left her in the car in front of the station and went in alone. She marched past that busybody at the desk and down the hall, singing out crisply so he'd hear if he'd a mind to, "Chief in?"

Jean Martell fussed and fumed after her, but sure enough, the chief opened his door and peered into the hall. Jean faded into the distance. The chief held the door for her. Age had certain advantages, after all. She plopped the unwieldy parcel on his desk and perched on the edge of the chair opposite.

"Open it," she ordered.

She watched him fumble with the paper, saw the rich wood gleam through. "It was my husband's. Made special. I filled it for you. Not Cubans. Wouldn't want to go breaking any laws, you know."

Was that a smile? Sarah thought so. He opened the humidor, took out a cigar. She'd thrown in Arthur's gold lighter and the cutter, too.

"Mind if I smoke?" he asked.

"No, not at all."

He cut and lit like he'd done it a few times before, like Arthur himself might have, even. He leaned back in his chair, and the old familiar smell filled the room.

After some seconds Sarah cleared her throat. "I caused you a lot of trouble, I know. If I could do it again—" She hesitated. If she had it to do again, what would she do? What would bring the girl back?

The chief leaned forward in his chair and squinted hard at her. "Sarah, you were an old fool for a while back there. Don't be one now, too. What happened to Carrie Suggs had nothing to do with you. This is a very good cigar. Thank you."

With some effort Sarah straightened her ancient spine and met the chief's squint head-on. "You're welcome."

Of this, at least, Arthur would approve, she knew.

33

Now, forward with your tale

It was an unusual sight, Evan Spender all alone on the steps of Beston's Store, but not an unwelcome one, unless you were, like Pete, one of the few dozen Nashtoba residents still without phone service. The island of Nashtoba had still only partially recovered from Charlotte. The power was back, but the phones weren't. The roads were cleared of silt, but the washouts remained. Some foliage still clung to battered branches but was salt-burned brown.

Pete climbed the steps and sat. "Any news on the wedding front?"

Evan rolled his eyes at the still-perfect, still-blue sky. "Still thinking, she says. What's thinking got to do with it, I'd like to know?"

Pete tried to look like he had no clue where that idea might have come from.

"How's the tyke?" asked Evan finally.

Pete shook his head.

"She's young. Give her time."

When Pete didn't say anything to that either, Evan seemed to think a change of subject was due. "And Polly? She's moving back, is she?"

"Eventually. We need the help at Factotum." And with Lucy. But there were a few things to be done first, although the plan was essentially in place. The Clausens had arrived, taken one look at their displaced boat barn, and disowned it completely. Pete and Connie had decided to move it onto their southeast corner, the upstairs to serve as an apartment for Polly, the ground floor to serve as a new home for Factotum, thereby allowing Pete and Connie to reclaim their own ground floor. They were already bursting at the seams again. It was amazing the size and number of accoutrements required by one little five-year-old girl.

"Don't imagine Polly will be bothering you two much when she comes," said Evan. "Every time I see the chief seems like he's just talked to her."

Again, Pete remained silent. Partly because it was nobody's business what was going on with Polly and the chief, but partly because he had, in fact, no clue what was going on with them. They may be talking to each other, but they sure weren't talking to Pete.

After some further silent examination of the sky, Evan moved on to another new topic. "Old Fern's finally sold up, I hear. Going back to Texas. And young Web appears to be taking to that museum like a duck to water."

True, thought Pete. He and Connie had brought

Lucy in there the day before, and while Lucy was busy showing off for Connie all the shells she'd learned to name, Pete had been accosted by the new director. He needed the trails cleaned up after Charlotte. Could Factotum? Sure, said Pete. An awkward minute had passed while Pete wondered if there was some tactful way to raise another subject, but before the minute was up, Web had brought it up himself. He'd seen Pete on the water that day before the storm. Whose boat? Pete had told him. And had ventured to add that he'd seen Web, too, had seen him trailing smoke . . . ?

Web Three had laughed. Not smoke, ashes. The minute he'd withdrawn from school he'd burned all his papers and tossed the ashes into the bay.

A funeral of sorts, Pete supposed, but sans body.

Evan harrumphed loudly beside Pete, bringing him rudely back to the present. "So you and Connie going to try again for that honeymoon?"

"Not for a while," said Pete. "Not till Lucy gets settled in." And that was going to take time, as Evan had said himself not long ago. Time. Pete looked casually at his watch and then again, not so casually. Christ. Lucy got home in fifteen minutes and it was his turn for bus duty.

Bert Barker and Ed Healey came up the store steps as Pete barreled down them without stopping.

"Well howdy-doo to you too," Bert sang out.

"Sorry," Pete called over his shoulder. "Gotta run."

The two men peered after him. "Have you noticed he's looking pretty peaked lately?" asked Ed.

" 'Course he's looking peaked," said Bert. "What do you expect? Damned fool just got married."